'TIS THE DAMN SEASON

FIONA GIBSON

Boldwood

First published in Great Britain in 2024 by Boldwood Books Ltd.

Copyright © Fiona Gibson, 2024

Cover Design by Debbie Clement Design

Cover Photography: Shutterstock

The moral right of Fiona Gibson to be identified as the author of this work has been asserted in accordance with the Copyright, Designs and Patents Act 1988.

All rights reserved. No part of this book may be reproduced in any form or by any electronic or mechanical means, including information storage and retrieval systems, without written permission from the author, except for the use of brief quotations in a book review.

This book is a work of fiction and, except in the case of historical fact, any resemblance to actual persons, living or dead, is purely coincidental.

Every effort has been made to obtain the necessary permissions with reference to copyright material, both illustrative and quoted. We apologise for any omissions in this respect and will be pleased to make the appropriate acknowledgements in any future edition.

A CIP catalogue record for this book is available from the British Library.

Paperback ISBN 978-1-83617-215-4

Large Print ISBN 978-1-83617-216-1

Hardback ISBN 978-1-83617-214-7

Ebook ISBN 978-1-83617-217-8

Kindle ISBN 978-1-83617-218-5

Audio CD ISBN 978-1-83617-209-3

MP3 CD ISBN 978-1-83617-210-9

Digital audio download ISBN 978-1-83617-211-6

Boldwood Books Ltd

23 Bowerdean Street

London SW6 3TN

www.boldwoodbooks.com

For Anna, Pete and the hens

1

ELEVEN DAYS UNTIL CHRISTMAS

'Can we go home now? *Please*?'

Shelley stops in the busy shopping mall and glares at Joel. Fairy lights sparkle overhead and 'Do They Know It's Christmas?' is being piped out from somewhere – the bowels of hell possibly – accelerating Shelley's heart rate like a double caffeine shot. 'Just need to get a few bits,' she says. 'Honestly, it won't take too long.'

'I *hate* this,' he whines. 'We've been here for hours!'

'Joel, we only arrived forty minutes ago—'

'I'm hungry and I need a drink—'

'We won't be much longer—'

'I *really* need something to drink,' Joel insists, gasping now, as if they were traversing the Kalahari Desert and not an east London shopping mall long overdue a refit. 'Why do we have to do this? On a Saturday as well. All these people! I hate it!'

'For God's sake.' Shelley rounds on him. 'You think *I* love it?'

'I'm tired and I want to go home.' Joel looks at her imploringly. Then he makes his body go floppy, as if his spine has suddenly melted and he is on the verge of collapse.

Trying to blot him from her vision, Shelley marches on determinedly, rattling through the kind of mental lists that have cluttered her brain throughout every December since she first gave birth. Travel mug for Fin (can his preferred type *really* cost forty quid?) and that special razor Martha wants, plus roll-on perfume, sheet masks, pillow spray containing some crucial ingredient that Shelley has now forgotten, and something called a 'pore blurrer'.

At seventeen years old, Martha's pores are invisible to the naked eye. It's Shelley's pores that need blurring, she decides crossly. She's been tempted by something her friend Pearl, a former beauty editor and product aficionado, has been raving about. 'The Miracle Filler', it's called. But are things really so bad that, at fifty-two, Shelley's face needs to be *filled,* like cracked mortar?

As she drags the whining Joel past a desolate branch of Claire's Accessories, her brain flips back to her Christmas list. A sweater for Fin, or will he despise it on principle? Socks! Non-moulting scarf for her mother-in-law, because last year's choice shed turquoise fluff all over her good jacket and apparently she's still picking bits off...

Shelley glares at her shopping companion as he lopes along at her side. Now her list swerves down an alternative route. *Strong booze, cigarettes, divorce lawyer...*

Unfortunately, she can't placate Joel with a Chupa Chups lolly or even a visit to Santa's grotto, set up in a saggy velour tent outside Dr Noodles. Because Joel isn't a small child, being dragged around the shops by his mum. Joel is Shelley's husband, aged fifty-two and a highly successful freelance graphic designer and father to their teenage daughter and son.

For the seventeen years they've been parents, Joel has cunningly avoided any involvement with Christmas at all. Or indeed parenting, pretty much. However, it's the festive season that always threatens to tip Shelley over the edge. In the early years, when Shelley was at home full time with the kids, it *sort of* made sense, as Joel would be working flat out to meet Christmas deadlines (he never works at a normal rate; it's always 'flat out'). By the time Martha and Fin were at school, and Shelley had returned to work, Christmas had well and truly become her department.

Really, *everything* is Shelley's department. If their lives together were one of those vast, old fashioned department stores, Shelley would be in charge of ladies' fashions, bedding and electricals, plus the restaurant, staff, cleaning and building maintenance. What Joel does, as he points out regularly, is earn money to keep them all. The *real* money, that is. Shelley's contribution, from working as a receptionist at a local care home, is barely acknowledged.

'Can't you do it all online?' Joel asked this morning, meaning the Christmas shopping.

'No, I can't,' Shelley insisted. 'I need one day – just one day, Joel, with you helping me – looking around the real shops.'

And now, as they head home on the Tube, laden with bags, Shelley senses Joel's spirits rising. 'Thank God that's over,' he announces loudly, for the benefit of the whole carriage. '*Please* promise you'll do it all online next year. Don't make me go through that again.' Rather than deigning to reply – which would only encourage him – she watches her husband catch the eye of the young man in a mustard beanie hat sitting opposite. And she reads the silent exchange between them.

Joel: Women, eh! Christmas!

Beanie man: You poor bastard, mate.

Joel: But I did it 'cause I'm a good guy!

Beanie man smirks in a way that Joel interprets as male-to-male camaraderie, when in fact he is probably thinking, *Stop grinning and staring at me, weird old man!*

Back home, Shelley and Joel dump the numerous bags in the hallway. Before she has even pulled off her jacket, he's zoomed to the kitchen and snatched a beer from the fridge as if it's essential to life. Then he marches past her, cantering upstairs with his beer, leaving her standing with the shopping bags clustered around her feet.

Shelley blinks down at them and then glares upstairs. It wouldn't have killed him to help her carry them up to their bedroom, where Christmas presents are being stored. Presents, incidentally, that include carefully chosen items for Joel's mum and dad – to which the non-moulting scarf will be added – plus his brother, his brother's wife, their three children and a couple of elderly aunties. They, too, come under the banner of 'Shelley's department'. Joel is too busy being God, installed up in his studio in the converted loft space of their somewhat scuffed and shabby terraced home.

'Martha? Fin?' Shelley calls out. No response. The kids must be out, so at least their presents can be squirrelled away without any interference. 'Joel?' She stares upstairs. '*Joel!*'

After a few moments he appears on the landing, looking distracted and clutching his phone. Joel is obsessed with his phone and checks it repeatedly during mealtimes and sometimes, on occasion, during sex. In those rare moments when he isn't holding it, his hand still forms a phone-holding shape. Shelley worries that he might need an operation to correct it.

'What is it?' He frowns.

'Could you help me upstairs with this lot?'

'Can we do in a bit? Just sending some emails—'

'It's just, if the kids come back they're going to see—'

'Can I do it when I've finished?' He disappears back up the wooden staircase to the loft. Simmering with irritation now, Shelley lugs the shopping upstairs in two loads, and then heads to the kitchen to prepare dinner.

The sink is piled high with dirty dishes. Shelley's family seem to be under the illusion that this is a magical sink that cleanses its contents without any human involvement, like those freaky public loos that sluice everything down when you've gone out.

She re-fixes her blonde ponytail and tears into the washing up. And now she remembers that Joel has invited 'the boys' around tomorrow for mince pies, mulled wine and their annual festive table football tournament. Shelley likes Joel's friends, gathered from his various magazine jobs and a football team he belonged to, briefly. She's happy for him to invite them all round, as it's usually a jolly occasion. But they're not ready this year. Not a single decoration has been put up yet, and there isn't a tree. There aren't even any mince pies, for crying out loud. They're Joel's friends! Couldn't he have sorted this?

She scampers upstairs and bursts into Joel's studio. He springs back in his chair as if she's pulled a gun on him. 'We need to get a tree,' she announces.

'What? What kind of tree?'

What kind does he think? An apple tree? A weeping willow? 'A Christmas tree! You've got the boys coming over tomorrow—'

'We can get it tomorrow morning,' he says with a shrug.

'Can't we just do it now? So we can decorate it in the morning and do the room? Make it look festive for everyone coming? The man's there till around seven...' The Christmas tree man, she means. He's been selling real pine trees all week from a pop-up shop in the old launderette.

'We don't need it all decorated for tomorrow. It's *ages* till Christmas.'

'It's not ages, Joel. It's eleven days—'

'Fucking hell, are you counting?' he splutters.

'It's just, I'm working four days next week—'

'So am I! I'm working *all* the days!'

'Yes, so if we don't do it this weekend that's another week gone—'

'Oh, for God's sake.' Joel places his phone face down on his desk, a vast expanse of vintage teak the size of Kent. He won't admit how much it cost. 'It's a business expense,' he'd insisted. Whenever he looks cross when Shelley buys anything other than the cheapest white wine, she is tempted to tell him it's necessary for the smooth running of their family home. So that too is a *business expense*. 'All this fuss,' he grumbles now. 'Every year it's the same—'

'Joel, I didn't invent Christmas. I'm not the Virgin Mary.' What is she saying? Is she going mad? Inexplicably, Shelley's eyes prickle with sudden tears as she looks around Joel's immaculate workspace.

There are several computers and tablets; state of the art technology that no one is allowed to touch. A new laptop is Joel's prized possession. He also lied about the cost of this; Shelley knows because she checked. Not because Joel isn't entitled to buy whatever he likes. He earns the money, after all. And it's not just a laptop, it's a *vital tool*, he says. No, she only checked the price to confirm to herself that it really hadn't been £200, and that therefore, he must think her an idiot.

Her gaze sweeps across the rest of the room. There's his beloved football table, which Fin and Martha used to nag to play until Joel's rabid competitiveness drained all the fun out of it. In the corner, a fantastically expensive guitar, virtually unplayed, gleams from its stand, and the walls are hung with huge framed prints showcasing Joel's typography. 'FREE YOUR SOUL', one of them reads. Okay, Shelley thinks, but could you also get the ladder out and climb up through the hatch, like I keep asking you to, to free the Christmas decorations from the loft? She's about to ask again, but the way he is looking at her now – *Please go*, his look says – sends Shelley stomping back downstairs, calculating that in three days' time she'll be getting together with Pearl and Lena and then her equilibrium will be fully restored.

And then, she is sure of it, everything will be all right.

2

TEN DAYS UNTIL CHRISTMAS

Lena stares at Tommy and waits. She is waiting for his top lip to quiver, as it does when he's winding her up and trying to trap in a laugh.

Surely this is a joke. Tommy has always been a prankster – she'd fallen in love with that daft, larky side of him – and this is a good one.

So the old elm crashed through Mum and Dad's kitchen roof and now they're coming to us for Christmas!

Hahaha! Hilarious. Any second now, laughter will burst out of him and she'll play-wrestle him in mock-fury. *Don't you ever do that to me again!*

But Tommy still isn't laughing. And something hard and cold seems to clamp itself around Lena's chest as she registers his chalk-pale face, the sheen of sweat on his forehead.

'Tommy, *please* tell me this is a joke?'

'Of course it's not.' He looks down, frowning, his usually bouncy demeanour somewhat flattened. 'The whole kitchen roof's got to come off. They could've been killed, you know. If they'd been in the kitchen—'

'I don't mean the tree part,' she says quickly.

'It's going to cost tens of thousands—'

'Yes, and I'm really sorry about that. I meant the Christmas part, Tommy. Your mum and dad just announcing they're coming to us for Christmas Day, like it's a fait accompli. You're not serious, are you?'

He runs a hand over his abundant dark hair, swept back and flecked a little with silver. At fifty-one – a year older than Lena – Tommy looks startlingly youthful, considering he loves his red wine and the occasional illicit cigarette in the garden. In the genes, she reckoned when they started dating. The Huntley family goes back generations, as does Lena's of course; everyone's does. But whereas Lena considers her family to be very ordinary – she grew up in a tiny terraced house in Manchester – Tommy's family aren't ordinary at all. His family home, High Elms out in Berkshire, has a walled garden and a lake, and its bedrooms are named according to their colours: the yellow room, the blue room and so on. Lena's eyes boggled when she first saw the place.

'Sorry. I'm not joking, darling,' he murmurs now.

Lena stares at him across the kitchen. 'And you're okay with this, are you?'

Tommy's mouth twists. 'No. No, of course I'm not. It's completely bonkers. It'll be hell.' He closes his eyes and exhales, seeming so distraught that she can't find it in herself to be angry with him. It's not his fault that the elm toppled. Not his fault that his over-privileged parents believe they have the right to do whatever they want, without considering anyone else. Lena knows in her heart that Tommy is a good, kind man, and he'd never want to cause her any stress.

Four years ago, Lena had been out at a Vietnamese restaurant with Shelley and Pearl, her closest friends. They'd all been a bit tipsy when one of the men at the next table overheard something Lena had said, and there'd been a flurry of banter between the two tables.

After dinner, the groups had merged and they'd all clattered off together for a drink. And that had been that. Mutual attraction between Lena and the six-foot-three Tommy with brilliant blue eyes and a broad lopsided smile. He reminded her of those foppy heroes from Merchant Ivory films. She'd never met anyone like him before. Two years on, he moved into her somewhat compact two-bedroom flat in a 1960s block in Hackney. Not because her place was 'better' than his, but because Tommy was living in a commuter town and, much as she loved him, she wasn't prepared to give up the place she loved. Or, for that matter, London. Lena doesn't think she'll ever be ready for a life in the Shires.

'And they've literally got nowhere else to go?' she asks now, incredulous.

Tommy shakes his head. 'You know what they're like.'

'Um... yeah.' Lena *does* know.

'Cantankerous old buggers have fallen out with pretty much every living relative,' he adds. 'I'd dig up a dead one if I could.'

'Hmm.' Lena's mouth compresses into a flattened line. 'What about a hotel? Couldn't they go out for Christmas dinner?'

'Flat refusal. Mum hates hotel catering.' He mimics her strident tones: '"I'm not going to some grim carvery where the bird's been drying out under a heat lamp as if it's had a shampoo and set!"'

Lena sniggers. She doesn't mention the fact that her own parents love the Sunday carvery at their local pub. 'They wouldn't have to do that,' she points out. 'They could go somewhere really swanky—'

'Mum says absolutely no way. Anyway, Dad's tried. Anywhere decent was booked up months ago, apparently.' He looks at her in his cheeky way, trying to defuse things with humour. 'I did suggest they tried Nando's in Slough' – Lena splutters at this – 'but that was a no go. And it was all, "Don't you *want* us, Tommy? D'you realise what we're going through, with the house?"'

Lena nods as a thought occurs to her, accompanied by a tiny glimmer of hope. 'This means we can't have our wedding there.' At High Elms, she means. Not if the kitchen is lacking a roof.

'I'm sure it'll be fine,' he insists.

'But what if it isn't? Sounds like they're under enough stress as it is,' she says, trying to keep her tone light. What a shame, she decides privately, that they'll have to come up with an alternative plan. Tommy proposed on Lena's fiftieth birthday in July. After her divorce, she'd never imagined wanting to get married again, but here she was, saying yes because Tommy is wonderful and she loves him and would trust him with her life. His mother insisting that they have the wedding reception at High Elms is less wonderful, but Tommy was railroaded. 'It means a lot to her and it's only one day, darling.' And so, reluctantly, Lena agreed.

'They've already organised the contractors to start work,' he tells her now. 'They'll easily be finished by April. All done and dusted and back to normal again.'

Lena bites her lip. 'Okay. But I'm still not sure about Christmas with them, Tommy.' She glances around the living room that she'd furnished quickly and cheaply after her marriage breakup. She'd walked away from all of the mutually owned furniture that she and her ex had saved for over the years. The thought of living with any of that stuff – of seeing that chair, that lamp, every day of her life – repulsed her. Instead, determined to start afresh, Lena had dashed to IKEA and sourced a fair few pieces second-hand on Gumtree. She'd found the bookshelf abandoned in the street and dragged it in and given it a lick of jaunty turquoise paint. 'Hardly High Elms, is it?' she remarked once, soon after she and Tommy had got together.

'No, thank God,' he told her.

Now Lena opens the sliding door that leads onto a tiny balcony overlooking another sixties block. Their neighbours are lovely and there are fantastic little family restaurants nearby. Both Lena and Tommy love living here. But she can only imagine what his parents will think of the place. They have never suggested visiting before, and Lena can't understand why they're so intent on spending Christmas here.

Tommy comes out and takes her hand, beckoning her back in. 'We can make it work, can't we? Just for Christmas Day and the one night? They could have our room, and you and me could squeeze into the box room...' A hopeful smile. 'It'll be cosy, you and me all snuggled in together—'

'It's not the sleeping arrangements I'm worried about,' Lena cuts in. *It's all of it*, she thinks, although she doesn't say this.

'I know, sweetie,' Tommy murmurs. 'But we can evict them on Boxing Day. Fuck it, I'll drive them home myself—'

'It's not that I don't *want* them here,' she says firmly. No, actually, it is! Both she and Tommy are divorced – his was a lot more amicable than hers – and they have cherished the low-pressure Christmases they've created together. These past two years they have cosied up here, in Lena's flat, with wonderful food and wine and wall-to-wall movies. Lena's parents haven't minded her staying in London. She has four siblings and a gaggle of nephews and nieces so there's always plenty of activity going on in their

Manchester home. And Tommy's daughter Daisy has spent them with her mother.

Besides, Tommy's parents have given no indication that they actually *like* her. 'So where are you from, Lena?' William, his father, barked at her the first time she visited High Elms.

'Manchester,' she replied, 'but I moved to London when I was twen—'

'No, I mean *originally*.' William's gaze bored into her forehead over the silver candlesticks.

'Um, I was born in Manchester,' she said pleasantly, while Tommy patted his clammy forehead with a napkin and tried to veer them down an alternative path.

'Dad, I was thinking we could take Lena on the forest walk tomorrow. What d'you think—'

'I mean, where were your *parents* from?' William boomed.

'Well, my dad's from Bangladesh,' Lena explained in a perfectly level tone, 'and he met my mum, who's from Yorkshire, when he moved to England in the sixties.'

'*Ahhh*,' William said, apparently satisfied that he had managed to finally drag the correct information from her.

Then later, over after-dinner drinks, Tommy's mother started on her. 'So you don't have any *children*?' In the tone of, 'So I hear you don't wear any *knickers*?'

'No, I don't.' Lena's reserves of pleasantness were dwindling rapidly.

'Mum, I hear you're thinking of renovating the summer house!' Tommy announced.

Ignoring this, Annabelle peered expectantly at Lena, as if awaiting an explanation. Lena toyed with telling this pinch-faced woman the truth. That she and her ex-husband had tried to get pregnant, and when nothing had happened he had been unwilling to try IVF, so she'd had to let it go. And how it had turned out that the fertility issues were on her side, as throughout all of the trying and sheer desolation whenever her period arrived, he'd been shagging someone else. Clearly, Max's sperm had been plentiful and upwardly mobile as, before Lena had discovered what was going on, his lover had had a baby.

'We have four,' Annabelle boasted.

Well done! Lena wanted to applaud her. How fantastically clever of you!

'Mum, Lena knows all about our family,' Tommy said in a pained voice.

'All boys,' Annabelle trilled. 'Quite the little team!'

'Yes, I bet.' Lena eyed her almost empty wine glass, willing it to magically refill.

'...Been wonderful seeing them all grow up,' Annabelle went on, sipping her Chablis. Yes, so I've heard. Each one of them packed off to boarding school at seven years old. 'All excellent at sports!' Amazing really, as Tommy hated school sports due to that pervy teacher who'd make the boys line up and hold out their rugby shorts to check they weren't wearing pants underneath... 'We're so very, very proud,' Annabelle drawled, waggling her glass, which William beetled over to refill.

Then the talk turned to Catherine, Tommy's ex-wife – who had of course managed to produce a child – and of whom Annabelle is clearly very fond. 'How *is* Catherine, Tommy?' she asked, throwing Lena a quick look.

Lena turns away from Tommy now and looks down onto their street. It's a crisp, bright Sunday morning and across the road, a young couple are carrying a Christmas tree into their block. 'Darling, I'm so bloody sorry, I can't tell you.' Tommy stands behind her and wraps his arms around her waist, trying to coax her round to face him. But she isn't in the mood for hugs now. Lena disentangles herself and escapes to their bedroom where she grabs her phone, brings up the group chat with Shelley and Pearl, and types a message.

LENA

Just found out Tommy's parents are coming here for Christmas!

SHELLEY

WHAT?!

PEARL

That's crazy! What's going on?

LENA

Tree fell down. Loads of damage to the family pile. You could call it a natural disaster.

SHELLEY

Or an act of God?

LENA

Maybe it's punishment for me shoplifting a packet of Jelly Tots from the newsagent's in 1982?

SHELLEY

You can't allow this Leen. You've got to put your foot down.

LENA

No choice seemingly. Too early to start drinking?

SHELLEY

Never.

LENA

Hope we're still on for Tuesday night girls.
PLEASE SAY YES!

3

EIGHT DAYS UNTIL CHRISTMAS

'So, are you all ready for the big day?' the bartender asks. Shelley looks round at Lena and Pearl and the three women laugh. 'What?' He grins. 'What did I say?'

'Three champagne cocktails please,' Shelley announces.

'Oh, like that, is it?'

'D'you do pints?' Lena asks, leaning forward over the bar. '*Pints* of champagne?'

'Tense time of year then,' the neatly bearded young man remarks with a smile. They perch on stools as he makes their cocktails, taking in the glamour and opulence of the Rivoli Bar at The Ritz.

It's an annual tradition, coming here. Just one cocktail each; it's all they can afford. But they soak it all in: the polished walnut and glistening chandeliers and Christmas trees decorated in silver and gold.

From there, they stroll happily onwards to Soho where they squeeze their way into their favourite pub. It's noisy and scruffy, its gloss-painted walls deeply nicotine stained and hung with ancient tattered theatre posters. It has terrible loos and the burgundy patterned carpet is rather sticky. However, although the cocktails are always fun to kick off their Christmas night, here is where the friends really feel at home. Miraculously, as Shelley is served, a tiny table in the corner becomes free, and Lena bags it.

Soho has changed a lot since Shelley, Pearl and Lena worked together just a short hop away on a women's magazine in the mid-nineties. Chain coffee shops have proliferated, squeezing out the celebrated greasy spoon where they often converged for hungover lunches. Madam Jojo's has gone, and the piano bar next door, where they'd perched on stools at the piano and laughed away many a night. It hardly seems possible that thirty years have whipped by since they met in that cheerful buzzy office, filled with music and chatter and clouds of Shockwaves hairspray.

Lena was features writer and Shelley the editor's PA. Shelley had met Joel there. Joel the art director, loud and brash and wildly flirtatious with his risqué banter and bleached quiff. He'd slept with half the office before he and Shelley had got together. But he'd grown up by then, she decided. Got it all out of his system, she'd told Pearl and Lena, as if to convince herself as much as her friends.

Pearl was the magazine's beauty editor and never 100 per cent sure about Joel. However, she too had met her future husband on the magazine, soon after landing in London from the sleepy Cheshire village where she'd grown up. Shy, lovely, handsome Dean, who everyone had adored. They'd been mates at first, as everyone was on the magazine: a riotous gang. Dean had been a designer, laying out pages and always taking extra care when working on Pearl's beauty features. Dean always worked away quietly, in contrast to Joel, his boss, who liked to *perform* at work, showing off, making everyone laugh.

Pearl had always liked Dean, and it wasn't just Lena and Shelley who'd teased her about what was obviously a mutual attraction. *Pearl and Dean*. It had been the office joke: the perfect coupling that had yet to happen; that unmistakeable music blasted out frequently, long after the joke had worn thin. It didn't matter that Dean was three years younger than Pearl. They had fallen in love, and two years on they were married – Pearl in a vintage silk dress and Dean looking as if he'd raided his dad's wardrobe for a suit. The whole magazine staff had attended, and Joel had created a celebratory mock magazine cover depicting Pearl and Dean smiling broadly, cheeks pressed together, to mark the day. Beautifully framed, it was presented to them on their big day.

Pearl + Dean Special Wedding Issue!

Pearl was thirty-two when their baby, Brandon, was born. They wanted more children but a year or so later, Dean became ill. There was a year of hell, through all the chemo and radiotherapy. And it seemed hopeful for a while, but then the cancer came back, and Pearl's beautiful man faded and then died on his fortieth birthday. She'd lost the love of her life and Brandon, aged ten, had lost his much adored dad.

The years have spun by and finally, last year, Pearl started dating again, crumbling under pressure from Shelley and Lena to at least give it a go. After all, it had been over a decade. And three months ago, on Hinge, she met a handsome Belgian man named Elias.

'So he keeps hinting that he's planning this amazing present for me,' she announces now.

'What is it?' Lena exclaims.

'He won't say! He won't even give me a hint. He's going home to Brussels for Christmas and he's back on the twenty-seventh and says I need to pack a bag.'

'A bag!' Shelley grins. 'I wonder where you're going?'

'I don't know!' Pearl beams at them, cheeks flushed in the overheated pub. 'What d'you think Joel's getting you, Shell?'

'Oh, you know what he's like. Says it's all a load of commercial nonsense.' Her tone is breezy, accompanied by a shrug. 'Made such a fuss about shopping on Saturday, and then on Sunday he had his mates round for table football and he was laughing about the tree in front of them all—'

'What, your Christmas tree?' Pearl frowns.

'Yeah! I wouldn't have minded but I'd gone out and bought it and dragged it home myself, and stuffed it in a pot, and he reckoned it was wonky—' She breaks off, feeling unexpectedly emotional at sharing this.

'Christmas trees are *meant* to be wonky,' Lena says firmly.

'And he keeps saying why do I make such a fuss about Christmas?'

Shelley continues. 'And why not get everyone one of those charity presents? A goat or a donkey or a donation to a sewage system—'

'Joel wants a sewage system?' Pearl's eyes widen.

'God, no. He wants a guitar amp. A massive black box thing to keep up in his lair—'

Lena splutters. 'Maybe he could come over and do a performance for Tommy's parents on Christmas Day? Distract them from grilling me about where I'm "from"?'

'I can't believe they're coming to you.' Shelley shakes her head.

'I know. Rain water's pouring into the kitchen, apparently. Annabelle can't possibly cook Christmas dinner in there.'

'Couldn't they microwave a couple of jacket potatoes?' Pearl suggests.

'And what about their other sons?' Shelley asks. 'I thought there was a whole gang—'

'Team,' Lena corrects her. 'It's "Team Huntley", remember? And no, they can't go to any of the others because they're all off to some massive chalet in the French Alps for the whole of Christmas…'

'Well, couldn't they join them there?' Pearl looks confused.

'*Oh* no. They wouldn't want to intrude on the holiday, not when they've all worked so hard all year being Chancellor of the Exchequer and boss of the Bank of England and Mayor of bloody Berkshire.' She is exaggerating, but only slightly; in fact, Lena can never remember what any of them do. Only that they are terribly important and that all they ever seem to talk about is 'managing wealth'. When magazines started closing, Lena swapped careers from features writing to creating content for several linked charities. She loves her work, and the flexibility of freelancing, but she is definitely not in the managing wealth bracket. On occasion it's been more like managing the loose change she's managed to scrabble together from under the sofa cushions.

She pushes her short, choppy dark hair behind her ears. 'I actually feel like running away,' she admits.

'If you're going, I'm coming too,' Shelley announces. 'Joel wouldn't even get the decorations down from the attic. He said, "Why don't you just get some new ones?" And I said I wanted my grandma's baubles like we have every year. I ended up clambering up there myself, with Martha resenting holding the ladder for ten minutes, asking if I was nearly done yet because she was going out...' She laughs dryly, trying to make light of it. She didn't plan to pour out her woes on a night that kicked off with cocktails at The Ritz, and which they'd looked forward to for weeks. But still, her heart quickens in anger. *Her grandma's baubles.* Why couldn't Joel understand?

'You know,' Pearl says, 'we could go away. My cousin's always inviting me up to his place...'

'Oh, who's this?' Lena asks.

'Michael in the Highlands,' Pearl replies. 'I haven't seen him in years – decades actually. And he's not even a real cousin. He's my second cousin, I think – or once removed? Our mums were cousins, or second cousins. I was never quite sure. And he's quite a bit younger – five or six years or something like that. I used to babysit him occasionally.'

'You went up to the Highlands to do that?' Lena asks in surprise.

'No, they lived in Cheshire, like us, but in a much posher area. Michael went to private school. But he was nice, y'know? A sweet kid. We always got along well.'

'So what happened?' Pearl asks. 'Did you just lose touch?'

'Yeah, you know how it is. Our lives just veered off in different directions. I moved to London, and from what I heard he met this girl, and they got married and had this dream of living the rural idyll up in Scotland. They found this ramshackle place and did it all up and now it's a B&B.'

'Wow,' Lena murmurs. 'So did it work out for them?'

'The B&B has, as far as I know. The website's still up and running and his address is the same as it always was. But not the marriage, I don't think. At least, I assume they've split because the Christmas cards stopped coming from Michael and Rona. These past few years they've just been from Michael.'

The girls order more drinks, filled with excitement now about this new information. 'A single man, stuck way up there on his own,' Shelley muses. 'I'm impressed he gets it together to send Christmas cards at all.'

Pearl chuckles. 'I thought you were going to delegate this year, Shell? Get Joel to do them?'

She snorts. 'I gave him the box of the cards and the list of addresses and he wrote one, illegibly—'

'And he's meant to be the typography expert?'

'Allegedly. I had to take them off him—'

'You know what that's called?' Lena cuts in. 'Doing a job deliberately badly so you can get out of doing it? Weaponised incompetence.'

Shelley laughs and shakes her head quickly, as if wanting to dispel any thoughts of her husband right now. 'So can we see pictures of Michael's place?' she asks, and Pearl nods eagerly and pulls up the B&B's website on her phone. The three crane forward, taking in the heather-strewn landscape and the powder blue cottage nestling between purplish hills.

'Wow,' Lena murmurs. 'Imagine living way up there. So beautiful.'

Pearl nods, bringing up interior pictures of the B&B rooms. With whitewashed bare stone walls, they are flooded with daylight and furnished simply. Beds and easy chairs are strewn with woollen throws in deep violets and mossy greens. Bare floorboards are dotted with sheepskin rugs. The effect is at once stylish and modern, yet cosy too. Shelley peers at a double bed generously made up with fluffy throws and heather-coloured pillows and has a sudden yearning to spirit herself into it. She spots several pairs of green wellies, lined up neatly by the cottage's front door, and thinks of Joel's trainers: whacking great objects, like hovercrafts, kicked off in their hallway at home.

'It looks amazing,' she marvels. 'I'd love the three of us to go up and stay sometime.'

'Yeah, we'd pay of course,' Lena adds quickly. 'I mean, it's his business, isn't it? We wouldn't expect to stay for free.'

Shelley takes a big swig of wine. 'I want to be there right now, Pearl. Beam us up there. Call him now!'

Pearl laughs, and her auburn curls bounce around her cheeks. 'I'll message him sometime, see what he says. I haven't seen him since, God – he must've been about twenty. But he's never forgotten Brandon's birthday, even though they've never met. He still sends a card, even now. And he was so kind and thoughtful after Dean died.'

'He sounds *lovely*,' Shelley announces.

'I was just so impressed,' Pearl adds. 'Michael didn't know us as a family and he doesn't have kids. But when he heard about Dean he was on the phone right away. And then a few weeks later he called again and asked if he could talk to Brandon. He chatted away to this bereaved ten-year-old kid about what he was into and stuff. And that Christmas he sent him a Lego robot.'

Shelley's blue eyes glitter as she squeezes Pearl's hand. 'I really think we should go. How about early spring?'

'Count me in,' Lena enthuses. 'I can think about that little blue house while Tommy's mum's saying, "Oh, I didn't think you people celebrated Christmas?"'

'And I can picture myself thrashing through the heather with a bottle of Scotch when I've peeled the seventy-fifth potato and Joel's asleep on the sofa with his mouth open.' Shelley laughs. 'We *need* this to get us through Christmas.'

'We absolutely do,' Pearl says firmly. 'Leave it with me, girls. I'll sort it.'

4

Pearl's mood is high as the three friends part company that night. Never mind that the world she has built for her and Brandon since his dad passed away has recently been turned on its head. Because Brandon's girlfriend Abi has burst in on their world, arriving with a gigantic pink suitcase with no prior consultation and proceeding to bellow everything at maximum volume:

'Pearl, could you stick my pyjamas in with your next wash?'

'Pearl, that tinted moisturiser you left out in the bathroom. I used the last little bit. Hope that's okay!'

Tonight she senses a flicker of relief as she lets herself into her first-floor flat. Brandon and Abi are out. She knows they're not working tonight – they're both doing bar work – so it must be a night out. She hopes it's a late one, but is primed for them to burst in at any moment. In the meantime, she rounds up the socks and cotton buds and lacy knickers left scattered by Abi all over the bathroom floor. And that thing Brandon said, when she'd just moved in, pops into her mind.

'Just a temporary thing, Mum, to tide her over. She's had a really tough time.' It's been three months now and Abi is showing no signs of moving on. But then, she has nowhere else to go, and they are in love. At twenty-one, this is Brandon's first serious relationship and they think nothing of full-on snogging while waiting for their toast to pop up. Once, Pearl accidentally glimpsed Abi jabbing her tongue into Brandon's ear. Brandon who, just last week (it feels like) had an army of Bionicle robots all set up on the living room floor. Yesterday Pearl discovered a small gold vibrator placed casually on top of the potatoes in the vegetable rack. It wasn't hers.

Naturally, Abi will be here for Christmas. She's fallen out with her mother and it doesn't look as if there will be a reconciliation anytime soon. Occasionally, Pearl is tempted to call Abi's mother and offer a mediation service. Surely the rift can be healed?

Having gathered up the girl's detritus from the bathroom floor, Pearl stops and frowns at the glass shelf. She always applies her make-up in here, as the light is the best in the flat. And Pearl *adores* make-up. Even in her darkest days, she has never been 'not up to' applying a full face. Quite the opposite, in fact. However wretched she's felt, as she's worked through the steps – base, eyes, blush and lips – Pearl has always sensed herself settling, her heart rate calming and things being just that little bit better.

Now she notices that her favourite lipstick isn't in her make-up bag, where she's sure she left it. Instead, it's sitting out on the shelf. No longer a beauty editor, when she was festooned with free make-up samples from PRs, Pearl now works as a freelance make-up artist. These days she buys most of her make-up, although she has enough friends in the industry to be sent the occasional jiffy bag packed with samples. It's a delightful perk of her job.

However, this particular lipstick wasn't a freebie, and Pearl didn't buy it. This Tom Ford lipstick was a present from Lena, who knew she'd adore it and would never spend £48 on a lipstick for herself. The colour is Ruby Rush: the perfect warm red for Pearl's auburn hair and fair skin.

She pulls off its lid and frowns at the mangled state of it. Well, it certainly wasn't Brandon. Abi must have used it and jammed the lid back on, without properly twisting it back down. Should she say something?

No, she can't bear to be so petty. However, it rankles her, the way her flat feels invaded – and it's not restricted to her make-up or even the bathroom. The entire flat is strewn with Abi's puffa jackets and huge quilted bags with their flashy gold logos and jangling chains. The Småstad storage unit Pearl ordered, still boxed and propped up in the hall, is heaped with further jackets and scarves. Yet Pearl can't help feeling sorry for the girl. After the fall-out with her mother, she seemed a bit lost, despite the brazen attitude. And Pearl knows all about feeling lost.

Now, though, things are getting better. She's had a lovely night with her best friends, and things are good with Elias. So far, he's been unfailingly sweet and thoughtful, and gradually she's allowed him into her life. And who knows where things will lead?

She's not going to let a mangled lipstick ruin her mood.

Now, as Pearl pulls on her pyjamas, her phone dings with a text. It's Elias.

> **ELIAS**
> Hey gorgeous hope you're having a fun night out. Know it's cheeky and late but can I be cheeky and late? *winky face* Can I come over when you're back? It's about the surprise!

A rush of anticipation surges through Pearl's body, instantly dispelling any irritation over the crushed lipstick.

She replies, smiling as she types:

> **PEARL**
> Of course. I'm just home so come over. See you soon! Xx

5

SEVEN DAYS UNTIL CHRISTMAS

1.07 a.m.

Fifty-three years old and Pearl is in the throes of a sexual reawakening. She's already had two orgasms since Elias bowled up an hour ago, fresh from his Christmas night out with his consultancy buddies and expressing delight that they had her flat to themselves. Before she met him, it was more than she'd had – at least involving another human – across the entire previous decade.

Elias is a remarkably youthful-looking man of fifty-eight, with barely a wrinkle and an enviably toned physique. Pearl wonders if he's had work done and fears that his peachy complexion makes her look like a withered potato in comparison. Always impeccably groomed, he has a personal trainer and guzzles probiotics for his microbiome and drinks only *natural* wine, and in moderation (as far as Pearl is concerned there is nothing unnatural about any wine).

Pearl had never imagined that this kind of scenario would be possible because, until a few months ago, when she'd started dabbling with a couple of dating apps, she had been celibate since Dean died. Sometimes Pearl had wondered if she'd even remember what to do. And the thought of being with anyone who wasn't Dean seemed unthinkable and rather terrifying.

Going on a couple of dates in the summer merely confirmed that she was better off alone. There was the man in frankly hideous basketweave shoes who, after they'd agreed to meet for a coffee, proceeded to order an enormous salad and sat there cramming lettuce into his mouth in front of her. Then the cycling enthusiast with whom she re-lost her virginity, and who harangued her for not having a proper pension provision in place: 'And you, being freelance? What are you going to live on – supermarket own-brand food?' Pearl had wanted to cosh him with a tin of Aldi baked beans, but she couldn't, as they were in his flat. Instead, she messaged the group chat from his dismal maroon-tiled bathroom.

PEARL

He'd barely climbed off me and he started offering me financial advice!

It was a numbers game, her friends insisted. Don't throw in the towel after a couple of bad dates. And then she met Elias, who is currently lying naked beside her in her own bed. Opportunities such as this are rare and precious. Pearl loves her little modern flat, and feels lucky to have it. But sounds travel freely through the tissue-thin walls, and if Abi isn't clomping about in the colossal wooden-soled platforms she bought recently on eBay, she is blowing her nose on a tea towel or bellowing on her phone outside Pearl's bedroom.

Sex, when it happens, takes place mainly at Elias's apartment – a warehouse conversion next to the Regent's Canal, all stripped floorboards, exposed brickwork and squishy tan leather sofas. It's a novelty to have him here with her, and the flat to themselves. He hasn't even told her what the surprise is yet.

Pearl pushes back her mussed-up hair and stretches up to kiss his mouth. The post-coital Elias is extremely loving and sweet. He likes to cuddle and talk and run his fingers over her body, sending her tingling all over again. 'So you're not angry about your boyfriend turning up in the middle of the night?' he ventures.

She smiles. He's never referred to himself as her boyfriend before. 'I'm furious,' she teases. 'You do know I should be asleep by now.'

Elias chuckles. 'Not working tomorrow, are you?'

'No. I had all those jobs last week but there's nothing now till after New Year. I'm relieved, to be honest. Now I can just focus on Christmas.'

'Ah, that's good.' Gently, Elias lifts an auburn curl away from her finely boned face. 'You look so gorgeous like this.'

She smiles, still unsure of how to respond to his compliments. 'You're not so bad yourself.'

He traces his fingers over her bare shoulder. 'It's nice, being here together for a change.'

'It is,' Pearl agrees.

'So, it's okay for me to stay over?'

"Course it is,' she says, laughing. 'Did you think I was going to throw you out into the cold wet night?'

'Well, you might,' he teases.

'Brandon's fine with you, you know that.' In fact, they have already met several times and he is happy about his mother seeing someone. He'd encouraged it, even; another person along with Lena and Shelley, badgering her to start dating. She doesn't need to pretend to be a nun, and she suspects Brandon and Abi enjoy having the flat to themselves whenever she stays over at Elias's place.

'It won't be awkward over breakfast?' he asks now.

'Of course not. They probably won't be up anyway. But honestly, Brandon likes you.'

'Oh, I'm glad.' He smiles. 'So, d'you reckon the girlfriend's thinking of getting her own place?'

'Abi?' She shrugs. Elias has met her too, several times. 'She can't afford it. Neither of them can. They're just doing bar work at the moment, so money's pretty tight—'

'And she can't go back to live with her own parents?' He looks quizzical.

Pearl shakes her head. 'She's not speaking to her mum and her dad's never been on the scene.'

Elias frowns in sympathy. 'Hopefully they're both chipping in, though?'

She blinks in surprise. 'You mean for food and stuff?'

'Well, yes, that of course. But also rent?'

Taken aback, Pearl allows herself a moment before replying. Having grown up in a sprawling country home just outside Brussels, Elias has never married or had children. When he's not working from home – and his hours seem incredibly flexible – he's out taking arty architectural photographs around London. He seems to have spent his life pretty much pleasing himself.

'No, I don't charge them rent,' Pearl says, keen to change the subject.

He gazes at her, chin propped up on a hand. 'But they're both adults, aren't they? Both working—'

'Yes, but as I said, they're not rolling in money—'

'Well, neither are you.' He raises a brow, and she feels herself recoil from him. 'What?' He frowns.

'Nothing.'

'I'm sorry, I didn't mean—'

'No, it's fine,' she says firmly. 'But I'd better get some sleep—'

'Pearl, sweetheart.' He wraps his arms around her and pulls her close. 'I'm sorry. It's none of my business.' *No it bloody isn't!* she thinks irritably, extracting herself from his embrace and sitting bolt upright in bed. Mid-September, she met him. Just three months ago. Yet he feels entitled to comment on how she manages her life with her son?

'Pearl, I really am sorry,' he murmurs. 'I think you're a *great* mother. Everything you've coped with, doing it all on your own—'

'I wasn't always alone,' she snaps, aware of her eyes prickling.

He sits up and folds a hand around hers. 'I know that, honey.' Then he tips his head, gaze fixed on her until she looks at him. 'I haven't told you what your surprise is yet...'

'Oh.' She softens slightly. 'No, you haven't.'

He smiles. 'Remember I said you'll need to pack a bag?'

'Yes?'

'Hang on...' He swivels out of bed and fishes his phone from the pocket of the trousers he'd flung over the chair. Slipping back in beside her, he types something and taps the screen. 'I was thinking that after Christmas, when you've slaved away, no doubt making it a fantastic day for the three of you...' Elias glances at her and grins. 'Then you'll deserve a treat.'

He hands his phone to her, and Pearl peers at it. It's a home page for something called Moksha. *Where freedom beckons*, the text reads. 'What's this?' she asks.

'A club,' Elias replies.

'A club?' She frowns. 'Oh, I don't know, Elias. I haven't been clubbing for decades. How do people even dance any more? I'd feel like a complete idiot—'

'No, not that kind of club.' His eyes glint, and he chuckles. 'We'd stay overnight. It's in Somerset. And Somerset's lovely, isn't it? All cider orchards and rolling hills...'

She bites her lip and clicks on the 'about us' link. 'It says Moksha means "freedom" in Sanskrit.' She looks at him. 'Freedom to do what?'

'Whatever you want!' he announces. 'It's this private club, this little secret haven tucked away near the coast, for like-minded people to get together and have fun and—'

'These look like B&Q garden huts,' she cuts in, studying the accommodation page now.

'Oh, they're really snug and cosy,' he says quickly. 'Very tastefully done—'

'So you've stayed here before? You're a member of this club, are you?'

'Uh, yeah, I am.' Elias nods, and she navigates to the events calendar.

Fancy dress disco
Boxing day BBQ
Hot tub party
Spanking workshop

'Elias?' Pearl turns to him. 'This is some kind of sex club, right?'

'No, no, it's a naturist club,' he insists. 'But the no-clothes thing is optional. No one forces you. You wouldn't have to go naked if you didn't want—'

'Oh, great!' she exclaims. 'That's good to know!'

He peers at her as if she's misunderstood the concept. 'Honestly, Pearl. It's not weird or anything, it's just about being sociable and relaxed and having fun—'

'And spanking each other?' Her green eyes widen.

'That's just a bit of fun, it's all optional—'

'"Hot tub party",' she reads again. 'A load of horny strangers feeling each other up in a bubbling plastic pond?'

'You wouldn't have to do anything you wouldn't want to do,' Elias says sharply, seemingly outraged that she might be suggesting otherwise. 'You could just... relax.'

Pearl glares at him. 'It doesn't sound very relaxing.'

'I think it is,' he says sulkily.

'So, if it's all optional, and I opted *not* to take part, what would I be doing while all this spanking and shagging was going on?'

He exhales. 'Whatever you like.'

'Right, like knitting or reading *Woman's Weekly*—'

'I just thought it'd be fun, to give you a bit of a break—'

'And we'd go after Christmas?'

Elias nods. 'If we go for a Twixmas deal, they're doing three nights for the price of two...'

'*Right.*' She hands him back his phone. It's not that Pearl is a prude, or that she has a problem with people getting naked in a field bordered by shabby wooden huts just outside Weston-super-Mare. She just doesn't want to join them. But that's not the real issue either. These past three months have turned her world on its head, in a good way. Elias is handsome, attentive and kind, and Pearl has told herself that this is good for her – to allow herself to grow close to someone again. He might not be 'the one' but Pearl doesn't want a *one*. That had been Dean and no one will ever replace him. Pearl had just wanted to feel alive – and, yes, like a sexual being – again.

'Pearl? What d'you think?' The mouth that caused her to orgasm just thirty minutes before is now set in a petulant pout.

'It's nearly two o'clock. Let's go to sleep.' She turns away from him and clicks off her bedside lamp.

'If you don't think it'd be fun,' he mutters, 'we could do something else.'

'I'm really tired, Elias.'

He sighs forcefully and switches off the lamp on his side. As his breathing slows and deepens, Pearl lies with eyes wide open, still facing away from him. She doesn't want him to see that they are now filled with tears. Was she an idiot for thinking that Elias knows her well enough to suggest something she'd genuinely love to do? She flinches as the front door opens, banging back against the wall as Brandon and Abi clatter in. 'I'm starving!' Abi bellows. 'Are there any of those crumpets?' More banging and crashing. It sounds as if burglars are smashing up the kitchen.

Elias groans. 'Jesus Christ.' Pearl lies very still, feigning sleep. 'Do they really need to do that?' he mutters.

'Just go to sleep.' She wishes now that she could make him disappear through the power of concentration alone.

Because there's something Pearl wants to do right now. Elias is right, in that she does deserve a treat. She *has* to get away – before Abi mashes up all of her lipsticks and she goes quite mad. Not to a frothing sex pond near Weston-super-Mare, but to somewhere far, far away, with people who really love her.

Now it sounds as if Abi is battering the kitchen worktop with a mallet (she is probably only buttering a crumpet). Elias grunts and tries to tug Pearl's share of the duvet off her.

This is it, she decides. He can find someone else to 'relax' with in a garden shed in Somerset, because they are over. She made a mistake, by allowing him into her life.

Elias is snoring softly now, properly asleep. Although it's the middle of the night, and it won't be seen until morning, Pearl is seized by an urge to fire off a message.

Taking care not to disturb Elias, she reaches for her phone and types:

PEARL

> Hi Michael, hope all's well. Am sure you're super busy with Christmas but thought I'd drop you a note. I know it's been years since we've seen each other but you've always said I should come up and visit. I'd really love to do that sometime. Could I bring a couple of friends, if that wouldn't be too much of an imposition? Love Pearl xx.

She sends it and, and in a blink, her phone pings with a notification. Michael has replied.

6

2.17 A.M.

> **PEARL**
> Wow, you're awake! Sorry, hope I didn't disturb you.

MICHAEL
Not at all. Bit of a night owl these days. How are you? How's Brandon?

> **PEARL**
> We're good thanks.

MICHAEL
It's terrible but I've lost track of his age. I'm guessing he's outgrown those Lego robots now? What were they called again?

Pearl tries to close her ears to the muffled sex noises now coming from Brandon's room.

> **PEARL**
> Bionicles. Yes he has but the one you sent was his favourite! He's twenty-one would you believe?

> **MICHAEL**
> Wow. So you'd like to come up and stay?

> **PEARL**
> That'd be great if you have any space?

Now Abi is panting loudly like an enthusiastic golden retriever. Pearl tries to shut off her ears as she stares at the screen. *Michael is typing.*

The sounds intensify. Pearl wonders if in fact the girl is having an asthma attack. Should she call 111? Bang! Crash! 'Hold it. Hold it right there!' Abi commands. Perhaps they're building the Småstad?

> **MICHAEL**
> ...you're really welcome anytime I have rooms free.

> **PEARL**
> We'd pay of course. We wouldn't expect to stay for nothing.

> **MICHAEL**
> Don't be crazy. You're family! In fact, my family room's free this coming weekend right up until Christmas. And the double. Can't imagine anyone'll book now. But you're probably mad busy at this time of year...

As Pearl blinks at the message, figuring out how to respond, Elias mumbles something under his breath. Then, just about audibly: 'What's that noise?'

'Just something outside,' she replies, relaxing only when his snores resume.

> **PEARL**
> Wow thanks! Yes it's probably impossible but sometime soon, definitely. Can't believe I've never seen your place. Can I talk to the others and get back to you?

> **MICHAEL**
> Of course. Night then.

PEARL

Good to be in touch again and let's chat soon. Goodnight x.

* * *

11.15 a.m.

PEARL

Girls I bring good tidings!

LENA

????

PEARL

Michael's up for us going to stay!

SHELLEY

Brilliant! Shall we book a date? When are we thinking?

PEARL

He won't take any money from us as long as he has rooms free. He's adamant about that. Says he actually has space this coming weekend right up until Christmas! Could we possibly do this?

LENA

You mean go BEFORE Christmas? Like this week?

PEARL

I'd be up for it if we could pull it together. Shell when d'you finish work?

SHELLEY

Thursday's my last day. Then off till 27th. How about you Leen?

LENA

Yeah I could get all my work done. We could do this.

SHELLEY
We actually could!

PEARL
Was hoping you'd say that girls. REALLY need to get away.

SHELLEY
All OK? Something up?

PEARL
Weird thing with Elias. Think it's all over.

LENA
Oh no what's happened?

PEARL
He seems to think I'd like a Twixmas deal at a spanking club in Weston-super-Mare.

SHELLEY
WHAT???

LENA
OMG.

PEARL
But it's not just that. It's this place too. Feels like it's closing in on me. So how about we head to the Highlands this weekend? Say four nights, Friday through till Christmas Eve?

LENA
And miss the whole pre-Christmas thing? You mean duck right out of it?!

PEARL
Exactly. How would that go down with Joel and the kids Shelley?

SHELLEY
Like a cup of cold sick.

LENA
Can we talk later? Got work call in a min.

SHELLEY
At work too but free later. Exciting!!!

* * *

6.09 p.m.

Abi is hogging the bathroom. It's probably only been half an hour but it feels like *weeks*. With Brandon out at work, Pearl jiggles in the hallway, trying to hold in her pee as his girlfriend's shower goes on and on and on.

'Abi?' She knocks on the door. 'I really need the loo.'

'Won't be long,' she bellows. 'Sorry, think I used up all your conditioner!'

Pearl doesn't care about the conditioner because her bladder might possibly explode very soon like a water balloon.

She knocks again – politely, as Pearl hates being impolite. If it were Brandon in there, she'd have no problem hammering on the door. But she still regards Abi as a guest. 'Abi?' she calls out sweetly. No response. Abi is singing loudly – Amy Winehouse's 'Tears Dry on Their Own' – and apparently enjoying herself hugely in there.

In actual pain now, Pearl hurries to the living room and looks around wildly for something to pee in. Anything will do. Any kind of receptacle that won't leak. The wastepaper basket? No, that's wicker – it'd drip out everywhere – and she can't bring herself to use a kitchen item like a saucepan or the salad bowl. She'd run out to the library at the end of the road but it'll be closed, she realises. And she's not sure she'd make it that far anyway.

A large, round red plastic object catches her eye beneath the sparkling Christmas tree. It's the tub of Celebrations that Nadira, their kind upstairs neighbour, brought down for them last night. 'Don't eat them all at once, guys!' she instructed with a grin. Pearl is in too much pain now to acknowledge the small stab of guilt as she tugs off the lid and tips out the few remaining chocolates onto the floor.

She tears down her jeans and knickers and almost weeps in relief as she squats over the tub. This is me, she reflects: fifty-three years old and peeing in a Celebrations tub because I can't gain access to my own bathroom. Once she's finished, she holds the position for a few moments longer, drip-drying. It's good for the thighs, she supposes, squatting so close to the ground. People go to classes for this stuff.

Pearl tries to see the positive in the direst of situations. When she had counselling after Dean died, her therapist encouraged her to acknowledge her achievements; to take a pause and notice how far she'd come. She tries to do that now, recognising that if it weren't for her enviable pelvic floor, she might have wet herself there in the hallway. And that there's something almost *festive* about peeing in a Celebrations tub.

Finally, Pearl stands up and pulls up her knickers and jeans and picks up the tub.

'Oh, Pearl. I'm really sorry!' Abi has appeared, swathed in a turquoise bath towel and with Pearl's spotty shower cap on her head.

'Oh, it's okay—' Pearl reddens, assuming Abi is apologising for hogging the bathroom until she follows her gaze to the floor. Now she sees that, out of all the Celebrations, only the mini Bounties are left. 'I *love* Bounties,' she fibs.

'No, no, it's the loo. Don't know what happened. It just kind of pinged off to one side...'

'What did?' Pearl is still clutching the tub of warm, steaming pee. Quickly, she jams the lid on it.

'The toilet. The seat, I mean. It broke.'

'Oh! I'll just take a look at it.' Pearl glides past Abi, transporting the tub with the care and reverence that she'd bestowed upon the platter of fairy cakes she'd carried to the front table at her school's Harvest Festival.

In the steam-filled bathroom, she locks the door and regards the loo seat. It has indeed come away from its fittings, as if sat upon roughly by a very large, drunk cage fighter. Perhaps Brandon can fix it. Perhaps *she* can. She could look it up on YouTube: 'How to fix a broken toilet seat.' Also: 'How to remain perky and pleasant when under duress.' Because now Pearl fears that, after Elias, and now this, her perky pleasantness has all but dwindled to nothing.

And there it goes – the final trace of it, along with her pee, as she tips away the tub's contents and flushes the loo.

7

A little way east, Shelley is also having bathroom-related issues. Having just come in from work, she was eager to jump into the shower and sluice off the horribleness of the day. They are making cutbacks at the care home and two of her friends' jobs are definitely going. Beth and Anja were in tears at coffee break, and Shelley wonders how long her own position as a receptionist will be safe. She'd only taken the job as a tiding-over thing, but has grown extremely close to the tight-knit team, as well as many of the long-term residents and their families. They've almost become like family to her too.

Peony Lodge isn't one of those dismal homes where the residents are parked in a huge semi-circle around the TV. There are art, yoga and music sessions and frequent trips out. It's a proper *home*, bright and cheery and buzzing with activity, and Shelley is proud to be a part of it.

She can't shower yet, because Joel is languishing in the bath. However, the flurry of messages this morning has triggered a little hum of excitement in her, and Shelley manages to shake off her irritation. She pulls out her ponytail band in the kitchen and runs her fingers through her shoulder-length hair. Once a natural light brown, it's been highlighted for so many years she has no idea what her natural colour might be now. It's the only money she spends on herself really, and those two and half hours spent with James every couple of months represents a certain kind of bliss. James enjoys hearing about her travails with Joel and the kids and they have a laugh together. Shelley always emerges from his salon feeling restored, not just hair-wise but *all*-ways-wise.

Now she remembers that she left a bowl of home-made chilli defrosting in the fridge for tonight. So at least she won't have to make dinner from scratch.

She opens the fridge. Her gaze lands on the bowl which had indeed contained chilli, but now looks as if it has been lapped at by a dog. Joel must have scoffed it while she was at work. And maybe the kids had some too? Martha and Fin's secondary school is at the end of their road and they often pop home at lunchtime.

The logic of dumping the bowl back in the fridge, with the smeared equivalent of a teaspoon of chilli left it in, is beyond her. But Shelley isn't feeling logical now, on this drizzly Wednesday afternoon, with Christmas hurtling towards her. These past few years, her mum and stepdad have spent their Christmases at home in Cornwall. But as is the custom, Joel's parents will be here for the big day. A glum couple, fixated on terrible happenings in the news, Brian and Babs will ensure that war, murders and soaring crime rates are hot topics for discussion at the festive table.

Shelley's thoughts switch back to the excitable message exchange between her, Lena and Pearl this morning. She's hasn't had time to process whether it really might be possible to run away to the Highlands this coming weekend. Of course she wants to very much. But she can only imagine how her family would react.

The front door opens. Shelley hears a schoolbag being thrown down on the hall floor before her daughter flounces into the kitchen. At seventeen, Martha is a tall, gangly beauty; all long, slender limbs and a mass of glossy dark hair that's rarely combed, but always looks fantastic. With her earbuds jammed in, she avoids eye contact as if she has better things to do than interact with her mother.

'*Hi*, love,' Shelley says pointedly.

'Hi.' Martha opens the fridge. 'Oh,' she mutters, as if unimpressed by the options available to her.

'Did you eat the chilli, Marth? It was meant to be for dinner—'

'That wasn't me,' she snaps.

'Okay,' Shelley starts. 'I only asked—'

'I didn't touch it!' Martha slams the fridge door shut and immediately stabs at her phone, perhaps to alert her lawyer over the wrongful accusal. Then she swans out of the kitchen and a few moments later Fin mooches in, making straight for the enamel bread bin.

'Hi, honey.' Shelley smiles.

'Hey, Mum.' At fifteen, Fin is less outwardly hostile than his sister but tends to keep himself to himself. He is also ravenous every second of the day, as if harbouring a tapeworm. He yanks the lid off the bread bin and glares into it.

'There's no bread.'

'No, I forgot to pick some up,' Shelley says mildly. 'Did you eat that chilli, Fin?'

'What chilli?'

'The chilli that was there in the fridge, for...' She starts to tell the back of his head as he leaves the room. 'Fin!' she calls after him. 'You will remember to tidy your room, won't you? Remember Gran and Granddad will be staying in Marth's room on Christmas night. So there'll need to be space in yours for the airbed—' She breaks off, realising that she may as well be shouting into outer space.

She stands alone in the middle of the kitchen of their terraced house, wondering what to make for dinner now.

I know, she decides. I know what I'll make.

Shelley opens the fridge and takes out the chilli bowl that no longer contains chilli and dumps it on top of the dirty plates and mugs and glasses that have accumulated in the sink while she's been out at work. Then she returns to the fridge and lifts out the unopened bottle of sauvignon.

'I know what we'll have for dinner,' Shelley announces out loud. She reaches for a wine glass from the cupboard, fills it to the brim and takes a fortifying gulp.

'That you back, Shell?' Joel calls out from upstairs. 'I was gonna say. The tree's still wonky. Looks drunk!' He guffaws, and as Shelley tips more wine down her throat, she wonders how this has happened to her.

How she's become the one in charge of Christmas – indeed of everything here – when no one else in her family seems to care that it's happening. As if she is in fact *Mother* Christmas, insisting on putting up decorations and fairy lights and having a tree, when clearly, her husband and offspring couldn't give a stuff.

Is she silly for trying to make it jolly and fun? For buying chocolate tree decorations even though the kids are nearly grown up? And for rushing out for mince pies for Joel's mates, *and* making mulled wine, which he refused to do, saying he didn't know how? 'You just throw spices in and heat it in a pan, Joel. An infant could do it.' *Aw, couldn't you do it, babe? I'm juggling so much stuff right now...* What, precisely, was he 'juggling'? Phone poking and enjoying languid baths?

Maybe it was also silly of her to 'drag' Joel around the shops, as he put it, when it would have been so much easier to order everything online. And perhaps, instead of pulling out all the stops to produce her usual all-the-trimmings Christmas dinner, with the home-made cranberry sauce her mother-in-law guzzles by the spoonful, she should just bang a ready-roasted chicken on the table and be done with it?

Rubbing at her tired eyes, Shelley installs herself at the kitchen table. It's cluttered with papers and the kids' school stuff, and jars of peanut butter and Branston Pickle with the lids left off. She glares at it all, then goes onto the group chat.

Several new messages have appeared since this morning.

> **LENA**
> Tommy's parents are saying they always have beef as well as turkey. Keep telling T we can't fit all that into my little oven but he says we'll manage somehow. Why does he agree to everything they say?

> **PEARL**
> He's just trying to keep the peace.

> **LENA**
> It feels like a terrible test they've set us to prove he's marrying the wrong woman. You know they'd love him to get back with Catherine?

PEARL

Ignore them and stuff the beef! No pun intended...

LENA

I've never dreaded Christmas before. I want to run away.

PEARL

Let's do it. Let's run away together.

Shelley is poised to add her message when Joel appears in the doorway, a vision of still-wet hairy legs in a Muji waffle dressing gown. No, not a dressing gown. He's told her off about calling it that. 'Makes me sound like I live at your care home,' he'd retorted. 'It's a *robe*.'

'What's for dinner?' he asks now.

Shelley blinks at him, still clutching her wine glass. 'I don't know,' she replies.

Joel looks at her expectantly, as if she doesn't know *now*, but at any moment will come up with several options. Shelley just sits there, drinking wine.

'Well, *is* there anything?' he prompts her.

She places her almost empty glass on the table. No, *how was your day?* No, *any news about the redundancies?* He knows she's been worried, that it's all been bubbling away these past few weeks, the staff room humming with rumours and huddled conversations. At least, she's been telling him. Sometimes it feels like talking to a brick.

'I don't know, Joel,' she replies.

This seems to confuse him. 'You don't know?' Then, as if he's only just noticed: 'Drinking already?'

She looks at him; this tall, good-looking and confident man, on whom she'd nurtured a crush from the moment she started working at the magazine. He'd already been out with Petra and Charlotte, and probably some others in the office that she and her friends didn't know about. Then finally, one evening, he and Shelley had ended up sitting together on the coach back to London after an office day out in Margate. There'd been a lot of drinking that day.

'I've always fancied you,' he told her. 'I think you're amazing.' Ridiculously, she'd assumed she was too low down in the food chain to warrant attention from the loud and glamorous art director. She wasn't in the fashion, features or art departments. Not one of the creative team who came up with the brilliant ideas that made the magazine such a success. She didn't interview pop stars or choose cover models or direct fashion shoots. She was just the editor's PA, and Joel had never paid much attention to her before.

'Yes, I *am* drinking,' she announces now, necking the rest of her wine before adding, 'And no, I have no idea what we're eating tonight.' Then she turns away from him, blocking his waffle-swathed form from her vision as she types:

SHELLEY

Girls I'm definitely up for this trip. Friday through to Christmas Eve. No one'll miss us will they? I know I could drop dead right here and Joel and kids would step over my rotting corpse. So let's book flights.

8

FIVE DAYS UNTIL CHRISTMAS

The plane climbs through a thick duvet of cloud, emerging into clear blue above. On a paint chart it would be almost *too* blue, too intense to live with. But way up here it is perfect, a world away from bathroom hoggers and grumpy teenagers and the looming spectre of in-laws. Shelley, Lena and Pearl are installed in row twenty-one, as excitable as teenagers on a school trip, while still a little stunned that they are doing this. So close to Christmas too; it feels reckless and perhaps a little mad. They had bagged cheap flights to Glasgow and will pick up a hire car at the airport. It has all seemed ridiculously easy to arrange.

The bright winter sun has burnt off the three friends' grievances even before drinks are served. Now Lena thanks the flight attendant as she hands her a wine, and looks at Pearl and Shelley. 'This feels like a dream,' she announces.

Pearl laughs. 'It really does. So what was the reaction at home?'

'Tommy was all for it,' Lena replies. 'Thought it was a great idea. Even offered to pay for my flight, as an extra Christmas treat, but I wouldn't let him.'

'He must feel bad about his parents descending for Christmas,' Shelley remarks.

'Oh, he does, definitely.' She grins. 'But I'll be ready for them after this. So how was your lot?'

Shelley smiles. 'The kids were all, "Yeah okay Mum." You'd think I'd just said I was going upstairs. And Joel thought I was joking. Then it was, "You're seriously going to leave us here with everything to deal with?"'

'So he's finally noticed Christmas is happening?' Pearl teases.

'Yep, that woke him up a bit. Started on about there being so much to do – as if Christmas is normally thrown together in the last few days. But it's virtually all done,' she adds firmly. 'I mean, everything apart from dropping off cards to the neighbours and picking up the turkey and wrapping the last of the presents. And they're for his mum and dad. That's not too much to deal with, is it?'

'Of course it's not,' Lena asserts.

'It's just, he hates wrapping, says he can't manage the corners—'

'This is *exactly* why you should be here with us,' Pearl announces.

'Yeah.' Shelley nods firmly. 'But he did keep asking if I was "all right"...'

'In a "have you lost your mind?" kind of way?' Pearl sniggers and sips her coffee.

'Exactly. Never mind the Christmas part. He reckons only a crazy person would go to the countryside of their own accord.'

'I think "the countryside" doesn't exactly convey it,' Pearl adds. 'This is the Highlands, remember. It's not like a little jaunt around the leafy lanes of Kent...' Of the three, she is the only one to have grown up in rural surroundings. Her Cheshire village consisted of a cluster of cottages dotted around a picture-perfect village green. Her family's pink thatched cottage was the stuff of postcards, the epitome of the English country idyll. But Pearl had yearned to escape to London, and by twenty she had landed a junior job on the magazine where she met Shelley and Lena. Besotted by the world of make-up, Pearl had been thrilled to have access to the beauty halls of Selfridges and Liberty – even if she could only try out the testers. And quickly, her sleepy village upbringing faded from her mind. 'It's crazy that I've never been to Scotland,' she adds. 'You two have both been, right?'

Lena nods. 'Me and Tommy had that weekend in Edinburgh. First time we'd been away together—'

'—When you spent the whole time in bed and staggered out at ten at night, desperately needing food?' Pearl teases.

'We saw the castle!' she protests. 'We went to a couple of comedy shows—'

'And I've been to Glasgow,' Shelley cuts in, 'that time Joel did a talk about magazine covers at the School of Art.' He hadn't really wanted her to come, she remembers now. 'It'll be cold and wet and there are *gangs* there.' She'd looked at him incredulously. Shelley might have grown up in an unremarkable Essex town, holidaying at Butlins. But she knew that Glasgow was a modern cosmopolitan city. She'd been pregnant with Martha at the time and was feeling bovine-level cumbersome with her swollen feet and enormous boobs. When she'd shown him her new maternity bra he'd reeled back, horrified. 'Fuck's sake, Shell. What's that? A contraceptive?' What did he expect her to wear in her third trimester – an underwired half-cup in transparent lace? 'Bring out the big guns,' he'd muttered before loping away. It was ridiculous to worry that Joel would try to get off with an art student the minute he was out of her jurisdiction. However, she'd tagged along on the trip, feeling like an unwieldy accessory he'd have happily left behind in a coffee shop if he could have got away with it.

'So, what d'you think it'll be like up at Michael's?' Shelley asks Pearl now.

'That's the thing. I've no idea,' Pearl admits. 'Only what I've seen in photos.'

'There's a village though, right?'

'I'm sure there must be. At least a few shops. I don't know how he'd run a B&B otherwise.' In fact, Pearl wonders now if she should have done a little research into their trip. But at home, with Abi forever firing questions at her, she could barely think. Where was the jumper de-bobbler? Could she pick up some kombucha next time she was out? Was there any oat milk left? As if Pearl possessed special powers that enabled her to see into the closed fridge, and do an inventory of its contents.

And then there'd been the minor matter of finishing with Elias. Which had been easy, as it turned out. 'I'm not really sure I want to be with anyone right now,' she told him.

'Great. Fine.' He'd swept out on a gust of haughty disappointment, as she wasn't the up-for-larks, sexually liberated woman she'd led him to believe she was. Now Pearl can admit to herself that she hated the way he made a little slurpy noise every time he took that first sip of hot coffee.

'I just want to get away from it all,' Lena announces. 'D'you think Michael will take us out on long, hearty hikes through the hills?'

'I'm sure he will,' Pearl says firmly.

'And we can stop off at a cosy village pub with a crackling fire and a little dog lying in front of it,' Lena adds, warming to the theme.

'And have fantastic, hearty pub lunches,' adds Shelley, giddy with the thought of leaving domestic responsibilities behind. Joel and Martha had mocked 'her' tree (why was it *hers?*), still listing tipsily to one side in its pot in the living room. They hadn't laughed quite so much when it became apparent that dinner *really* wasn't happening on Wednesday night. Like a student newly moved into halls, Joel had finally knocked together a basic supper for himself and the kids. Clumsily hacked cheddar, burnt under the grill; there you go kids! Resentment on toast. Blame your mother. Shelley had made do with a sack of Kettle chips and that bottle of wine. The next night, aware of trying to atone for her sins, she'd rustled up a crowd-pleasing lasagne.

'Things are going to change at home after this,' she muses aloud. 'It's so weird, y'know. We're not even properly away yet, and already I can see what an idiot I've been.'

'You're *not* an idiot,' Pearl insists. 'You just hold it all together at home. They're going to realise that, while you're away.'

'It'll do them good to fend for themselves,' Lena adds.

'Well, let's see.' Shelley smiles, hoping they're right. Then as they descend towards Glasgow Airport, Joel and the kids shift away from the main centre of her brain. At the airport they stock up on thank you gifts for Michael, hoping that wine, chocolates and a bottle of Hebridean gin will feel adequate, considering his generosity in hosting them. By the time they pick up the hire car, Shelley's crumb-strewn kitchen has melted from her consciousness and she can barely contain her excitement.

The Highlands! The images Shelley holds in her head have been informed by Hollywood movies and Netflix series, featuring crumbling castles and mist settling over shimmering lochs. Yes, there'd been that trip to Glasgow seventeen years ago when Joel had complained about 'watery' scrambled eggs at the hotel breakfast buffet and sampled too many single malt whiskies in the bar. But Shelley knows nothing of Scotland's wilder side.

Gradually it begins to unfold magnificently as they head north. Pearl has offered to drive. Although it hasn't been stated as such, she has fallen into the role of unofficial trip leader, with Michael being her not-actual-cousin.

'So, what's he like?' Lena prompts her.

'Honestly, I don't really know much about him these days,' Pearl admits. 'But he sounded lovely on the phone, just as he always was. And he's excited about us going up.'

'Maybe he'll be glad of the company,' adds Shelley from the back seat. 'You reckon he definitely lives on his own?'

'Yes, I think so,' Pearl replies. 'Like I said, the Christmas cards just come from Michael now. He doesn't have kids and he didn't mention Rona or any other partner when we spoke.'

'Will there be any B&B guests there?' Lena asks.

'Doubt it,' Pearl says. 'Not at this time of year. Who goes away the weekend before Christmas?'

She glances at Lena to her left, and Shelley in the rear-view mirror. There's a beat's silence before they all burst out in unison: 'WE DO!' And now they're all laughing, a trio again just like when they were young and enjoyed virtually limitless freedom, if only they'd known it. When a product called The Miracle Filler hadn't even been invented, let alone been considered as a viable solution for facial cracks.

In truth, all three know that it *is* a bit bonkers to absent themselves five days before Christmas. Yet at this precise moment each woman believes that it might possibly be the best thing she has ever done.

9

Although none of the women are true Londoners, over three decades the bustle and noise has seeped into their bones, and they are immune to it. To Lena, even her Manchester suburb feels subdued in comparison when she visits home. But not like this. The wildness of the empty landscape seems to catch in her throat. They fall silent as all around them are purplish hills, swooping down into valleys where rivers meander and fields are dotted by sheep. In the distance, a sliver of water gleams in the fading light. Further away still, craggy outlines of mountains are dusted with snow.

'Just *look* at this,' Lena breathes finally.

'I know. It's incredible,' Shelley exclaims, face close to the window. 'Can we stop and take photos?'

'I think we should press on,' Pearl replies. A confident driver back home, she is unfazed by driver aggression as she zips to jobs with her make-up kit stashed on her ageing Mini's backseat. There is no driver aggression here. Just the sudden squawk of a bird – a crow maybe, or a hawk? They have no idea. The only birds they notice in London are pigeons. But mostly, there is just silence as Pearl drives with the intense concentration of sitting her test. They have left the main road for a single-track lane with passing places. It twists and turns, weaving its way through thick dark forests. Dusk has fallen rapidly and by four-thirty it is properly dark, the moon a low hanging bauble in the inky sky.

They pass through a village of huddled stone cottages, crammed right at the roadside, lights glowing invitingly inside. There's a rickety-looking wooden village hall, all in darkness, and a red phone box. A tiny village shop looks as if it has already shut for the day. There's not a soul to be seen.

Now Michael's directions lead them onto a bumpy unmade road where they climb sharply upwards. To their left is what appears to be a sheer drop, with no fence or barrier. Just a steep wooded hillside and the loch far below, shimmering in the moonlight. 'We must be pretty close,' Pearl announces, relieved as the road levels out, cutting across what appears to be bumpy heather-covered ground. She picks up speed, but then slows abruptly. Being able to navigate the North Circular has not prepared Pearl for sheep blocking the road.

At a halt now, she looks round at her friends. 'What are we meant to do?'

'Let's just wait,' Lena suggests. Three plump sheep watch them with interest, showing no sign of moving on.

'Shall we... shoo them away?' Shelley suggests, although she doesn't fancy confronting them herself. She's hoping Pearl or Lena will do it.

'They'll move soon,' Lena says with authority. But they don't move, and no other traffic comes. 'Beep the horn,' she commands, but Pearl won't do that.

'It might scare them.'

'No, it'll just make them move!' Lena remembers how Pearl and Dean's enormous tabby cat, Albie, had reigned over their home, appropriating a velvet armchair as his throne. Pearl would refuse to move him, even when a human wanted to sit there.

Shelley lowers the back window and juts out her head, gasping as the bitingly cold air hits her face. 'Move along please!' she calls out. No one does anything she asks at home, so why is she expecting a better result here? 'Pearl, you're the country person,' she announces. 'Jump out and move them.'

Pearl splutters. 'We had guinea pigs, Shell. You think I grew up on a farm?'

'Rev the engine then,' Shelley urges her. So Pearl revs and Shelley shouts some more from the window and Lena tries to google 'What to do with sheep on the road' – but there's no signal. Then headlights appear in the distance, growing brighter as the vehicle approaches. It's a jeep, they can see now. It stops and a man climbs out and suddenly the sheep scatter, tumbling away into the darkness.

The man seems to regard their car with suspicion, as if they have contravened some country code. He comes around to the driver's side and Pearl lowers the window. 'Hi!' She affects polite brightness as if she has pulled into a drive-thru Costa.

'You all right there?' The man tips his head and frowns.

'Er, yes,' she starts. 'We're just looking for Shore Cottage...'

'Michael's place?'

He has a neat dark beard and a thick woollen hat pulled low. With a nod, he indicates to the right. 'You're right at it.' *Obviously,* his tone says.

'Oh,' Pearl exclaims, registering the narrow track now, and a small wooden sign, low to the ground and barely visible – let alone legible – in the dark. 'Thank you *so* much,' she gushes. With a shrug he saunters back to his jeep and waits for Pearl to turn into the track.

'We didn't need to pass the sheep.' Shelley grins.

'D'you think we seemed like locals?' Pearl chuckles, her shoulders unclenching as the bumpy track curves around to a parking area surrounded by what seems like an extensive garden. And there it is: a sizeable pale blue cottage perched a little way above the water, illuminated by a single outside light above the front door. Shore Cottage isn't on a coastal shore, but on that of the loch. And now the door opens and a black and white collie bounds out. Then Michael appears; a tall and fit-looking late-forties man with broad shoulders and tousled wavy hair.

'Hi, Michael!' Pearl climbs out and he beams at her, and they hug.

'Great to see you, Pearl. Journey okay?'

'Yes, easy,' she says breezily. She pulls back, filled with warmth at seeing him again after so long. Pearl's village childhood was so uneventful, dominated by church fetes and her mother's talk of the bowling club, that visits from Michael's family always felt like a treat. Her mother would launch into vol au vent production on an industrial scale, and as the adults settled with gin and tonics, she was always happy to take Michael out to play.

Introductions follow as Lena and Shelley climb out of the car. Although friendly, he seems to switch into a more businesslike mode, as if greeting regular B&B guests. 'Good to meet you,' he says. There are handshakes now, rather than hugs, and Pearl reminds herself that they are not in huggy London now. On make-up jobs no one seems to greet anyone with less than a full-on embrace. 'Here, let me take those bags,' he says, reaching for their cases.

'No, we're fine, honestly,' Lena insists.

'And who's this?' Shelley bobs down to greet the excitable collie.

'That's Stan.'

'He's beautiful!' She laughs as the blur of fur and tongue flings himself at her.

'Stan, hey. C'mon now,' Michael says firmly, and they all head into a cosy dining kitchen.

'How long's it been since we last saw each other?' Pearl asks him.

'Oh, well over twenty years. Closer to thirty, I reckon.' He shakes his head. 'Terrible, isn't it?'

'It really is. But you've hardly changed at all.' It's true. His mid-brown hair is flecked with a little silver and he's more powerfully built than Pearl remembers. His life up here clearly involves a lot of physical work. But that aside, he doesn't look so very different from the last time she saw him.

'And neither have you,' he says.

Pearl laughs off the compliment, her gaze skimming the bluey-green Aga, the softly worn oak table and shelves neatly stacked with crockery and cookware. Stan has already installed himself in a basket in a corner. Although the kitchen feels rustic, there are contemporary touches in the form of abstract paintings in muted greens, and a sparkling beaded curtain hangs in a doorway. Eclectic is how Pearl would describe it; a favoured magazine term back in the day.

'Your place is beautiful,' Lena announces.

'And I *love* that curtain!' Pearl indicates the glittering beads, red and orange and gold, like a sunset.

'Oh, that?' Michael shrugs. 'Rona wanted it, but then she decided it really belongs here. We bought it in India,' he adds.

'It's all so homely,' Shelley enthuses. 'I bet your guests love it.'

'They seem to,' Michael says lightly. 'I just want people to kick back and feel at home here. They're mostly walkers and outdoorsy types and they don't expect luxury. Let me show you your room,' he adds.

As Michael leads them out of the kitchen and along a short corridor, Pearl senses relief settling in her chest. She hadn't known for sure how it would be to arrive here en masse. The adult Michael is a little shy, she surmises. Or perhaps over the years he has developed a way of dealing with guests when they arrive. Welcoming, yes – but in the manner of a professional host. That's fine, she decides. They'll respect his space and take care not to create extra work for him.

Michael stops, looking apologetic as he shows the three women into a spacious room with a double and a single fold-out bed. 'I'm sorry the three of you are all crammed in here together,' he says. 'It's not what I'd planned. But I had a last-minute booking and they wanted the family room. I could let you have the bigger room tonight, and then move you into here when they arrive tomorrow—'

'All that extra work?' Pearl exclaims. 'This is fine, Michael. Honestly, there's plenty of space for us…'

'Two of you don't mind sharing a double?'

'Of course not,' Lena says firmly.

'We've had holidays when all three of us have crammed into a bed together,' Shelley adds. 'And this is *beautiful*.' She looks around the simply furnished room, taking in the whitewashed bare stone walls, the soft mohair blankets and sheepskin throws.

'Well, if you're sure. It's a couple with just the one child,' he adds. 'So it shouldn't be too rowdy…'

'It'll be lovely to have people around,' Pearl says. 'We're just grateful to be here, like you wouldn't believe.'

'Great.' Michael pushes his hands into his jeans pockets, seeming relieved. 'So they're arriving tomorrow afternoon. There'll be another guest too, in the smallest room. All staying Saturday and Sunday night...'

'So there'll be a houseful.' Lena turns to him with a smile.

'Yeah.' He nods. 'But I always kick them out straight after breakfast and they're not allowed back in until five.'

'Really?' Shelley blinks in surprise, and he chuckles.

'No, not really. That was the old-fashioned way of doing things...'

'You'd be slung out all day, whatever the weather,' Lena agrees. 'I remember that. We stayed at a place in Skegness when I was a kid. We'd all be shivering on the beach, desperate to be let back in.'

'Things are a bit more modern now,' Michael explains. 'Guests are welcome to come and go as they want, and there's always a fire on in the lounge. Plenty of books and films and games in there if the weather's bad. Which, to be honest, isn't unusual up here. Anyway,' he adds quickly, 'would you like some time to settle in?'

'That'd be great,' Pearl says, turning to her friends as he leaves. 'This place,' she murmurs. 'I can hardly believe it.' She rushes to the window and stares out into the moonlit night. The sky is scattered with stars and the loch gleams like silk. 'Come and see this,' she says, and her friends cluster around her as they all gaze out.

She turns to Lena, whose eyes are large and bright with excitement. But Shelley, she notices, looks a little tense. 'You okay, Shell?' she asks.

Shelley nods. 'I'm fine.' Then, after a pause: 'I just... hope everything will be okay, y'know?'

Pearl frowns in concern. 'What, here?'

'No, at home.' Shelley glances distractedly around the room. 'I know what Joel's like. He'll be holed up in his studio the whole time I'm away. Living on beer and cereal, I'd imagine. I just hope he remembers he has kids.'

''Course he will,' Lena says firmly. She winds an arm around her friend's shoulders and pulls her close. 'He's perfectly capable when he wants to be. And really, what can go wrong in four days?'

10

If Joel ever feels guilty about what's going on in his life, he's come up with a nifty list to justify it. It's not just a mental list, tucked away in his brain. He has actually typed it out in Times New Roman (italics), a pleasingly crisp yet classic font designed in the 1930s – a font which, irritatingly, Joel has yet to better. As well as being a graphic designer, Joel also fancies himself as a writer (all those years spent working on magazines) and a bit of a philosopher too. He enjoyed compiling the list and definitely felt better by the end of it. Stored on his Mac in his studio at the top of the house, it goes like this:

1. It doesn't affect my family. I am still a good husband, a good dad.

2. If it wasn't happening, I wouldn't feel right. I'd be miserable and harder to be around. So really, Shelley and the kids benefit.

3. Because of this, I am actually nicer to Shelley than I might be otherwise. So again, she benefits.

4. Shell takes me for granted. Hardly ever interested in sex.

5. We only have one life to live and everyone owes it to themselves to squeeze the maximum fun and joy out of it. Once your one life is gone, it's gone.

Joel was especially pleased with that one. He is thinking of creating a poster using those words.

6. I work so hard and funnel so much of my money into this family that I deserve some kind of reward.

And that's it. That's how Joel justifies his behaviour to himself. While he isn't entirely sure that it would stand up in a court of law, he has played the scenario over and over numerous times since it all started six months ago, and the list always helps to settle his nerves.

That's why he is re-reading it now, on a cold, wet Friday night in their little corner of east London. He is feeling antsy at being left in charge here, and is wondering if there's anything else he can add to it.

Installed at his desk, on his fantastically expensive ergonomic chair, he glances down to assess the state of his stomach. There had been a bit of a paunch developing there, which Shelley had prodded at playfully. 'It's lovely,' she insisted. 'A lovely squidgy daddy-tum.' She'd laughed and hoiked up his self-designed T-shirt (inspired by Soviet-era propaganda poster art) and blown a raspberry on it. But Joel doesn't want a daddy-tum. And thankfully, due to his perpetually highly charged state – not to mention all the extra-curricular physical activity going on – things are definitely looking firmer in that region.

He starts to add another point to the list.

7. It motivates me to take care of myself and keep in shape. Another win for Shelley—

'Dad?'

Joel freezes as if the police had burst in. 'Fin! What d'you want?' He quickly minimises the document.

His son's gaze shifts from the screen to his father's perspiring face. 'Nothing.'

Why are you creeping in here then? Joel wants to snap. Instead, he stands up and rotates his shoulders as if loosening the joints after a punishing evening's work. Then he makes for the open-tread wooden stairs, hoping his son will follow in his slipstream.

'What were you doing?' Fin asks mildly as they trot downstairs.

'Just working on some ideas for a project,' Joel replies. When have his kids ever been remotely interested in what he does? He's just the money machine here. As long as he keeps on landing lucrative jobs, no one cares.

'What's for dinner?' Fin looks at him as they arrive at the kitchen.

'Haven't thought about it,' Joel says tersely.

A silence hovers. 'How long's Mum away?'

'Four nights. She's back on Christmas Eve.' Fin seems to pale and shrink into himself, as if this isn't the news he wanted to hear. Joel isn't best pleased either, although he plans to make the most of his relative freedom while Shelley is away.

'Where's she gone again?' Fin asks. This is all very different, his dad being left in charge of things.

'Scotland,' Joel replies.

'Whereabouts in Scotland?' Fin squints, as if having trouble with the concept.

Joel emits an audible sigh. He grew up in the furthest reaches of east London, in a suburb so dull it makes his scalp itch to think of it. Apart from their annual family package holidays to Spain or Greece – and that long-ago excursion to Glasgow when Shelley had to sit down on the old-lady chair in John Lewis and ask for water – he has barely been out of London at all. As far as he is concerned, the UK is divided into two sections: 'London' and 'Outside London'. The latter, he can't see the point of at all.

'Someplace in the middle of nowhere,' he replies, although he doesn't really know.

'Why's she gone there?'

'Don't know. Just an urge, I suppose.' With a snort and an eye roll, Joel tries to engage his son in a silent man-to-man exchange. *Women, eh?* But

Fin isn't biting. 'Why don't you go and watch TV?' Joel suggests impatiently.

Fin blinks at him. He doesn't 'watch TV'; he gains all of his visual stimulation via his laptop and phone. His dad might as well have suggested he pop off and listen to the wireless. But he leaves the kitchen anyway, and soon Joel becomes aware of a mumbled conversation between Fin and Martha in the living room.

Feeling weighted down by having to care for his kids, Joel boils enough spaghetti to fuel a football team and grabs a jar of sauce from the cupboard. *Sun ripened Isle of Wight tomatoes and fragrant basil. Made with love,* the label reads. Joel isn't making dinner with love. He slops out ill-tempered spaghetti for his near-silent kids, slumped gloomily at the table. It's a relief when dinner is over, and first Fin heads out to his mate Ajay's, and then Martha announces that she too is meeting 'people', no further information supplied.

Alone now, Joel prowls around the Victorian terraced house that they almost bankrupted themselves to buy when Shelley was pregnant with Fin. It's as if he needs to reassure himself that no one is hiding away in any of the rooms or cupboards. He even checks the tiny downstairs loo and the cupboard under the stairs. Although he is often alone here during the day, when Shelley is at work and the kids are at school, tonight's aloneness has taken on a different quality.

There's something almost *thrilling* about it. It's like those rare occasions when his parents went out to meet friends at the pub, a fake Tudor monstrosity with a terrible font on its signage close to Epping Forest. Left home alone, the teenage Joel would raid their drinks cabinet and concoct audacious cocktails incorporating all the spirits, topped up with the sangria they'd brought back from Lloret de Mar in a bottle shaped like a bull.

Tonight's aloneness is like that. It feels shiny, like a gift. Because for one thing, it's evening; the start of the last weekend before Christmas. Better still, Joel doesn't have any outstanding work to do, and he isn't about to tackle the dishes. Why should he clear up after his kids, like a servant?

No, tonight Joel has another plan. Leaving the dirty pasta bowls on the table, he bounds upstairs for a swift shower and then, in the bedroom, surveys his naked form in the full-length mirror. He has definitely trimmed down in the belly region and he's not in bad shape for fifty-two. In fact, if he stands up straight to his full six feet and sucks in his stomach, he's actually still pretty hot.

Shelley might not think so, judging by the way she clambers into bed in her flowery pyjamas that remind him of his late nan's curtains and immediately pops her reading glasses on. But someone else does. Someone who seems pretty impressed by his semi-fame as a top graphic designer and who would never wear spectacles in bed.

The thought of this person triggers a spontaneous stirring of Joel's loins. That's what she does to him. It's as if he's a teenager again, hair-triggered to respond to the slightest sexual provocation: watching *Top of the Pops*; glimpsing the bra section of his mum's Grattan catalogue. Even Margot from *The Good Life* could set him off when his hormones were at a rolling boil. But tonight, determined to keep himself for the delights ahead, he tries to dampen his ardour by focusing hard on decidedly non-sexual things: the damp patch on the bedroom ceiling; Shelley reminding him to sluice out the black wheelie bin because something is rotting in the bottom of it. Yep, that's done it. He picks out a plain dark-blue shirt and putty-coloured trousers and his favourite new trainers. Having dressed quickly, he squirts on the new fragrance that was gifted to him, as an extra thank you for his packaging redesign.

Frowning, he messages his kids to say he's meeting a friend for a drink tonight. Do they have their keys?

Yes, replies Fin.

Ye, says Martha.

Thus settled, Joel steps out into the dank December night, mentally adding an extra point to his secret list.

Shelley's fucked off to Scotland – five days before Christmas! – without even clearing it with me. So what does she expect?

11

Shelley is wary of the over-praising of men for doing ordinary things. The fanfare and wild applause when, say, a father helps his young daughter up onto the slide and then waits to catch her at the bottom. 'Aren't you a marvellous dad!' an elderly lady exclaimed once, when Joel had done precisely that. 'You deserve a medal!'

What about me? Shelley thought. What about the millions of times she'd brought Martha and Fin to the park in the rain, and pushed those swings while Joel stayed at home, having said he had 'stuff to get on with'? Why hadn't anyone rushed over and said *she* deserved a medal? Yet despite this, there is something about Michael and the way he seems to run things here – singlehandedly, it appears – that Shelley can't help but be impressed by.

'So, if guests want the dinner option, we eat here all together,' he explains as they rejoin him in the kitchen. 'But you don't need to do that. It's your weekend and you've come a long way for this. Just come and go as you like—'

'We'd love to eat with you,' Shelley cuts in, turning to her friends. 'Wouldn't we?'

'Of course,' Lena says. 'But only if it's no trouble...'

'Only if you have space for us,' Pearl adds. 'And if you let us cook.'

'Yes, just tell us what to do,' Lena insists, even though her culinary skills are decidedly limited. All those years with her faithless ex-husband, she had vowed to crash-course her way through Jamie Oliver's early works in preparation for the family they planned to have. However, she had never quite got around to it.

'Honestly, it's no trouble,' Michael says firmly. He hands them generous glasses of wine and pours a small one for himself. 'I've been doing this for so long, it pretty much runs like clockwork. I have my systems,' he adds with a smile.

'So how many will there be tomorrow night?' Pearl asks.

'Um, the Sampsons are a family of three, and then there's the single guy, Niall-someone – a hillwalker, I'm guessing – and you three, and me. So that's eight. That's pretty normal. There aren't many other options for eating around here,' he explains, turning away to tend to their supper.

Although all three offer to help, Michael insists that everything is in hand. He sets the table with charmingly mismatched china, and lights the cluster of creamy candles sitting in a bowl surrounded by holly sprigs. Chatter flows easily as their glasses are topped up. 'You've brought way too much,' Michael insisted earlier as he unpacked their gifts. 'But thank you.'

Now he's back at the stove, busying away without an iota of fuss. Shelley can't help observing, in the manner of an examiner at a home economics practical exam, as first a whole baked salmon emerges from the Aga, surrounded by perfectly roasted fennel and tomatoes, to be scattered with fresh herbs. *Top marks!* A tray of roasted baby potatoes follows, and a green salad is tossed and served in a huge earthenware bowl.

There's no banging or crashing or swearing here at Shore Cottage. Crucially, the kitchen hasn't been destroyed in the process. *Excellent presentation and thoughtful, methodical processes. A-plus!* Somehow, Michael seems to be capable of cooking, serving and clearing up after himself, all while sipping wine and chatting with his guests.

As they eat, Shelley replays Joel's performance in making that mountain of over-fired cheese on toast the other night. There'd been an explosion of crumbs, a liberally buttered worktop – and a bleeding finger, for crying out loud, as if a toddler had been let loose with a knife. But then, this is Michael's job, she reminds herself. Clearly, he is well practised at welcoming in strangers, and asking everyone about their jobs, families and lives. She also notices that, while he tops up their glasses, and makes sure there is a chilled bottle of wine on the table – they are on their second already – he is spinning out a single glass.

'Have some more,' Pearl urges him. 'It's only us. You can kick back yourself tonight.'

Michael hesitates. 'Oh, why not? This is a night off for me.' He chuckles. 'I tend to forget what that actually is.'

'It must feel like you're always *on*,' Lena suggests, 'when you have guests.'

'Yeah.' He nods. 'It's funny, because most of them are lovely and we keep in touch. And I have my regulars who've come back again and again. But even so...' He tails off.

'You're still hosting,' Shelley suggests.

'Yes, exactly.'

'But d'you enjoy it?' Pearl probes him. 'Running this place, I mean?'

'Oh, yes,' he says, and she catches a moment's hesitation. 'Like I said, most of the guests are great. But there's the odd rude one, you know? Demanding types. A bit, "Hey!"—' He clicks his fingers sharply, mimicking a rude customer in a restaurant.

'I hate that,' Lena exclaims. It had been a trait of her ex-husband's and she'd pulled him up on it many times. All through university Lena had juggled numerous waitressing jobs and was familiar with diners forgetting that she was an actual person.

'Oh, it's par for the course,' Michael says lightly. 'I guess I've become pretty immune to it.' A small pause settles, and Stan stretches and yawns, limbering up as he gets up from his basket. When he potters over it's Shelley he makes for, nuzzling her hand.

'Stan,' Michael starts, but Shelley assures him it's fine. Keen to have someone at home who'd be happy to see her, she has mooted the suggestion of getting a dog. The kids were keen and immediately checked out some rescue centres' websites. But Joel proclaimed that, as the home worker, he'd be lumbered with all the walking and care. So she let the idea drop.

'So, Michael,' Pearl says, emboldened by wine now, 'please tell me if I'm being nosey here.' She pauses. 'But I just wondered—'

'How come I'm running this place by myself?' His brows raise and he smiles.

She squirms a little. 'It just seems like a lot to manage.'

Michael sips his wine. 'It wasn't planned like this,' he starts. 'Can you believe I'd never been to the Highlands before I saw this place?' Pearl shakes her head. 'It was all Rona's idea,' he explains, looking around at all of them. 'We were still young, mid-twenties, neither of us massively happy in our jobs down south. She'd always had this fantasy of finding a little place in the middle of nowhere and turning it into the perfect B&B—'

'And it is!' Shelley beams at him and raises her glass.

Michael laughs. 'I don't know about that. But we started looking around, and we had a sort of exploratory holiday up here and we found this cottage. We took it on as a rental at first, and then the owner asked if we'd be interested in buying...' The 'we' hangs significantly. Clearly, there is no 'we' now. '...We'd become friends with her by then,' he continues to his rapt audience. 'Lovely lady, she was. She didn't have any family of her own and I think she'd become pretty fond of Rona and me. So we bought it at a bit of a bargain.'

'Sounds like it was meant to be,' Shelley offers, and he smiles wryly.

'We thought so at the time. But for Rona, it wasn't. She hated the isolation here, the constant cooking and gardening and ironing of sheets—'

'You iron sheets?' exclaims Lena, who doesn't iron anything at all.

Michael chuckles. 'A necessary evil, I'm afraid. So Rona started commuting to a job in Inverness, but that didn't work out either. And then she headed back south – that was around ten years ago – and that was the end of us really. And it's been a one-man operation ever since.'

The three women allow this information to settle. 'And how long have you been here?' Lena asks.

'Over twenty years altogether,' he replies. 'God, that's scary.' He gets up from the table, and as everyone leaps up to help, it's clear that they are getting in the way, and that Michael is perfectly capable of stacking the dishwasher himself.

Politely, he ushers them through to the cosy low-ceilinged lounge where a real Christmas tree is decorated with multicoloured glass baubles and twinkling lights. The mantlepiece is decked with pinecones and sprigs of fir and holly, with strings of tiny warm white lights twisted through.

'Oh, this is so gorgeous,' Shelley announces, briefly remembering buying this year's tree from the guy in the old launderette and hauling it home by herself. And how was she greeted, after all her efforts? With mockery and criticism that she hadn't managed to put it up straight. Here a real fire is flickering, and Stan flops onto a floor cushion in front of it with an audible sigh. Like the kitchen, this room is a delightful mishmash of old and new, with a softly worn leather sofa and stylish contemporary easy chairs. There are deeply tufted woollen rugs and more exposed stone walls.

Minutes later Michael joins them with the wine in an ice bucket, and sets it on the low table. 'So, I'm guessing you'll all be up for a full Scottish breakfast,' he says. 'I mean, the full works with Shore Cottage eggs.'

'Oh, you have hens?' Shelley asks in surprise.

'Yep, eight girls. I hope you like eggs?'

'Love them,' she replies as Stan, perhaps overheating a little, jumps up and pushes his way in between her and Pearl on the sofa.

'Stan, down—' Michael starts, but Shelley stops him.

'He's lovely. Please let him stay here. How long have you had him?'

'Couple of years,' Michael replies. 'He was on a local farm but useless as a working dog. They wanted to get rid of him, so...'

Shelley ruffles the soft fur behind his ears, wanting to ask so much more, and not just about Stan. She is naturally curious, and something about Michael's situation here twists her heart. How must it be, living for years alone, miles from anywhere near the end of an unmade road? But she is also conscious of *inventing* a story for him; that here is this somewhat tragic middle-aged man, desperately lonely, despite the steady stream of guests.

And actually, there is nothing tragic about Michael at all. At least, not in so far as she has gleaned tonight. So why does her mind run away like this?

The answer seems to hit her squarely in the gut as Stan's sandpapery tongue laps at her hand. Emboldened by wine now, Pearl has asked

Michael how he might possibly meet anyone, living out here, miles from anywhere.

'Well, there sort of is someone,' he replies.

And as he starts to share his story, Shelley decides that it's not Michael who's the tragic one. It's her.

12

'We're being far too nosey,' Pearl declares, although she is hungry for details. She wants to go to bed satisfied that Michael has the happy relationship he deserves.

'No, no, it's fine.' He hesitates and looks around the room, as if not sure how to put it. 'I've been... sort of talking to someone.'

'Oh, someone local?' Lena asks.

'Not exactly. She's in the States, upstate New York...' He gets up to poke at the fire momentarily. It's clearly a distraction from delving into further details. Pearl feels bad now for even bringing up the subject of dating.

'How long's it been going on?' asks Shelley, who has no such qualms.

'Erm, around nine months. First time we did a call, we talked for three hours.'

'So... you haven't met?' she ventures.

'No, not yet.'

'She's in the States,' Lena reiterates, but Michael shakes his head.

'She's actually on a layover in London around now. Just about arrived, I should think. She's a flight attendant,' he adds.

'How long's she there for?' Shelley asks eagerly.

'Until Monday. So, three days. A last-minute thing. A colleague didn't want to do the London flight so Krissy took it. They do that sometimes, apparently. When they get their rosters and there's a flight someone doesn't want to do.' He breaks off and smiles. Now he's warming up, Pearl decides as she tops up everyone's glasses. She had worried that they might be a little much, the three of them as gang. But at nearly midnight Michael is showing no signs of wanting to call it a night.

'I've learnt a lot about rosters,' he adds with a grin.

'So, what's she like?' Pearl asks.

He shrugs, and for a moment it's as if he's a teenage boy being grilled about his first girlfriend by his aunties. 'Just a really lovely person. We seemed to click,' he adds. 'You know when you feel like the conversation could go on forever?'

Pearl nods, realising she never had that feeling with Elias, and wondering how she'd got it so wrong. 'How often d'you talk?' she asks.

'As often as we can. Most days, when she's not working—'

'We're grilling you.' Pearl catches herself. 'I'm sorry—'

'It's okay, honestly.' He laughs.

'—But I have to ask you one very important question,' she adds. She laces her fingers together and leans towards him.

His brown eyes catch the light of the fire. 'What's that?'

'Er... why are you here, Michael?'

He frowns, as if not getting it. 'You mean, why aren't I in London?'

'Yes!' she said emphatically. 'You should've told us she was coming over. We could've planned our trip for the new year, or spring or even later—'

'I actually didn't know,' he cuts in, 'when we arranged your visit. And also, there are guests coming—'

'But the family only booked in at the last minute,' Lena reminds him.

'Yes, but the other guy booked weeks ago and I didn't want to mess him around,' Michael states firmly. 'He seemed especially keen to stay here. Said it was exactly the kind of place he'd been looking for...'

'Well, I think you should have,' Pearl announces with uncharacteristic boldness. 'A weekend in London with Krissy, who you talk to almost every day?' *And who you're besotted with,* she wants to add.

Michael looks around at the three friends and shrugs in a 'what-could-I-do?' kind of way. 'Just bad timing. But it's not really, is it?' he adds quickly.

'It's great you're here. I couldn't believe it, actually. That you could come up before Christmas.'

'Neither could we.' Shelley laughs.

'Can we see a picture of her?' Pearl asks. Michael looks surprised, but then goes to fetch his phone. They all crowd around him on the soft leather sofa as he brings up photos of Krissy. She's strikingly beautiful, in her mid-forties perhaps – although they are all holding back from demanding further information. Her hair is glossy and dark, her skin creamy, her eyes big and brown. And something seems to happen to Michael as he talks about how she has brought up her son alone, and the child stays with her mother when Krissy is working. How she has worked hard all those years in order to raise him, and lives in a little wooden house by a river. He seems to light up, and appears a little surprised by his own effusiveness as he slips his phone into his pocket.

'She sounds lovely,' Shelley announces.

'She is. But she also lives over three thousand miles away.'

Michael gets up then to let Stan out into the garden. As cool air gusts in, Shelley's mind flickers to her terraced house and her life there. It's okay most of the time. She loves her friends and her job, and Martha and Fin of course, even though they've turned sour, like milk – Martha especially. And mostly, Shelley does the proverbial rolling-up-sleeves thing, and they all get by. But occasionally, she is startled by something – like a dazzling light shone into her eyes. And she can't tell anyone – not even Lena or Pearl – that when the light shines, she *knows* it. That falling in love with Joel was a mistake.

Of course, if she hadn't, there would be no Martha or Fin. But her mind doesn't work that way when the light dazzles.

And here is a man who grafts away alone, and has a chance of happiness. What was that thing she'd spotted on Joel's desk, when she'd ventured in to dust his studio? He'd written it on a scrap of paper and left it there.

Once your one life is gone, it's gone.

Probably just a doodle, she'd surmised. And she thought it should be '*has* gone', rather than '*is*.' But never mind that now, because the sentiment seems to ring loud and clear in her head.

Michael could go to London to see Krissy.

She looks at Lena and Pearl, who are admiring the hand-made ceramics dotted around the snug little room, and agreeing how perfect the cottage is. 'Girls,' she starts, biting her lip. 'I've had an idea.'

'What is it, Shell?' Lena looks quizzical.

'You're going to think I've gone mad,' Shelley replies. 'But what if we can persuade Michael to go to London? D'you think we could look after things here?'

13

There are so many things Joel loves about London. The way it makes him feel, for one: buzzy and connected and at the centre of the world, as if every other place is a mere offshoot. He loves living in a city where there is the Tate Modern and the Royal Academy and the Barbican, although he rarely visits these places. In fact, the part of London he is especially keen on currently is a little one-bedroomed flat in a converted church in Finsbury Park.

The flat belongs to a photographer called Carmel Levine. Carmel doesn't care that Joel is married and she isn't remotely interested in his kids. He'd known her a little through a fashion magazine he'd worked on – the last staff job he'd had, before he went freelance – and then run into her by chance at a friend's private view in Shoreditch. Joel had only gone along for the free booze.

He had always found her attractive, but that night she seemed especially so. Gone was the sharp brown bob; she had let her natural silver grow out, and it was warmer – *sexier*. Coupled with her customary red lipstick, it gave her the air of a French film actress, and Joel was delighted that she was giving him so much attention that night. He'd always assumed that this confident six-footer with the body of a runway model thought he was a bit of a buffoon. However, that night they'd flirted wildly and gone on for more drinks. Then they'd headed back to the flat where Carmel lives alone.

The sex had been, to put it mildly, astounding and a world apart from Shelley in her nana-curtain pyjamas. They fell into a pattern of meeting once a week or so, always the same routine: quick pint in the pub at the end of her road and then back to her place.

There, things have been somewhat *less* routine. Out of bed, Carmel is all husky laughter and affectionate touches with everyone she encounters. In bed that first time, she had him blindfolded and lashed him to her bedhead with a pair of stockings. Since then he's become accustomed to hearing her rummaging about, assembling her array of props, switching things on, ripping the packaging off various gizmos. He marvels at how a woman can exist in a compact little flat like this one, yet produce so much stuff. Where does it all go, he wonders? Is there a secret sex toy vault under the floor?

Tonight Joel lies on Carmel's bed with her silk-lined leather blindfold pinching a little above his ears, virtually quivering in anticipation as to what she might be about to do to him. As long as it doesn't give him an electric shock – or mark him – Joe doesn't mind. That first night he'd gone home with a tiny scratch on his left buttock. He'd been paranoid and wondered how the hell he might cover it, or explain it away. But of course, Shelley pays no attention to his bottom or indeed any of his bodily parts and hadn't noticed anything untoward. Too busy reading her doorstopper novel with her glasses on.

Now Joel can hear distant potterings and surmises that Carmel has gone to the kitchen. Could they *possibly* get a move on here? He actually has a home to go to! Briefly, he wonders if the kids are home yet and, if so, what they'll think when he's not there. But Carmel was in the mood for chatting tonight, and shunned his repeated suggestions of going straight to bed. Instead, she took what felt like forever over a couple of large glasses of red wine.

He won't be home too late, Joel reassures himself. It was only midnight last time he looked, and he'll be back in twenty minutes in an Uber—

Instantly Joel's travel-related musings evaporate as suddenly Carmel is on top of him, flicking him sharply with the leather fronds of her whip. He is hard instantly and now inside her. And somehow it all happens too fast, maybe due to his desperation to see her, what with his house being empty and being able to do what he likes for once, and all the preamble chit-chat about her recent shoots and the funny thing her assistant did, and has he been following a certain political story in the news?

No, he hasn't been following the news! He's been following his penis to Flat 2, Rowan House, London N4 – and he needs her too much. That's the problem.

Carmel clambers off him without comment and Joel tugs off the blindfold. His heart seems to sink as he registers her blasé demeanour as she shrugs on her silk robe and belts it tightly. At her wardrobe mirror, she smoothes her hair and leans in, checking her face – as if she is having a quiet night in alone. While Joel doesn't expect rapturous applause for his performance tonight, he'd appreciate *some* acknowledgement that something has happened.

He sits up and pats the space beside him on her bed. 'Come back here, babe,' he murmurs.

She glances round at him. 'Shouldn't you be getting home?'

For a moment, Joel feels quite used. 'Shelley's away,' he announces.

'Really?'

'Yeah, she's in Scotland till Tuesday. On a jaunt with her mates...'

'Very nice,' Carmel says, displaying an utter lack of interest.

Joel frowns at her. 'D'you realise what this means?'

Carmel looks at him and smirks. 'You can live on bowls of Weetabix.'

'I don't live on Weetabix!' he exclaims. 'I can cook, y'know. I'm pretty *domesticated*...'

'Oh, really?' Her nostrils flare. 'So, what *does* it mean then?'

'It means I can stay with you for the whole night. Not tonight,' he adds quickly, hauling himself out of her bed now. 'I told the kids I was only going out for a drink so I'd better get back.'

She regards him dispassionately. He doesn't expect her to start asking about Fin's and Martha's interests or wanting to see their school reports. Yet it feels a little off, that she doesn't even acknowledge this unavoidably significant side of his life. Whenever he mentions his kids he sees her eyes glazing over as if she is rapidly slipping into a trance. He might as well be talking about radiators.

'Okay,' she says mildly.

Joel gathers up his clothes from her bedroom floor and dresses quickly. 'Tomorrow I could, though.' He is already forming a plan to tell his kids that there's some event way across town. A major exhibition opening, with an after party. Conveniently, he'll be staying over with friends close by.

The prospect of spinning a yarn to Martha and Fin troubles him no more than lying to Shelley. When they were younger, the kids adored him, screaming in delight whenever he chased them around the park, being a bear. Now though, they regard him as an embarrassing old man. He's registered the eye rolls as he's told them about the raves he used to go to; how wild it was with the smiley T-shirts and dancing in fields. He put on a track once – 'Loaded' by Primal Scream. He started throwing shapes in the kitchen and popped a Cheerio into his mouth, joking that it was a disco biscuit. 'That was a silly name for ecstasy,' he explained as they gawped at him. 'Not that I ever did drugs, kids! Just say no!' He might as well have been dancing naked, judging by their horrified expressions. Maybe they'd understand it more if he was wearing the right outfit? He rushed off and came back wearing his favourite trousers – his phat pants, banana yellow with a squiggly pattern – and Martha looked as if she might throw up.

'All right,' Carmel says now.

'All right?' Joel repeats. 'Is that it?'

She blinks in surprise. 'What d'you want me to say?'

'I just thought…' He frowns, trying to mentally bat away the sulk he can sense about to come over him like a wave. 'I just thought it'd be nice to wake up together. That's all.'

'Oh, okay.' She shrugs and nods, in that couldn't-care-less way, like when the guy in the newsagent asks you which lighter you'd like, and frankly you have no opinion whatsoever. 'That'd be nice,' she adds.

Joel inhales slowly. 'I thought you'd be pleased.'

'I *am* pleased. It's fine! Let's have a sleepover!' Amusement dances in her dark brown eyes. 'So, when is this momentous occasion happening?'

'Tomorrow! I just said.' The thing with Carmel is, you can never tell when she's taking the piss.

'Okay. Great.' No-need-to-ask-which-colour-of-lighter-I want-just-gimme-one-that-works.

He sits heavily on the edge of her bed and pulls on his new trainers, aware that he is definitely sulking, and also aware how unattractive it must be. Then he kisses Carmel goodbye and travels home in an Uber, ashamed now of his behaviour, as if it was an embarrassing jacket – called 'The Sulk' – that he can't shrug off.

He'll make it up to her tomorrow night, he decides. Tomorrow, they will spend the entire night together, and Joel can't wait.

14

FOUR DAYS UNTIL CHRISTMAS

It's too much, Michael insisted last night. He couldn't expect them to look after everything here. It was a lovely idea, and fantastically kind of them – but no.

However, as a trio, Pearl, Lena and Shelley are quite a force, and they insisted that everything would be fine. That as a make-up artist, a charity's content writer and a care home receptionist they were fully equipped to look after his guests.

He'd looked baffled at that part. 'We're used to *people*,' Shelley insisted. 'And we're hard working and organised and can cope with whatever's thrown at us.' *And two of us have kids,* she wanted to add. *D'you think we're not used to dealing all kinds of demands?*

By the time a third bottle of wine was finished, Michael had agreed to at least check if flights were available. And to okay a visit with Krissy, of course. So first he messaged her, and then set down his phone and looked at Pearl. 'She really wants me to come down,' he said. 'She'd wanted to suggest it but thought there was no chance. She knows I can't just up and leave this place on a whim.'

'Well, you can now,' Pearl said firmly as he got up, and they hugged. Then Shelley hugged him, and Lena too. It was clear then that Michael was unaccustomed to such displays of affection and he quickly stepped away, professional-host demeanour now firmly back in place.

'Are you absolutely sure about this?' he asked.

'Of course we are!' Shelley beamed at him.

'It's not just the wine talking?'

'No,' Lena insisted. 'It's crazy you being here when you could be there. Imagine how you'll feel if you don't do it?'

Michael still looked doubtful. 'Okay then, if you're absolutely set on this.' His gaze skimmed the room. 'There's a lot to go through, to tell you about. But I think we'd better do that in the morning, if that's all right?'

''Course it is,' Pearl said firmly. 'Now off you go and book your flights.'

And now, on a bright and frost-sparkly morning, Michael greets them a little blearily in the kitchen. 'How are you?' Pearl asks as he pushes back his rumpled hair. It's outgrown its cut, but it suits him.

'Okay. I'm all good.'

She smiles. 'So you've booked your flight?'

'Yep, I have. Nothing from Inverness, and nothing available from Glasgow to Heathrow either. That's where Krissy's staying – at an airport hotel. But I managed to get one from Glasgow to Stansted so that'll do fine...' He pauses, looking apologetic. 'I need to head off pretty soon. Can I show you everything? I'm sorry, I don't think there's time for me to do the full Scottish breakfast. But there's plenty of bacon and eggs and—'

'Please don't worry about that,' Lena says quickly. 'We can look after ourselves.'

His looks suggests that he is still uncertain about leaving. But he murmurs, 'I'm sure you can,' and then, as if to distract himself, he gives Stan his breakfast. 'Dog food's in the utility room. A cupful, twice a day—'

'We can look after Stan,' Shelley says impatiently.

'Right. Okay. You'll find fire lighters and tonnes of old newspaper in there too. For the fire...' He catches himself. 'Sorry, I'm stating the obvious.'

'Michael, we'll figure it all out,' Pearl says. 'Why not give us a whistle-stop tour and then you can go?'

So that's what he does, taking them out into the rambling garden with its vegetable patch and herb pots and several rickety outbuildings. The frosty grass crunches underfoot and their breath forms puffs of white in the sharp morning air. Beyond the garden a misty haze hangs low over the still waters of the loch.

Stan potters around them as Michael leads the three women past the raspberry canes to the bottom of the garden. Here the hens live in a little wooden house and a wire mesh-covered run.

'Oh, they're gorgeous!' As Shelley bobs down to ground level, her instinct is to capture them in photos. With plumage ranging through pale beige, rust red and black with white speckles, she hadn't realised they were quite so beautiful. 'Look at their little pink combs and dangly bits under their chins!' she announces, but Michael is in no mood for such fripperies.

'So, their food's in the big tub in the shed...' He indicates a hut almost entirely swathed in ivy. 'There's a tap there too. All you need to do is keep their feeder and water dispenser topped up, and make sure their water doesn't freeze...'

'Don't they get cold?' Lena asks, shivering now in her lambswool sweater and jeans.

'They don't mind it,' Michael replies. 'They just puff up their feathers and they'll go into the house if they want to.'

'So we don't put them to bed?' Shelley asks.

'No.' He frowns, as if unsure whether she is joking. 'You don't put them to bed. Their run is secure so as long as you keep the door shut, they'll be fine.' He strides away now, checking the time as he goes, with Stan, Pearl, Lena and Shelley in pursuit. 'That's the woodshed.' He indicates another wooden structure, roofed but open to the elements at one side with logs neatly stacked. 'Plenty of logs and kindling – and the axe if you need it.' Pearl arranges her face to suggest that, as a London-dwelling make-up artist, chopping logs is par for the course in her normal day.

Michael stops. 'You're okay, aren't you, with lighting a fire?'

'Of course,' Shelley announces, remembering Guide camp fire duties in something like 1983. She's confident that it will all come flooding back. Back indoors, Michael whisks them into the large family bedroom with its en suite, all made up and ready for the Sampson family, and the smaller room for a man called Niall Dixon, all of whom are due to arrive in the early afternoon. The guests' shower room is gleaming, and heather-scented toiletries are lined up neatly on the shelf.

'What else?' Michael murmurs distractedly. 'Yes, breakfasts. You'll find everything you need in the pantry and fridge. Bacon, eggs, cereals, bread, preserves...'

'And dinner?' Pearl asks, sensing his growing agitation as he marches back to the kitchen. The same thing happens to her when it comes to going away. It always has, since Dean died and suddenly she was in sole charge of taking Brandon on holiday. Somehow her husband had become Keeper of Passports and Booker of Flights, and he'd always have researched places to go and things to do. All Pearl had to do back then was pack. And now here she was, 100 per cent responsible for Brandon having a holiday to remember.

Michael turns to her. 'You know I mentioned my systems? It might sound obsessive but I need to have everything organised up front. It's how I've operated since I realised I'd be running the show myself.' The women nod, listening with rapt attention. 'So,' he continues, 'everything's home cooked from scratch and frozen in portions, okay? It's all labelled very clearly. So it'll just need defrosting and re-heating in the Aga...'

'Erm, where are the controls?' Lena eyes the enormous appliance somewhat warily.

'There aren't any. It's on all the time. You don't need to do anything...' He catches Pearl frowning at the confusing array of hotplates and doors. 'Here's your boiling plate and simmering plate,' he explains, 'and that's your roasting oven, your simmering oven, your slow cooking and warming ovens...' She nods sagely, wondering what bright spark at the Aga factory came up with the idea of not labelling any of the oven doors. It seems like a cruel joke, like being instructed to drive a car without anyone explaining what the different pedals do. Still, they can google it later. They'll find their way around this cast-iron beast and, more importantly, they'll have helped to orchestrate Michael getting together with his long-distance love.

He pats it affectionately. 'That all okay?'

'Yep, absolutely,' Shelley chirps. 'Or we could just give them fish and chips?'

Michael frowns. 'I'm afraid the nearest chippy's over an hour's round trip.'

'I was joking,' she mutters, but now Michael is hurriedly wrapping up his instructions. 'Now, for dinners, if you look on the chalkboard in the utility room, everything's detailed there. What they're all having, I mean – for Saturday and Sunday night. I send out the menus well before guests arrive. So they've already made their choices.' He pauses as if to check that all of the information has been absorbed so far. 'Okay?' he says.

'Yep, got that.' Pearl senses herself snapping to attention.

'There's plenty of veg and salads in the pantry and fridge,' he adds. 'I'm licensed to serve alcohol with dinner and there's plenty of wine and beers, if they want it. Of course, help yourselves to anything...' He rakes back his hair. 'I'd normally bake a loaf but I'm sorry, there hasn't been time. Oh, and there's a folder in the lounge, full of info on walks around here. And there's Wi-Fi of course. It's patchy but it works...' He looks at the three women in their jeans and light knitwear. 'Did you bring warm enough clothes? There are jackets and wellies in the utility room. And hats, gloves, torches...'

'In case there's a power cut.' Shelley nods.

'Well, in case you need to go out after dark.' For a moment, Michael looks uncertain that he can trust them at all. 'And there are plenty of waterproof trousers,' he adds.

'Waterproof trousers?' Pearl laughs. 'I don't think so...'

'You might need them.' He smiles briefly. 'Okay, I think that's everything. I hope you have time to explore. There's my boat, if you get the chance to go out on the loch. Oars are there too. It's down on the beach. Sorry I won't be here to take you out on it...'

'Next time,' Pearl says firmly.

He nods. 'So, you'll tell the guests I've had to go away?'

'Yep,' Lena says. 'We'll see them off on Monday morning, like you said...'

'And I'll be back on Monday afternoon. So at least we'll have a bit of time together.' Michael swings his small rucksack onto one shoulder and, with Stan bounding at his side, he strides out and dumps it on the backseat of his car. Pearl, Lena and Shelley all hug him, and he reciprocates somewhat stiffly. 'Call me any time, if anything happens. I mean anytime at all,' he adds.

'We will,' Shelley gushes. 'We promise.'

The tension leaves his eyes as he seems to believe, finally, that Shore

Cottage B&B might possibly operate for two nights without him. 'I can't thank you all enough,' he adds. 'It's so incredibly generous...'

'Honestly, it's nothing,' Pearl insists.

'But you do realise we're going to leave you a terrible Tripadvisor review,' Shelley teases. '"Host buggered off to London leaving us to look after ourselves!"'

Michael laughs. 'I know I've just thrown an awful lot of information at you. But if you could remember to ask the guests to write in the visitors' book—'

'*Bye*, Michael.' Shelley grins, and he climbs into his car and lowers the window.

'Have a great time, won't you? Really, I just need you to hold the fort.' And with that, and a quick wave goodbye, he pulls away up the gravelled track, and then he's gone.

15

Tommy isn't one of those hapless men who exists on bowls of cereal whenever his partner is away. He has several friends who fit this description: full-grown adults with whom he went to boarding school. Men who have somehow reached their fifties and can still barely boil an egg. They boast about it, affecting a 'wife's-away' swagger as if maintaining a smooth-running home is baffling and actually beneath them. Briefly liberated, they allow the washing up to accumulate to gargantuan levels, to be attacked like an enemy battalion as 'the wife' drives home from her weekend in the Cotswolds with the girls.

Now Tommy looks around the living room, trying to reassure himself that everything is just so. At least, his and Lena's version of just so – because this little 1960s flat has been furnished on a budget. 'I needed to start afresh,' she'd explained the first time he came here. 'I couldn't be surrounded by all the stuff Max and I had chosen together.'

Tommy admires her ingenuity and he loves this place, because it's Lena's. However, now he worries that it might appear a little shabby – studenty even – in the eyes of someone seeing it for the first time.

He re-plumps a tangerine cushion unnecessarily and picks a tiny speck of something off the candy-striped rug. Burrowing into the muddle under the sink, he manages to locate a duster and runs it over the extendable table where they sit to eat, and where Lena often works. While she does her copy writing mainly from home, as a manager at a high-end recruitment company Tommy is expected to be present in the office. Just as well, as it would be a squeeze for both of them to work in the flat.

Tommy straightens up the books on the over-crammed bookshelf. There are loads about society and politics and world affairs; brainy stuff of Lena's that Tommy wouldn't even pretend to understand (his taste is more pacy thrillers). He wonders what she's doing now with her friends in the Highlands. He remembers visits up there when he was a child, to an aunt and uncle who had a terrifying housekeeper called Miss Maud. Lena has messaged Tommy to let him know they arrived safely, and that everything is wonderful. That was last night. He yearns to hear her voice, but she's told him the signal is patchy, and he doesn't want to be the pesky boyfriend constantly calling to remind her that he exists. But still, he misses her already.

Tommy checks the time on the cheap digital clock on the shelf, wondering if he should have told Lena what's happening today when he messaged. But for some reason, he didn't. He held the information back because he wasn't sure how she'd react. And he doesn't want anything to unsettle her on her trip. Anyway, there was no need to mention it because there's nothing to tell! Absolutely nothing at all! Yet Tommy feels uncomfortable now, as if he has lied by omission. Which he has of course. This is Lena's home, so of course he should have told her.

He worries now that if they speak while she's away, and he tells her after the event, she'll wonder why he didn't mention it earlier. And then what will he tell her?

And now Tommy realises he is absent-mindedly polishing the flex of the wobbly desk lamp. He throws down the duster, marches to the living room window and rubs a smear off it with the cuff of his sweater sleeve.

Calm down, he tells himself. This is not a big deal, you great big idiot. Just calm down and get a grip on yourself.

* * *

Across town, lying flat out on his sofa, Joel replies to Shelley's message from earlier.

JOEL

> Glad you're having fun! Sounds amazing. All fine here don't worry. Remember to take loads of pics!

Fin wanders into the living room and looks quizzically at the Christmas tree that's leaning even more drunkenly than before. Then he glances over at his father, stretched out in a tracksuit and slippers, poking idly at his phone. At fifteen, Fin is starting to formulate some understanding of how a marriage works, and he's noted a marked difference in his dad since his mum went away yesterday morning.

The main thing is, his dad is no longer hiding away upstairs in his studio. It's like the re-wilding thing, Fin reckons, that happened during Covid. Goats venturing off mountains in Wales and wandering through towns, nibbling hedges. Deer strolling through an east London housing estate. Fin is a smart kid and he's figured out that, if you remove the main controlling factor – traffic, society, his mum – then environments re-shape themselves and everything is different. It's a little unsettling, especially his dad being downstairs so much. But now that he's adjusted a little, Fin is finding this new state of affairs pretty interesting. It feels as if there might be cameras concealed around the house, filming a documentary entitled 'Home Without Mum'.

'All right, Fin?' Finally his dad seems to notice that he's there.

'Yeah, I'm all right.' Fin glances briefly at the parcels all arranged under the tree by his mum. They look so enticing with their gold ribbons and bows, and Fin is still young enough to be excited by presents. He has already fondled and rattled a fair few, trying to guess at their contents. 'What're you doing tonight again?' he asks.

'What?' Joel sets his phone face down on the sofa. 'Oh, um... I'm going out actually. Just to a boring gallery opening thing.' As if he has only just remembered. 'Why d'you ask?'

'No reason!' Fin says in an overly casual manner.

Joel peers at him suspiciously and sits up, tugging down the tracksuit bottoms which had ridden up over his calves. It's not the kind of cheap tracksuit worn by local lads who hang around their nearest shopping centre. This is leisure wear, vastly expensive and bought by Joel in the hope that he might have the opportunity to wear it *at leisure* with Carmel at some point. He is growing a little frustrated by these dive-in-dive-out-again sessions, and occasionally he wonders if that's all he is to her: some kind of sex machine. Which is why he has built up tonight – 'our sleepover', as she mockingly called it – into such a monumental event.

'So, what are *you* doing tonight?' Joel asks, keen to switch the focus away from himself.

'Nothing!' Fin starts to leave the room, but Joel calls him back.

'Hey, hang on a minute. You know I've told Martha that she needs to be in tonight, don't you? To look after you. So if you go out you've got to let her know—'

'I don't need looking after,' Fin retorts.

'Yeah, I know son.' Joel's tone softens and he pulls an it's-not-me-it's-your-mum face, despite Shelley currently being 500 miles away. 'It's just, I'd feel better, okay? I know it's silly. Please humour your crazy old man...'

Fin grunts. 'Yeah, okay.' Then, frowning: 'You were out last night as well.'

'I know.' Joel chuckles. 'Two nights in a row. Just like the old days, heheh!' Tension flickers in Fin's pale blue eyes now, as if he's afraid that his father might launch into the dancing-and-disco-biscuit routine that he subjected them to a few weeks ago.

'You weren't on about Martha babysitting me then,' Fin reminds him and stalks out of the room.

Joel jumps off the sofa and scrambles after him. 'No, but tonight I might end up staying out west. It's such a pain getting home at that time—'

'At what time?' Fin stares at him.

'I don't know,' Joel blusters. 'Late, probably. I think there's an after party.'

'An after party?' Martha crows from the landing. 'At an art exhibition?'

'Well, *after* it,' Joel mutters, blushing.

'I thought you said it was going to be boring?' Fin remarks.

'It will. It'll probably will be deathly dull. You know these things.' His kids stare at him. They don't know these things.

'If it's going to be so bad,' Martha says with a sly edge to her voice, 'then why are you bothering going?'

'I just feel obliged to,' he says hotly, as if he is the teenager being grilled.

She smirks. 'Dad, you look really freaked out. Like, you're sweating. Are you worried about us being home without you?'

'No, of course not.'

'We'll be *fine*,' she declares. 'I'll put him to bed at seven-thirty—'

'You will *not*,' Fin exclaims.

'Six-thirty then.' She sniggers.

'Shut up, Marth!' He runs upstairs to meet her on the landing where they launch into a ramshackle play fight which Joel senses is being acted out for his benefit.

'Stop it, you two.' He glares up as they swing each other around ineffectually. 'Is this what's going to happen when I'm out tonight?'

They stop instantly. 'No,' Fin mutters.

He can sense Martha studying him from her vantage point. 'So, you won't be back until morning, then?'

'Maybe. Not definitely. But it's a possibility...' Joel winces as if to underline the fact that the event he's conjured up is an utter inconvenience to him.

'Are you going to "get on one", Dad? Like, take a pill?' Martha teases, and his cheeks flare.

'Don't be silly. It's a cultural thing.'

'Oooh,' she teases. '*Cultural!*'

Ignoring this mockery, he pushes back the slightly thinning hair that he still wears a little bit spiky, styled with gel. 'I'll message to let you know if I'm staying over. Is that all right?' he asks.

She gazes down at him with an inscrutable look on her face. Smart, sassy Martha, who seems to have given up on school of late, but could run rings around many of her teachers with her intellect. 'Sure, Dad,' she says, eyes glazing now, signalling that she has lost interest in his evening plans already.

'So, lunch!' Joel announces with uncharacteristic enthusiasm. 'How about I order us a Nando's?'

'For *lunch*?' Martha gasps.

'Can we have KFC?' Fin asks, and Joel sees a glance exchanged between brother and sister.

'All right,' she concedes, as if it's her who's paying.

'Okay, why not?' Joel swaggers up to the landing and pulls up the menu on his phone. An extensive order is placed – mains, sides *and* desserts, for lunch! Are they taking the piss? Then the kids disperse to their rooms and Joel heads back to his preferred stretched-out position on the sofa, telling himself that sixty-five quid should settle his guilt about heading over to Carmel's tonight. He'll leave them money for a McDonald's later too. They'll be wishing their mum went away more often.

Now Joel checks his phone again for the umpteenth time, to see if Carmel has messaged – she hasn't – and reassures himself that Fin and Martha are capable of looking after themselves for one night. In recent times, Joel and Shelley have occasionally left them alone, when there's been something like a big birthday party out of town (there's been a raft of fiftieths lately). Shelley has checked in with the kids throughout the evening, and everything has been fine. But on this, the last Saturday before Christmas, something feels off kilter. Slightly anxiety-making, as if Joel would actually be better off cancelling his overnighter with Carmel and staying at home instead – or at the very least popping an extra Citalopram. Because something is happening inside his brain, whether serotonin-related or due to something else. And he can't put his finger on what it is.

He leaps up when the delivery guy arrives and summons his kids downstairs for their feast. However, even as Martha and Fin tear into their chicken and fries like starving street dogs, the conscience-clearing effect hasn't quite worked in the way that Joel hoped it would.

Food devoured, the kids scarper, leaving him with an explosion of boxes and smeared paper napkins and greasy bones. Joel is seeing Carmel tonight so he should be delirious with excitement. But something is sitting uneasily in his gut, and it's not just the fried chicken. For the first time since the affair started, Joel seems to have swallowed a side order of guilt.

He goes through to the hallway and calls upstairs. 'Martha? Marth, can I have a word please?'

She emerges, radiating suspicion, from her room. 'What is it?'

'Nothing, hon. Nothing really. I just wanted to say thanks for looking after Fin tonight—'

'That's all right.'

'No, love, I really mean it,' he says, wanting so much for things to feel right here, so he can be free to enjoy the night. 'I appreciate it,' he adds. 'You really are a brilliant girl. Thanks so much for holding the fort.'

16

'This can't be right,' Lena mutters out loud. They mustn't have been listening properly when Michael was dispensing instructions. No wonder, with the workings of a five-oven Aga being explained in under a minute and then him rushing off, anxious to catch that flight.

Lena exhales forcefully and, for the third time, she rummages through the entire contents of Michael's freezer in the utility room. There are vegetables and raspberries and fish fingers and oven chips and a small supermarket-brand broccoli quiche. In the bottom drawer she unearths individually wrapped choc ices and a few loose sweetcorn niblets. But none of the promised home-cooked dishes for them to defrost in time for dinner tonight.

'Are you sure they're not there?' Pearl crouches beside her.

'Yes, unless I'm going completely mad.' Lena looks at her in panic as they both straighten up and assess the situation. 'So much for Michael's systems. What are we going to do for dinner tonight?'

Pearl grimaces and now Shelley joins them in the utility room. 'There are no labelled meals?'

'No!' Lena announces.

'Oh, God.' Pearl's gaze flicks to the wall-mounted chalkboard on which Michael has written the guests' meal choices.

SAT 1 mush 1 chick 2 lamb. All crum.
SUN 1 chick 2 sal 1 mouss. 2 A pie 2 stick.

'What does it all mean?' Lena stares at it.

'Well, there's chicken and lamb...' Pearl suggests as if they are at the initial stage of a crime investigation.

'Yes, I get that,' Lena says impatiently. 'But what kind of chicken and lamb? And what's "mush"?'

'And "crum", "stick" and "mouss"?' Shelley frowns at the board.

'Mousse?' Pearl offers.

'Maybe,' Lena says, 'but what kind, and where the heck is it?'

'There must be some other place.' Shelley looks around the room in panic. Fridge, freezer, cupboard and a rack of hooks piled with jackets; that's about it. There's another fridge in the kitchen but they have already checked it out. She glances briefly at the pile of wellies in a giant wicker basket, and then opens the rickety cupboard. Here are the promised waterproof trousers – several pairs all neatly folded – plus a selection of woolly hats, scarves and gloves. But of course there's no pie in there, nor a mousse.

'Shit,' she murmurs. 'But look, we've got time. The family's not arriving until two-ish so we have hours to figure something out.'

Lena checks her phone. 'Well, *two* hours, Shell. It's nearly twelve already—'

'Yes, but dinner's not until evening, is it? So there's no need to panic.' In her seventeen years of virtually single-handed parenting, Shelley grew accustomed to her kids' friends bowling up unexpectedly, and could stretch out meals to almost biblical degrees. Great cauldrons of chilli and rice were her speciality. Those gargantuan dinners are a thing of the past now, as apparently Martha and Fin would find it mortifying to have their friends sit and eat at their family table. In fact, Shelley is no longer allowed to interact with their friends at all. But she is still programmed to serve the needs of famished children, and is unfazed by the prospect of catering on an industrial scale. 'We can go through what there is,' she continues, 'and figure out what we can cook. We'll just say there's been a change of menu—'

'We can't do that!' Pearl exclaims.

'Why not?' Shelley asks.

'Because they've *chosen* their meals.'

'Well, they can un-choose them! Not the end of the world, is it? How many times d'you eat out and they say sorry, the thing you wanted is off—'

'But not everything,' Pearl protests. 'I've never gone out to dinner and *everything's* been off—'

'Well, it is now,' Shelley says firmly. 'Everything's off due to unforeseen circumstances. They'll just have to deal with that.'

Pearl's green eyes widen. 'But what'll we say?'

'That there's been a problem with our suppliers?' Lena suggests, also looking somewhat stressed.

'Yes, a logistical thing,' Shelley decides. 'There's been a rock fall, a landslide. Surely that happens around here.'

'So how are we going to put it?' Pearl asks. '"Dinner tonight will be an unusual pairing of melted choc ice and crumbled fish finger"—'

'Pearl, it'll be okay,' Shelley says firmly.

'We can garnish it with sweetcorn,' Lena mutters, but Pearl frowns, in no mood for jokes.

'There *must* be another freezer somewhere.' She strides out of the utility room and into the kitchen. To think, just few hours ago she was working through the various steps of her morning skincare routine (she has brought all of her products decanted into mini containers). Then she'd applied light make-up and sent a quick message to Brandon:

PEARL

> Hope all okay love. Happy for you and Abi to get a Deliveroo later if you like.

It's Pearl's account, and despite his girlfriend running roughshod over the flat, she knows he wouldn't order anything without checking with her. She's lucky, she thinks, to have such a decent young man for a son. He wouldn't have guzzled all the best Celebrations. That was definitely Abi's work. For eleven years she and Brandon have been a tight little band of two, and now they are three. When her patience twangs she reminds herself how blessed she is, to have had him all to herself for so long.

However, Pearl doesn't feel blessed now. The beaded curtain jangles as she sweeps it to one side and steps into the pantry. Here the shelves are neatly stacked with tins, cereals, baking ingredients and Kilner jars of pastas and grains. A rush of anxiety quickens her heartbeat and she tries to quell it by breathing slowly and deeply, the way her therapist suggested. In the couple of years after Dean had died, she was prone to panic attacks. Once, when buying a new school uniform for Brandon, she literally couldn't breathe. Things are better now but she is still prone to a certain jumpiness.

She glances at the well-stocked wine rack, seized by an urge to grab a bottle and start early. What was Michael thinking, leaving them to figure all of this out? But then, it was Pearl and her friends who'd persuaded him to go to London. Virtually forced him, really. He'd trusted them to manage things here, and Pearl is determined not to let him down.

'There's plenty of veg in here,' she calls out, eyeing the laden vegetable rack. Lena and Shelley peer in through the sparkly beads.

'Great,' Lena says without enthusiasm.

'And there's bread in the bread bin.' Pearl steps out of the pantry and looks hopefully at her friends.

'Hallelujah!' Shelley announces, and then the three women fall into a grave silence.

'I think I should message Michael,' Pearl murmurs as Stan nuzzles at her hand.

'Yep, definitely,' Lena says. 'Just ask him where the stuff is...'

Pearl goes to fetch her phone from their room, and has just fired off a message – *Sorry to bother you Michael but we don't seem to be able to find the frozen meals* – when tyres crunch on gravel. It's raining heavily and through the downpour she sees that a scruffy buff-coloured Range Rover has come to a halt.

'Someone's here!' Shelley calls from the kitchen. 'Is it that single bloke? That Niall guy? If so he's awfully early...'

'Maybe it's just a friend of Michael's?' Lena suggests as Pearl hurries through. They all peer out of the window and see a tall, slim man with cropped dark hair and spectacles climbing out of the vehicle. He pulls up the hood of his dark green jacket and looks around, as if taking in unfamiliar surroundings.

'That must be Niall.' Pearl quickly rearranges her expression to project what she hopes is calm professionalism. In her working life as a make-up artist Pearl has encountered all kinds of challenging situations. When her assistant was sick she made up seven models singlehandedly for a department store fashion show. She has made a tearful bride feel like the most beautiful woman on earth, and on the morning of Dean's funeral she applied the immaculate make-up which would carry herself – and by extension, her distraught ten-year-old son – through the most harrowing of days.

They might have no meals prepared but there is nothing Pearl can't handle, she reminds herself. So with Lena and Shelley in her wake, she grabs one of the outsized umbrellas stashed in the bucket at the front door. All crammed beneath it, the three women step out of Shore Cottage to greet their first guest.

17

The intercom buzzes loudly. Tommy flinches and quickly stuffs the grubby yellow duster into his trouser pocket as he stabs at the button. 'Come up, come up. Second floor!' he shouts into it. He is aware of fixing on a stupid grin as he opens the front door and hovers in the doorway.

Of course his daughter knows which floor he lives on! At sixteen she is perfectly capable of making her way here by herself by Tube and overground, and has done so numerous times. But today Catherine, his ex-wife, has decided to accompany her. Tommy reckons it's the first time she has visited Hackney by choice, rather than simply passing through it. It's hardly her kind of milieu. 'Just fancy a jaunt out,' she'd announced yesterday – but Tommy knows that Daisy must have mentioned that Lena is away, and Catherine is keen to see where he's living and where her daughter spends the occasional night.

Fine, he told himself. Nothing wrong with that. But now his heart is clattering as they trot lightly upstairs, and Tommy is still cursing himself for telling his daughter which floor he lives on as they appear on the landing. There are hugs as he booms 'Hello!' with the delivery of a children's entertainer.

'Hi, Tommy.' Catherine beams fondly as he ushers them into the flat, asking whether they'd like tea or coffee or anything else after their journey.

As if they have traversed the Alaskan tundra rather than merely popping over from Kensington.

'Just a water please,' Daisy says.

'Sure, honey.' When Tommy first moved in here, his daughter enjoyed staying the odd night in Lena's box room. But those overnight visits are rare now, such is the busyness of a well organised and activity-packed life.

'I'd love a coffee, if you're sure?' Catherine smiles, already gazing in interest around the living room.

'Sure, sure! Just sit down, make yourself comfortable...' He catches her look of bemusement before he darts to the kitchen.

'Isn't this sweet?' he hears her announcing. 'So quirky. So *individual*...'

He fills a glass with tap water, spraying his newly pressed shirt from the tap and remembering that Catherine always serves water in a jug, with ice and lime and sprigs of mint. There are no limes or mint here. No ice cubes either. Why is he worrying? Daisy is always perfectly happy with a plain glass of water, and surely Catherine won't notice that the ground coffee he and Lena use is Tesco own brand? Tommy makes a cafetière of coffee and carries through their drinks, plus a plate of Lena's favoured gravelly oatmeal biscuits. He sets them on the coffee table which, earlier this morning, was cluttered with books and newspaper supplements and Lena's scribble-filled work notebooks. Now it is bare, gleaming from a liberal spraying of Mr Sheen.

'Thanks.' Catherine picks up her coffee mug with a smile. 'They're nice inside, aren't they, these ex-council blocks?' As opposed to how they look on the outside, he thinks she means. Her gaze skims Lena's assortment of framed pop art prints.

'Yeah, it's pretty nice,' Tommy agrees. 'So, how're things?'

'Oh, just rattling along,' she says, pausing to nibble at a biscuit. 'Sorry to hear about the terrible thing at your mum and dad's. Absolutely awful, and so close to Christmas too!'

'Yeah.' Tommy nods, unsettled by the sight of his ex-wife sitting here on Lena's sofa. 'No one was hurt, thankfully.'

'Yes, that's all that matters really. But such a shock for them. I did give Annabelle a call and it sounds like they're rallying.'

'They are, yes.' His parents are good at rallying – when it suits them.

Not so much when he'd called them from boarding school with the exciting news that Simon Carver had tried to smother him with a pillow in the night. *I'd better go, darling. Daddy's taking us out for the day and he's giving me one of his looks!*

Catherine glances at her daughter, who is perched on the saggy blue sofa at her side. Well on her way to becoming a confident and self-possessed young woman, Daisy agrees that her grandparents are indeed 'amazing to cope with everything at their age'.

'I don't know how they do it, Tommy,' Catherine adds.

'I know. They're incredible.' He wonders now how long his ex-wife is planning to hang around today. It's not that they don't get on. They have always got along, apart from the terrible eighteen-month period during which their marriage had fallen apart. Tommy and Catherine had grown up in the same little corner of rural Berkshire where all the young people had socialised together. Birthday parties had morphed into house parties whenever an opportunity presented itself, and someone's parents were away.

Catherine hadn't even needed an empty house in order to host a gathering. Her mum and stepdad – firm friends of Tommy's parents – would welcome the entire local population of under-eighteens to run amok in the pool. A blind eye would be turned to illicit booze stashed in bushes and joints smoked in the summerhouse. 'Just high spirits!' her mother would proclaim as someone vomited on the lavender border.

Tommy and Catherine's first kiss had happened at such a party. By seventeen they were a couple, and married by twenty-four. Crazily young, he realises now. But once Tommy's mother had set her eye on the prize – the Huntleys and Chesswoods merged by matrimony – there was no stopping her, and Tommy and Catherine were in love.

However, by the time Daisy was eight, the occasional bickerings had intensified and were happening daily until one disagreement merged into the next and they were all worn out. Tearfully, Catherine told Tommy she wanted a divorce. Although devastated, he still remembers that his overriding emotion had been one of humiliation – not because he didn't agree that this was the best course of action, but because he had failed. However, as soon as they had parted ways, and legal matters were settled amicably, something seemed to switch in both of them. They both adored their academically brilliant daughter and were united in their commitment to doing what was best for her. Tommy has always respected Catherine as a woman and a mother. And as soon as the pressures of marriage were off, it was as if they were able to *like* each other again.

'Dad, you said Grandma and Grandpa are coming here for Christmas?' Daisy prompts him now.

'That's right.'

Catherine's mouth twitches in amusement as she stretches out her long slender legs. In dark jeans and a pale grey cashmere sweater, with her wavy chin-length fair hair worn loose, she is never anything other than elegant. 'D'you think that's going to be... okay?' she asks.

'Well, it'll have to be,' Tommy replies brightly.

'Is Lena all right with it?' The two women have met just once, when he and Lena picked up Daisy for a day out. As Catherine welcomed them in, and the women greeted each other in a burst of effervescence, Tommy could sense every nerve in his body jangling.

'She's fine,' he says firmly. 'She's looking forward to it.' *Especially my father grilling her about where she's 'from'.*

'Well, I don't know,' Catherine observes. 'It feels like a lot for the two of you to take on in this little place. Couldn't they have gone to Charlie or Harry or Ben?'

'Apparently not,' Tommy says, his mouth twisting. 'But honestly, it'll be great! They'll be perfectly comfortable here and we'll try not to poison them.'

Catherine chuckles and gets up and looks out of the window. A rogue thought pings into Tommy's brain: *They could come to you! They adore you and you have plenty of space. And now you've binned that hapless composer you'd hooked up with, there'll be no one else to get in the way.* This is madness of course. You don't foist your parents on your ex-wife so you can enjoy a cosy Christmas with your girlfriend, no matter how well they all get along.

'Isn't it a beautiful day?' Catherine is still looking out onto Lena's balcony where several pots contain long deceased plants. 'I was going to catch up on some work at home,' she adds, 'but it seems a shame to waste it.'

Daisy jumps up from the chair. Her fair hair is longer and her jeans baggier than her mother's. But she's still a miniature Catherine, pretty and blue eyed and pink-cheeked. 'Why don't we all go out together?' she announces, turning to her dad. 'You mentioned that pizza place near Vicky Park?'

'Oh.' Tommy blinks in surprise.

'No, no, this is your time together,' Catherine insists. But she doesn't follow this up with a, *Well, I'd better be going.*

'That's a good idea,' Tommy says, then turns to Catherine. 'Um, you're welcome to come if you like?'

'That'd be great,' Daisy enthuses. 'Please, Mum. You've never been to Victoria Park!'

It's just a park, Tommy wants to clarify. Just a normal east London park with a lake and people wandering about with dogs and it's nothing special!

'Okay,' Catherine says brightly. 'If you're sure I won't be getting in the way...'

"Course you won't,' Tommy assures her. So off they set, and as they reach the park gates, he starts to relax. He loves his life with Lena. Often, when he wakes before she does, he studies her fine features, her long dark eyelashes and perfect mouth, and he can't believe he had the good fortune to meet her. That night out with his friends – the wife's-away cereal munchers – changed his life. His confidence had been shot to pieces when he and Catherine split, and over the past four years Lena has helped to piece him back together again.

However, being with Daisy triggers a different sort of feeling in him. And Catherine too, he realises now as they follow the path towards the lake. Lena is great with his daughter, asking her all about her friends and her studies and occasionally picking up books for her that she thinks she'll enjoy. However, while Daisy is perfectly pleasant in return, Tommy senses her holding back, erecting a little barrier between them.

That's okay, he's reassured himself. Lena is his girlfriend and they're getting married – but Catherine is Daisy's mum. And now, as they cut alongside the lake towards the new pizza restaurant, and then step into the glass structure and inhale delicious aromas of oregano and freshly baked dough, Tommy experiences a feeling that eludes him, most of the time.

It's a *family* feeling. A sense that, although their marriage didn't work out, he and Catherine have made a great success of raising their daughter together and maintaining a friendship too. How many couples can say they've managed that?

Alongside swigging gin and lamenting over his divorce, a favoured pastime of Tommy's mother's is to pit her sons against each other. Charlie's done this, Harry's done that. Ben's been invited to a garden party at the Palace! Although comfortably off, and nowadays extremely happy, for much of his life Tommy has felt like a failure. However, sitting here choosing pizza with Catherine and Daisy is creating a feeling in him that he's doing okay. And that he isn't such a failure after all.

Bright winter sunlight is streaming into the restaurant, and an enormous tree is almost entirely covered in tiny silver baubles. Christmas music is playing; that jingly tune about Frosty the Snowman that's pretty corny really, but which Tommy finds very jolly and festive.

'See my new phone, Dad?' Daisy whips the device from her pocket and shows it to him.

'Very nice!' He examines it dutifully before handing it back to her.

'Early Christmas present.' Catherine winks at Tommy across the table.

'Oh, of course.' He knows the deal. He'll pay for it and is perfectly happy to do so.

'Mum,' Daisy commands, 'go round there and sit next to Dad. This camera's amazing. So much better than the old one. Let me take a picture of the two of you...'

'Oh, d'you have to, darling?' Catherine laughs and jokingly covers her face with her hands.

'*Please* Mum. We're never all out together like this.' So, with an indulgent smile, Catherine quickly smoothes her highlighted hair and gets up and sits next to Tommy.

'Closer!' Daisy waggles a hand as if directing a shoot.

Tommy looks at Catherine and edges a little closer, causing his chair to grate noisily across the floor. 'God, you two. Why are you so awkward?' His daughter laughs, and Catherine laughs too and puts her arm around Tommy's shoulders. He feels himself flushing and his heart rate accelerating as she pulls him closer, pressing her cheek against his.

'Smiiiile!' Daisy sing-songs.

Obediently, they both smile on demand, and before they have resumed their original positions at the table, Daisy has posted the picture on her social media.

She holds out her phone so they can see it. 'What a lovely photo!' Catherine exclaims, peering closely. 'Not too bad for a couple of oldsters, are we, Tommy?' But Tommy isn't registering whether or not they're ageing well. He is thinking, *It's only pizza, don't panic; there's nothing wrong with popping out for a spot of lunch!* And of course Lena won't mind that the minute she's gone off to Scotland he's on Instagram with his cheek jammed against Catherine's, with the caption 'Rare pic of parents together!!' accompanied by a flurry of red hearts.

18

Pearl is almost disappointed by how little care or attention Niall Dixon seems to need or want. Together with Shelley and Lena she had quickly beckoned him out of the torrential rain and into the warmth of the cottage. But he seemed a little baffled by Pearl's rushed explanation that they would be looking after things during his stay, and clearly wasn't in the mood to chat. She registered intensely blue eyes behind his wire-rimmed spectacles and offered him a hot drink, which he declined politely.

'I stopped for one about an hour ago,' he explained.

'So are you here on a walking trip?' she asked, insisting on taking his wet jacket from him and hanging it on a hook near the Aga to dry. Pearl can't help wanting to take care of people to the point of fussing sometimes.

'Kind of,' Niall replied. 'I'd planned a hike today but...' He nodded towards the window. It was as if it was being hosed from above.

'Not the weather for it,' Shelley suggested.

'Exactly. So I'm sorry to arrive early,' he added. 'I can go for a drive if you like?'

Pearl assured him that his room was all ready, and that he was welcome to settle in right away. 'It's not like those olden-day B&Bs where you're slung out into the rain until teatime,' she joked.

'I'm glad to hear that.' He smiled then and Pearl noticed how it lit up his face briefly, and his demeanour relaxed. He was a good-looking man, she decided, and could be anything from late-forties to mid-fifties. She has never been any good at guessing ages. On her first date with Elias she'd been momentarily taken aback to see the startlingly youthful man waiting for her at the bar. But it turned out that he was five years older than she was. Combined with good genes, his lifestyle had seemingly taken little toll on his looks. And whereas Elias was slick and groomed and wore labels that Pearl had never even heard of, Niall was stubbly and wearing the kind of top you only find in those outdoorsy shops that she never frequents. She wondered briefly if he was in the habit of taking solo trips. He certainly seemed to be pretty self-contained and wasn't up for any more pleasantries in the kitchen. Perhaps the welcoming committee of three was a little too much. So Pearl showed him to his room and he has remained there ever since.

'So what are we going to do?' she asks now. The three friends have gathered around the kitchen table. An emergency summit meeting is happening to decide what to do for dinner tonight as, despite a second message from Pearl, Michael still hasn't replied.

'Would *you* be checking your phone if you'd just got together with someone you're crazy about?' Shelley asks.

'I still think we should try him again,' Lena says firmly. 'It can't do any harm and he'd rather know, wouldn't he? He wouldn't want us blundering through the weekend, destroying his reputation—'

'We're not going to destroy his reputation,' Shelley insists. 'We're all competent women. We can handle this.' She gets up to fetch matches and lights one of the creamy candles set in the centre of the holly garland on the table. All three watch it flicker, as if awaiting divine inspiration.

'Could we do something with chickpeas?' Pearl grimaces. 'Or divide that little quiche between seven? Shell, you're the queen of meal-stretching—'

'We could add lots of rice and pasta,' she offers. 'And aren't there potatoes?'

'Or we could do a giant vegetable curry?' Lena suggests, aware that she would have to delegate this task. When Tommy first moved in, she tried, gamely, to wow him with stir fries liberally doused in soy sauce. Ridiculously, she was ashamed of the fact that, since her divorce, she had become reliant on ready meals and things on toast. But Tommy hadn't moved in to enjoy a meal service, and pretty soon he assumed the role of cheerful home cook.

'There's oven chips,' Pearl remembers, 'and tonnes of breakfast stuff. We could do a bit of everything. A huge, terrible, mismatched buffet...' An image flashes in her mind of one of Brandon's many birthday parties, when Dean was still with them. Together they would lay on a fabulous feast virtually shimmering with artificial colourings. She fears that this version would be less fun. 'Bacon and chips and scrambled eggs,' she suggests. 'Spaghetti and butter as if they're all six years old. And could we concoct a dessert from frozen berries, choc ices and cornflakes?'

Lena pulls a nauseous face and Pearl bows her head, sensing the weight of responsibility pressing down on her now. It was her idea to come here. A mad idea conceived on a boozy Christmas night out – because she was feeling desolate. Not simply because Elias had tried to entice her to a garden shed in Weston-super-Mare, but because, after more than a decade alone, she had finally let down her defences and allowed a man into her life. And somehow that crazy idea to run away with her best friends has spiralled into this.

Why had she agreed that it was a great idea for Michael to go to London? She was swept along with it, a yes person to her very core. Like the way she'd agreed that of course Abi could move into their tiny flat. No, Pearl didn't mind that their houseguest needed the heating on full-bast all day long. It was *fine*, living in a permanent menopausal sweat! And no problem whatsoever to stop off on her way home from an all-day make-up job to pick up Abi's favourite yuzu-flavoured kombuchas that cost a zillion quid a can. As if this perfectly able twenty-one-year-old was incapable of self-propelled forward motion. What even *was* yuzu? 'A citrus fruit,' Abi had replied, as if it was obvious. Pearl has been messaging Brandon, to just keep in touch, as is her way. And now, despite his girlfriend's overbearing presence, she is overcome by an urge to spirit herself home.

'I have a better idea,' Lena says suddenly.

Pearl and Shelley stare at her. 'What?' Pearl asks.

'How about the pub?'

Shelley frowns. 'What pub?'

'I don't know,' Lena says impatiently. '*Any* pub! There's got to be one around here, hasn't there?'

'I've no idea!' Pearl exclaims.

'There must be,' Lena insists. 'Why don't we check that folder? The one with all the information?'

'But they're expecting home cooking,' Pearl cuts in. 'Not to be taken out to the pub...'

'No,' Lena says emphatically. 'I mean, we could get them to do meals *to go*. Portions of whatever they have on their menu—'

'Who's "they"?' Pearl splutters.

'The pub! The *pub people*. We could drive over and collect it and smuggle it in, and stick it in whichever oven we're meant to use...'

'The warming oven?' Shelley brightens. 'My God, we could do that. You're a genius, Leen.'

Pearl grimaces. She isn't a fan of subterfuge. 'They're bound to guess we didn't make it. Remember that time you heated up an M&S lamb curry, Lena? And you presented it to Tommy as your own work? He teased you for weeks over that—'

'Yes, but that was different,' Lena insists. 'That came out of a box and it had that boxed feeling...'

'And this won't?' Pearl crooks a brow.

'No, because it'll have been made in a little pub kitchen by a friendly lady in an apron.' Lena beams. 'Pub kitchen, this kitchen. What's the difference?'

Pearl breathes out slowly. 'But we don't know what they've ordered, do we? All that stuff about *mouss* and *crum* on the board.' She bites her lip, checking her phone. Still no message from Michael. 'Shall we just see what the pub does, and hope for the best—'

'Ah, sorry!' Niall has appeared in the kitchen doorway and looks around apologetically. 'Don't want to interrupt, but—'

'No, come in,' Lena says quickly. 'Come and sit down. We're just doing some, uh...'

'Forward planning,' Shelley cuts in. 'Would you like something now? You must be hungry...' *Please say no*, she wills him.

'Um, a coffee would be great, if that's not too much trouble?' His demeanour is more relaxed than when he arrived, and he's giving the impression that he's not averse to some company.

'Of course it's not.' Shelley fetches the stovetop coffee maker as he takes a seat next to Pearl.

'So, whereabouts have you come from today?' Lena asks.

'Derbyshire,' he replies.

'That's a long drive,' Pearl remarks. Niall nods and agrees that it is, although he has the look of man who's no stranger to lengthy journeys. His clear blue eyes are alert, his face lean and jaw darkly stubbled.

'So what are your plans while you're here?' Shelley hands him a coffee. 'Lots of walking, I guess?'

'Yes,' he says, 'but other stuff too. This is actually a work trip for me.'

'Really?' Pearl asks in surprise.

'Yeah, I'm writing about this area. And other parts of the Highlands too...'

'D'you work for a magazine?' Pearl asks.

'I'm freelance,' Niall says, 'so I'll write for anyone who'll have me. But this past year or so it's pretty much dwindled to a handful of regulars.' They quiz him further and he rattles off a list of publications, one of which Shelley recognises as a glossy monthly that Joel subscribes to. For its high-quality design, she's surmised, as he never wants to travel anywhere.

'So you get plenty of work?' Lena asks.

'Yes, thankfully. One editor in particular seems to think I'm the only person alive who understands "the north". And I'm talking north of Watford Gap,' he adds with a smile.

They chuckle and Shelley thinks of Joel's intense preparations for that Glasgow trip. He'd panic-bought an ensemble of thermal undergarments, including what she'd termed long johns but he had snarkily insisted were 'base layer bottoms'. It had been a summer trip and the sun had blazed incessantly onto her lumbering pregnant form.

'So you're the northern correspondent?' she suggests.

Niall grins. 'That's pretty much it. So, I suggested a whole supplement on the Highlands...'

'Great idea!' Pearl enthuses.

'Actually, my editor wasn't sure. He reckons it's all about serious hiking and climbing. For tough, gnarly outdoor types...'

'All walking poles and Ordnance Survey maps?' Pearl remarks. Although her parents – long gone now – had settled in Cheshire, her father had been Cumbria raised and loved nothing better than a hike up Helvellyn or Scafell Pike. Her devotion to the world of beauty had baffled him, but he'd been proud of her all the same.

'Exactly,' Niall replies. 'And his readers are more your urbane type. Exclusive Ibiza resorts, that kind of thing. But I managed to convince him.'

'Well, we're glad you did,' Pearl says. 'And look at us. We're not exactly gnarly outdoor types.'

He smiles at that. 'So, how did you three meet?'

'Actually on a magazine in London,' Lena tells him.

'Really? That's amazing!'

'I know, isn't it?' Shelley laughs. 'We led glamorous lives once. But that was a very long time ago...'

'I just meant with you all being up here,' he says quickly, 'running a B&B. It's quite the leap—'

'Oh, we don't really run it,' Pearl explains. 'Michael had to go away unexpectedly so we stepped in—'

'We're only holding the fort,' Lena adds, and he smiles.

'Well, I think it's incredible.' Whether he means Shore Cottage itself, or the fact that the three women have landed here, they are not entirely sure. Yet as they all swap fond tales of the glory days of magazine publishing – when editorial budgets were huge and jobs plentiful – Pearl finds herself picturing her younger self, having landed in London at twenty, a shy country girl knowing no one. She quickly built a career and has weathered the hardest of times. And recently, despite the wrong turn with Elias, she has felt things shifting, as if she is ready for something new. Perhaps being thrown into this bizarre situation is the start of it, and together they can pull this off after all.

'Looks like the rain's off,' Niall says. 'Think I'll take a walk down to the loch.' He pauses. 'Dinner's around seven, Michael said? Is that still okay with you?'

'Yes, absolutely.' Lena smiles confidently. 'Um... you did let him know what you wanted?'

'Oh, yes. I just picked from the menu on the website and emailed it through to him. He said it's a lot easier to know up front—'

'Yes, it really is. Thanks for doing that.' *So there's a menu on the website!* Three intelligent and resourceful women – yet they hadn't thought to look.

Pearl gets up and strolls to the utility room, as if there is something she needs to check in there. Out of sight from the others, she takes a quick photo of Michael's notes on the chalkboard, and then grabs a waterproof jacket from the heavily laden hooks on the wall.

Back in the kitchen, Niall drains his coffee and gets up from the table. Pearl pulls on the man-sized jacket that drowns her diminutive form and slips her phone into a deep pocket. ''Scuse me a minute,' she says, beaming round at everyone. 'I'm just going to pop out and check on the hens.'

19

Michael strides into the arrivals hall at Stansted Airport and stops suddenly. He realises what he's done. But he doesn't want to believe it. He checks his jeans and jacket pockets, frantically patting and delving and cursing under his breath.

He sets down his rucksack on the floor while all around him joyous reunions are happening. There are Santa hats and sparkly reindeer antlers and many, many hugs. Several bored-looking men are holding up name signs. A baby is crying and somewhere a man is calling after a child. '*Amelie, come back here right now!*' All of life is here, milling around him. But what *isn't* here is his phone, because his flight was delayed, and in his eagerness to disembark, Michael had sprung out of his seat the instant the seatbelt signs were switched off.

No, he can't blame the fact that he left his phone in the seat pocket on the delay. He can't even blame it on the life he has now; that it had been years since he'd flown anywhere, and that he has clearly become deskilled at travelling further than the hour-long round trip to his nearest sizeable supermarket. Michael likes to think he's on top of his life, and that the running of Shore Cottage is as smooth as one of his freshly ironed sheets. But pluck him out of his natural habitat – drop him onto a plane and ping him out at the other end – and he turns into an idiot.

That's why Michael left his phone on the plane. Because he's an idiot. This single thought burns neon-bright in his brain as he looks around wildly for some official person who can help him. He spots a tall woman in a bright blue skirt and jacket and teetering heels, her blonde hair scraped back severely from her face. He hurries over to her.

'Excuse me,' he starts. He waits for the woman to make eye contact but she seems to be scanning the hall. 'Erm, I've done a stupid thing,' he explains. 'I've just arrived from Glasgow and I left my phone on the plane—'

'Sorry, you can't go back and get it.' Briefly, she flicks her gaze at him.

'No. No, I realise that...' As if he was considering fighting his way back through security and onto the aircraft. He might live in the middle of nowhere with only Harry and Pam from the nearby farm for neighbours but he's *not* a bloody fool. No, he is! He is a bloody fool!

'If you go to lost luggage you can fill in a claim form,' the woman states in an automated voice.

Michael rakes at his hair. 'Yes, but you see it's not actually lost. It's just there in the seat pocket on the plane. Seat 17b...'

'That's the best thing,' trills this woman with an unseasonal tan and thick black fringes for eyelashes that surely must be glued on. Despite his phone emergency, Michael can't help but marvel at their size and density. He never sees eyelashes like this back home.

She turns away and trots away on her heels, and Michael thanks her, even though she has gone now. He inhales deeply and looks around at all the people pulling their luggage along, or standing guarding it, and for a moment, he thinks yes, he'll do as he's been told and go to lost luggage. However, that would mean waiting around. And Michael hasn't abandoned his B&B guests and Pearl and her friends and travelled 500 miles to fill in a form and for nothing to happen. He is running late already, and that would make him even later. So instead, as if being pulled along now by an invisible cord, he heads down the escalator towards the Stansted Express.

As the train rattles towards London, he starts to reconcile the fact that he is currently phone-less. That's okay, he decides. He knows which hotel Krissy is staying at, out at Heathrow. He too has booked a room there for two nights (he didn't want to take anything for granted). He can locate Krissy through hotel reception, and later he can call his landline at home just to check that they're managing okay up there.

Of course they are, he tells himself. He left them with clear instructions – he *thinks* – and it's not rocket science, making breakfasts and heating up dinners and keeping on top of the place. It's not that he's ungrateful. Far from it. Michael is still bowled over by their generosity. This force of nature, in the form of three women who clearly needed to escape the pressures of Christmas, have made this trip possible for him. He doesn't know how he can possibly thank them enough. However, if he can run Shore Cottage single handedly, those three obviously smart and resourceful women can probably do a far better job.

Feeling calmer now, he looks around the carriage, spotting more of those fringed canopies (is this what eyelashes are like now?). He also notices that some of the women's faces look very different to the faces he's used to seeing back home. It's their lips, he thinks. He knows from his young nieces that having lips 'done' is a thing now, but he has never seen any out in the wild. As a kid, Michael loved those sci-fi movies where people were frozen for decades in canisters. He wonders now if this is how it might feel to have been finally thawed and released into the modern world.

Michael meets people, of course, in the normal course of his life. He meets *tonnes* of people. Most evenings they're sitting there at his kitchen table and he's eating with them, topping up their wine and answering their questions about walks and the landscape and what it's like living so remotely – 'And don't you get *lonely* up here all by yourself?' People ask that a lot. The women anyway. And he assures them that he's never lonely, that he's fantastically happy up here, looking after his guests and maintaining his property and doing his garden until, mercifully, they head off to bed.

Michael never admits that some nights, when there are no guests, he calls Stan through to his bedroom and lets him sleep on the bed beside him, just for the comfort of having another living being close by.

Mostly, though, he is too busy to dwell upon the fact that, at forty-seven years old, his life is chronically empty. Because for most of the year, people are coming and going at Shore Cottage and it's his job to take care of them. However, they are not like the people he sees all around him now. His guests tend towards the hearty and robust, clad in big sweaters and waterproofs and woolly hats. And here, on this softly rattling train, everyone seems to be in dazzling colour.

Michael doesn't stare at anyone. He's not going to behave in a way that could have him arrested. However, as his heart rate settles to something approaching normal, he sits there absorbing it all. A young man is wearing a purple velvet coat with a fur trim, and the elderly lady sitting next to him is sporting leopard print trousers and glittery platform shoes. A teenage girl with blue hair is carrying a live chihuahua in a backpack. Another dog – fluffy, white – is being carried by a shaven-headed man in a front-facing carrier, like a baby.

Don't dogs walk any more? Michael muses, fascinated. Is he being terribly old-fashioned in expecting Stan to trot around on his legs? Michael grew up in a small but thriving Cheshire town, and he's visited plenty of cities. In their early days he and Rona Interrailed all over Europe and travelled around India. For her thirtieth birthday, hoping it would make things better between them, he took her to New York. Gamely, his parents came up from Cheshire to look after the B&B for five days. He's been to London too, several times – but the last time must have been twenty years ago. And now Michael is on his way to meet a woman he knows only through a screen and their chats, which go on for hours sometimes. A flight attendant called Krissy who is waiting for him.

Thankfully, he checked out the route from Stansted to Heathrow while he was waiting to depart back in Glasgow. So he knows what to do. He'll get off the train at Liverpool Street, and then he'll take the Tube to Paddington where he'll catch the Heathrow Express. For a man who left an iPhone on the plane, Michael is remarkably sanguine now. He is sure that this bright, sunny Saturday will only get better when he meets the woman with whom he's besotted, if it's possible to be besotted with someone you haven't yet met in real life.

As the elderly leopard print lady catches his eye and smiles, and Michael smiles back, he is entirely certain that it is.

20

'Do we do food?' the man repeats. 'Yes, we do lunches here. I can see what's left if you like?'

'I actually wondered if you do evening meals,' Pearl says. This is the fourth place she's called. The first and second, no one answered. The third was an answerphone and she decided there wasn't much point in leaving a convoluted message. With Niall having set off on a walk, she quickly conferred with Shelley and Lena, and they devoured a pile of toast in the kitchen while mooting the possibility of driving to the nearest sizeable supermarket to stock up on the necessary ingredients. At least they knew now what the guests had ordered, having located Michael's short but tempting menu on the Shore Cottage website.

It was like cracking an admittedly extremely simple code.

Mush = mushroom, ale and roasted chestnut pie.

Chick = chicken casserole with leeks, mustard and Shore Cottage herbs.

Lamb = lamb tagine with apricots and sweet potato.

Mouss = aubergine and butternut squash moussaka.

Crumb = hedgerow berry and toasted hazelnut crumble.

A pie = apple and cinnamon pie with creme fraiche or locally made vanilla ice cream.

Stick = sticky toffee pudding with caramel sauce.

So that's what Niall and the Sampsons were expecting to be served up to them over the next couple of nights. However, the thought of throwing that lot together to Michael's presumably exacting standards was somewhat overwhelming. Even as the more proficient home cooks, Shelley and Pearl weren't confident that they could pull it off. Especially in a limited time frame, finding their way around all those ovens, perhaps with Niall hanging out in the kitchen and the Sampson family due to arrive at any time.

'No, we don't do evening meals,' the man tells Pearl now. 'But we have rolls left. I could do you some rolls?'

'Sausage rolls?' she asks. Could they do something with a vast quantity of sausage rolls?

'No, *filled* rolls,' he replies with a note of bemusement. 'Ham, cheese or ham and cheese.'

'Oh no, it's dinners I'm after,' she says, striding to the bottom of the garden, which looks out onto the vastness of the loch. It is perfectly flat, a sheen of silver in the cool wintery sunlight. Beyond it, the hills are a haze of rust and purple, the few trees bare and silhouetted against the colourless sky.

'Sorry I can't help you,' the man says.

'Is there anywhere else around that does evening meals?' Pearl can hear voices and clattering in the background.

'You could try the Ferry Inn? For tonight, is it?'

'Yes.' Her voice rises in hope.

'Aw, you'll be lucky. Last Saturday before Christmas? They'll be rushed off their feet—'

'Oh, of course.' She pauses. 'You're sure you couldn't do anything else, other than rolls?' she asks.

The man chuckles. 'Crisps and nuts?'

Pearl forces out a dry snigger and thanks him. Shivering in the bitter cold now, with her auburn curls gusting into her face, she stops by the hen enclosure, wondering what to do next. Of course no pub around here will be able to rustle up seven meals according to her precise specifications.

Not even for *one* night, let alone two. They'll be crammed with revellers gearing up for the big day.

Pearl bobs down to watch the hens pottering around in their enclosure. So far, Shelley has assumed the role of Chief Keeper, topping up their food, and bringing out bowls of hot water in order to stop the water dispenser from freezing. 'What next?' Pearl asks the black and white speckled hen. 'What are we going to do, eh?'

She stands up, wondering whether it's worth calling the Ferry Inn and sounding like a fool, when she sees Niall strolling towards her. 'Hi.' He raises a hand.

Pearl smiles and drops her phone back into the pocket of her borrowed jacket. 'Enjoy your walk?' she asks.

'Oh, yes. It's beautiful down there.' He nods to one side, indicating the loch, and she follows his gaze. In London she rushes around, barely registering the weather or the colour of the sky. But up here it can turn from searing blue to a moody grey in a blink. Every time Pearl looks, the whole vista has changed.

'I haven't even explored yet,' she says. 'Tomorrow, hopefully.'

'Do try to take yourself off for a walk,' Niall suggests. 'The path down there runs right along the lochside.'

'I can't imagine anywhere more peaceful,' she says, although in truth there are times when she has felt more peaceful than this. 'So d'you know Scotland well? Being the northern correspondent—'

'Actually no.' He smiles. 'I've only been to the more obvious places. Edinburgh, Skye, parts of the West Coast. I'd always wanted to do a big trip up here, off the beaten track. Away from the NC500 crowd, y'know?'

'Oh yes,' Pearl enthuses, although she's not sure what the NC500 is.

'Making it a work thing gave me the chance,' Niall adds. 'And the reviews of this place are great. He's obviously trying to do something different here, offering home-cooked evening meals in this amazing setting. And that's great for visitors, isn't it? It's not as if this area is overrun with restaurants—'

'No, it's not.' She pales a little.

'But I haven't been able to find much written about it,' he adds. 'So I figured it deserved more attention.'

Pearl nods, certain that Michael will be thrilled with the publicity. But will a seasoned travel writer be fooled by hastily bought-in pub food, even if they can find somewhere that'll provide it? 'So you're putting together a kind of *cool* guide to the Highlands?' she suggests.

Niall nods. 'I guess that's about it.' Then: 'So what do you do, when you're not holding the fort up here?'

'I'm a make-up artist,' she says as they stroll back towards the house.

'Really?'

She catches his quick glance and laughs. 'I know. Hard to believe, isn't it?'

'Oh, I didn't mean—'

'No, I get it.' She smiles. 'I must admit, this isn't my usual kind of trip. These past few years it's been city breaks with friends or beach holidays with my son. So, how long will your Highland trip take?'

'Three weeks in all,' he replies.

She looks at him, curiosity piqued now. 'But you only drove up from Derbyshire this morning?'

'Yep, that's right—'

'But won't you be going home for Christmas?'

'Actually, no—'

'So you'll still be away, will you?' she goes on. 'Working on your Scotland guide, even on Christmas Day—'

'It's not really that big of a deal.' He shrugs. 'I don't think so anyway.'

'Er, no,' she agrees, realising she has overstepped the mark. Pearl is a naturally curious person. She is aware that any offspring less tolerant than Brandon would take exception to her constant casual quizzing. How did his pub shift go yesterday? Is that new guy working out? Which film did he and Abi see the other night? Sometimes he laughs her off – 'Enough, Mother!' – and she catches Abi's surprised look. *How come your mum is so interested in your life?*

'Christmas is overrated,' Pearl adds now. A meaningless comment, and does she mean it really?

'Well, I think I'll head in and do some work,' Niall says, a little abruptly, already making for the front door.

Pearl watches him go. Maybe it's not the done thing to quiz guests about their Christmas plans? She can't imagine Michael doing that. And now a gleaming white SUV is approaching slowly down the drive. The Sampsons are here, and there are *still* no firm plans for dinner. Pearl quickly hoists a smile, and Lena and Shelley emerge from the cottage, passing Niall, who's paused at the door. Stan bounds out towards the vehicle.

The passenger door opens and a wiry woman with cropped burgundy hair and tiny rectangular spectacles steps out. 'This is Shore Cottage?' she asks.

'Yes,' Pearl replies. 'You're at the right place. You must be Mrs Sampson—'

'Frida,' she says brusquely. 'Bit of a disaster here.' Her voice is sharp, with a hint of an accent that Pearl can't place. But she is clearly used to commanding attention. 'Are you in charge?'

'Sort of,' Pearl starts. 'I mean, we all are. Michael's had to go away but we're all here to look after you. I'm Pearl, and this is Lena and—' She glances back at her friends, but Frida has already cut her off.

'Could we possibly have buckets of warm soapy water and some rags?'

'Rags?' Shelley repeats.

'Yes, *rags*. Theo's been sick. We need to do an urgent clean-up job—'

'Oh, how awful! Of course,' Pearl says.

'Your roads are terribly twisty,' Frida announces, as if Pearl designed them that way herself, just to spite them. 'They haven't agreed with him at all.'

'Well, I'm sorry,' she says, feeling helpless. *Why not write a complaint in the visitors' book?* And as she catches Niall's eye at the door – whom she seemed to offend, simply by asking about Christmas – she wonders if she really is cut out for this job after all.

21

Shelley doesn't know what they can use for rags. Neither does Lena. Pearl has decided that, no matter how desperate things are, no one is mopping up vomit with her 'intelligent' hair towel (100 per cent plant based) or her organic muslin double action cleansing cloths.

The three women confer quickly, aware of Frida's laser glare from beside the car and the whimpering little boy in the back seat. Mr Sampson is still in the driver's seat, twisting round to try and placate his son. Shelley has already suggested they all come into the house, but Frida snapped that they 'can't leave the car in this state. It needs to be drivable tomorrow.'

'It'll still drive, won't it?' Lena mutters. 'It'll just whiff a bit.'

Now Mr Sampson climbs out of the car and rubs at his beard. Dark brown with a flash of white, it's like a very small badger.

'Anything'll do for rags,' he says apologetically. 'Anything at all. Sorry to show up like this. I hope we're not putting you out—'

'Not at all,' Pearl insists. She looks around at her friends, and at Niall. 'We need to find something,' she announces.

'Erm, I have some old towels in my car.' Niall looks hesitant. 'For my dog,' he adds. 'He wasn't a good car traveller either. I'll fetch them.'

'Thank you,' Pearl says gratefully. 'Frida, Niall's going to—' But Frida is now busy admonishing her husband.

'If you'd driven more slowly, instead of taking the turns like that—'

'More slowly? I was doing twenty-five miles an hour!'

'Yes, and look what's happened. Poor Theo! Honestly, what a start to our weekend away.'

Thoroughly scolded, Mr Sampson seems to shrink into himself in his beige trousers and lobster-hued sweater. But he brightens a little, thanking Niall and Shelley profusely, as towels and buckets of water are miraculously produced.

Although everyone hovers around, willing to assist, Mr Sampson – 'Call me Roger!' – dismisses their offers of help. Meanwhile, Frida opens a rear car door and murmurs to her son, before turning abruptly to Pearl. 'Could you take Theo inside?'

'Er, yes of course,' Pearl replies. Clearly, she has singled her out as the one in control here. In a flash of rebellion she wonders how Frida would react to a mishmash of freezer gleanings for dinner tonight.

Frida steps back, as if here to direct operations rather than do anything hands-on, and Pearl peers in at the child. Theo is hunched in a vomit-splattered fleece, jeans and wellies. Somehow, a sizeable amount has also landed in his hair. 'Oh, you poor boy,' she murmurs. From the other door, Roger is gamely trying to mop up his son's emissions, which have also doused the floor and the back of the driver's seat. Pearl is briefly reminded of the Jackson Pollock paintings at Tate Modern. 'Theo, would you like to come into the house with me?' she asks gently.

'No,' he mutters.

'Theo, go inside with this lady. Mummy will be in in a minute,' Frida announces, and reluctantly, he climbs out of the car.

As he steps carefully onto the uneven ground, Pearl takes in the pitiful sight of him. His face is as pale as milk and his full pink mouth is set in a scowl. She guesses he's around five or six, and if there wasn't sick on his dinosaur fleece, she would hug him. 'Perhaps Mummy could bring in your luggage,' she suggests, loudly enough for Frida to hear, 'and then you can get showered off in your bathroom and into some nice clean clothes. Would that feel better?'

Glumly, he stamps onto a frozen puddle, splintering the thin ice. 'Just take him in please,' Frida instructs, as if he were a jacket she was dropping off for alternations. Pearl glares at her. So she'd rather stay out here – doing what? Supervising Roger while her son waits indoors with strangers in his pukey clothes? At just gone 3 p.m. the light is fading already and Pearl's face is tight with the cold. The poor child must be freezing.

Pearl reaches down for his hand. She can handle it being a bit sicky. She's been a single mother since Brandon was ten and has had to mastermind all manner of clean-up operations.

Theo stands rigidly, staring up at her now. 'Theo?' she prompts him. He shrinks away, blue eyes round with fear as if she might be about to abduct him.

'Why are we here?' he blurts out.

'For a weekend away, darling, before Christmas,' his mother replies. 'So Mummy can have a little rest before the onslaught!'

His bottom lip wobbles, and he flinches as Stan trots towards him. 'Are you okay with dogs?' Pearl asks, and he nods.

'Can I walk him?' he asks in a small voice.

'Tomorrow, yes. We can take him out together.' He looks less than thrilled by this, so she bobs down to his level, trying to put him at ease, trying to be a *great* B&B host. 'So, where d'you want to be, Theo? If you don't want to be here?'

'Switzerland,' he mutters.

'We usually go there for Christmas.' Roger pops up from scrubbing. 'To Frida's parents at Lake Lucerne.'

Shame you couldn't be there now, Pearl decides.

'Theo, go inside with the nice lady!' Roger adds.

Niall has disappeared now, presumably to the sanctuary of his room, and for a moment it looks as if Theo will do as his father asks. But as Shelley and Lena approach, he stiffens again. 'It's so cold out here, Theo,' Shelley starts. 'Come indoors and we'll make you a hot chocolate—' But he scurries to his mother, his face crumpling at the terrifying sight of this bright and cheerful stranger with a blonde ponytail, and he bursts into noisy tears.

'Theo, just go inside!' Frida commands as Roger springs up again, brandishing a dripping towel.

'Could I possibly bother you for some more soapy water?' he asks.

'Of *course*,' Shelley assures him. And as the crying Theo troops in beside her, dragging his wellies across the icy ground, she wonders how this might possibly come under the banner of holding the fort.

* * *

Five hundred miles south, Shelley's daughter Martha is rather looking forward to being in charge tonight. At seventeen, she feels like a fully-fledged adult, so it's incredibly frustrating that she has to live by her mum and dad's rules.

Well, her mum's really. Her dad isn't bothered what she does. And today he's even more distracted than usual because he's desperate to go out.

Martha has observed him hopping around all day, being overly jolly. He bought them a KFC for lunch and now he's saying they can have a McDonald's for dinner later. *Very* unlike him. 'So, you're going to be okay tonight?' he keeps asking. 'Call me, won't you, if you need me?'

Martha has no intention of calling him, but she wants to be sure of one thing. Otherwise tonight could end up in disaster. So, while her dad is having a shower – he's been in there for ages already, singing excruciatingly – Martha steps quietly into her parents' bedroom.

There she sees her dad's bag sitting on the bed. That embarrassing man-bag in a dull shade of orange that he insists on wearing cross-body style every time he goes out. Why can't he be like other dads and just stuff his belongings into his pockets? Why, at fifty-whatever-he-is, does he try to be 'cool'?

As he wails away in the bathroom, Martha quickly opens the bag and peers inside, registering the contents. Immediately, her heart settles. What she's seeing there is *exactly* what she'd hoped to find. Boxers, toothbrush. Those pokey tooth-sticks he uses, leaving his blood-tinged split splattered all over the wash basin. Martha already knows for sure that she will *never* marry a man.

Keen to leave the room before her dad appears in his mortifying dressing gown, she is about to close the bag when something else catches her eye. At the bottom of the bag is a tiny matt black box, with a gold gift tag attached. She lifts out the box and opens it, and her heart seems to turn over when she sees what's inside.

The terrible singing has stopped now, which means he'll be out of the shower and drying himself. Martha quickly reads the gift tag, her brain spinning as she tries to make sense of what she is seeing in her dad's ridiculously loopy handwriting. Then she jams the lid on the box and stuffs it back into the bag, and hurries out of the room.

22

Everything feels better at Shore Cottage once the fire has been lit in the lounge. Soon it's crackling and glowing, and Shelley has only had to use an entire bucket of kindling, a mountain of newspaper and three fire lighters. Those Girl Guide skills were useful after all. Meanwhile, Pearl has made pots of tea and coffee, and a mug of hot chocolate has been handed to Theo. Further pantry excavations have revealed a large tin filled with cookies, which has perked up the freshly showered and changed little boy. Neither parent seems to care as he shovels them into his mouth, as if stoking an engine.

At least he's happy now, Shelley decides, and relief settles over her in the cosy lounge. Theo is sitting cross-legged in front of the fire, stroking Stan a little rough-handedly. Neither Frida nor Roger seems notice this either. His father is scratching his beard and poring intently over the hefty folder, filled with information about walks and places of interest, and Frida is sitting bolt upright, eyes closed. Clearly, watching Roger scrub out their car, making sure he didn't miss a bit, has exhausted her.

Shelley senses that the Sampsons might prefer to be alone now in the lounge. However, she is reluctant to leave as Theo's 'stroking' of Stan has ramped up into more of a vigorous sports massage, sparking a sudden growl.

Frida's eyes flick open. 'Oh, is the dog aggressive?'

'No, not at all,' Shelley says firmly. Then to Theo: 'Please be gentle with him. A nice soft, gentle stroke. That's what he likes...' When that doesn't work, and his parents are clearly oblivious to their kid manhandling an animal, she opts for the distraction technique she used to employ with her own children. 'So what d'you like doing, Theo?' she asks brightly. 'What kind of things are you into?'

'I like driving,' Theo replies, and his father looks up from the folder with an indulgent smile.

'He means he likes sitting in the driver's seat, hooting the horn.'

Ah, how delightful, Shelley muses. Ruining the tranquillity of the Highlands for all. That's something to look forward to tomorrow. She glances out of the window, where Pearl is pacing back and forth in the garden, wrapped up again in one of Michael's hefty jackets and lit only by the single outside light. A phone signal can only be found outdoors, and at 4.10 p.m. it's already properly dark. An unfamiliar thick woolly hat is pulled down low on Pearl's head, her auburn curls barely visible. But she's wearing lipstick, Shelley notes. Her mood-boosting I-can-do-anything red. Still determined to locate a takeaway dinner option, she is calling more pubs. But Shelley has given up hope now and, after just one short afternoon with the Sampsons, she has started to form an idea.

Now Lena appears, having insisted that this time she would check on the hens. Shelley suspected she craved a little respite from the guests. 'Would anyone like a drink?' she asks, and Frida seems to jolt suddenly into full consciousness.

'Oh, what do you have?'

'There's wine and beer,' Lena starts. She doesn't know if it's against licensing rules to serve drinks outside mealtimes – but sod it. The police are hardly likely to bowl up at Shore Cottage and they're going to have to get through this somehow.

'I'd love a white wine,' Frida says, 'if it's chilled...' Have they remembered to chill it? Lena isn't sure but, as if reading her mind, Shelley nods quickly.

'Red for me please,' Roger says, and drinks are poured, and then Niall appears, going to the window where he stands for a moment. 'It's snowing,' he remarks.

'Snow?' Theo asks excitedly.

'Yes, darling, snow!' Frida announces, as if she has made it happen. '*Just* like at Grandma's.' And Shelley, accustomed to welcoming anyone who comes into the care home, latches onto this as a conversation topic. Frida sips her wine, happily answering her questions about her childhood in a Swiss village, and how she came to meet Roger.

'I was travelling,' she explains, 'all over Europe, all by myself. And I met him in a hostel in Paris. We were so young, weren't we, Roger? Just nineteen, the pair of us. Twenty-one years ago with the world at my feet!' She shakes her head in wonderment. 'I wasn't sure I even wanted a child' – charming, Shelley surmises, with your son sitting in front of you – 'but eventually we thought, why not? We weren't getting any younger. And the very minute we'd decided, that was that!'

'How lovely,' Shelley enthuses, but Theo cuts in.

'Mummy, I'm hungry.' What, after eighty-seven cookies?

Frida frowns, and now Pearl strolls into the lounge, looking a little panic stricken. 'We'll be eating at around seven,' Shelley says quickly, 'but that's maybe a bit late for Theo?' She catches her friends' startled looks. *What* will they be eating at seven? 'Would you like some pasta now, Theo?' she asks.

'Oh, he hates pasta.' Frida grimaces. 'Unusual, I know!'

You could say that, Shelley reflects. Up until the age of seven both Martha and Fin would barely tolerate anything other than spaghetti, to the point that she imagined their developing bones to be 99 per cent durum wheat.

'Can I have a sandwich?' Theo asks his mother.

'I'm sure you can, darling.'

'Of course.' Shelley springs up. 'What would you like in it?'

'Well, what do you have?' Frida asks pointedly.

Oh, just the usual. Chickpeas, frozen sweetcorn, leeks? 'I'm sure we have cheese,' Pearl announces. 'D'you like cheese, Theo?' He nods mutely, and off she goes with the kid sloping along in pursuit.

There is bread, thank goodness, and a wedge of locally produced

Cheddar. As she makes Theo's sandwich he twirls around the kitchen, careering into cupboards, finally settling on swinging haphazardly on the beaded curtain. She smiles benignly, willing him not to snap it. Pearl remembers now that Michael and Rona had brought the curtain back from their travels in India all those years ago. 'Steady there!' she says. Theo laughs as he grabs an armful of strung beads, clutching them to his chest and leaning fully back with all of his body weight.

'I like this!' he announces.

'Yes, Michael does too. That's his curtain, Theo…'

'Who's Michael?'

'The nice man who owns this house. *Please* be careful…' Pearl always struggles with the concept of telling off someone's else's kid.

'Wheeee!' Every nerve in Pearl's body seems to twang as Theo is now swinging, feet off the ground, from the curtain. *I'm glad you're happy and no longer crying with sick in your hair. But why aren't your parents looking after you?*

'Here you go, love.' She hands him a doorstopper sandwich on a plate with firm instructions to take it back into the lounge. *Away from the curtain, please!*

Having come through to join her in the kitchen, Shelley and Lena exchange looks of panic. 'My God,' Lena murmurs. 'What a family. How long are they here for again?'

'Till Monday,' Pearl reminds her. 'So, look, we're going to have to serve up a fabulous meal in two and a half hours' time.' Beyond stressing now, she rubs wearily at her eyes. 'I've tried all the pubs. No one can do it. Shame really, because there are some amazing-sounding places. But they've all been fully booked for weeks. And when I asked if they could just knock out some takeaways—'

'No joy,' Shelley cuts in, and Pearl shakes her head.

'We'd better get cooking then,' Lena starts, but Shelley winds her arms around her friends' shoulders and pulls them to her.

'Hang on a sec,' she says. 'You haven't been drinking, have you, Pearl?'

'Not yet,' she says with a dry laugh.

'You don't mind driving, then?'

'No, of course not. But where to?'

Shelley looks at her friends as Stan trots in to join them, clearly having tired of Theo's attentions. 'Okay,' she starts. 'What we're going to do is this. We're going to tell our guests that there's been a *technical hitch...*'

'What kind of hitch?' Pearl's green eyes widen.

'We can't cook dinner tonight. The Aga's fucked—'

'What?' Pearl gasps.

'Not really,' Shelley says quickly.

'Agas don't break, do they?' Pearl frowns. 'They go on and on forever, like tortoises—'

'Not this one, darling. Not tonight. Because we're not using that thing.' She glances briefly at the cast iron hunk. 'This isn't our place,' she states firmly, 'and we're doing our best for Michael. And tonight, no matter what they've ordered, *everyone's* having fish and chips.'

23

Something feels different at Carmel's this time. It's the way she greets him, Joel thinks. Is he too early at 5.30 p.m.? The kids were obviously unconcerned whether he was at home or not – or living or dead, probably. So he'd come out with some guff about heading over early to the gallery opening 'to help set things up'.

'All right,' Martha said nonchalantly. Things felt a little funny there too. A bit *too* quiet, too calm – almost eerie. But hovering about was making things worse, so Joel had left them a couple of twenty-quid notes – guilt money – and taken the Tube to Finsbury Park.

Carmel hadn't fancied the pub this evening. 'Just come to mine,' she'd said. Disappointing, Joel thought, as he'd enjoyed the prospect of spinning things out, luxuriating in the many hours they would have together tonight, all the way through to Sunday morning. He'd panicked slightly about morning breath. But in his nifty burnt-orange man-bag, Joel has packed breath spray along with his toothbrush, inter-dental sticks and a clean pair of boxers and socks. There's also a small Christmas present in there for Carmel. Small but very expensive. He'd also wanted to pack another outfit to wow her with tomorrow, but thought it might arouse suspicion if he turned up at home tomorrow in different clothes. Silly really. Joel suspects he could wander in sporting a gorilla costume and his kids would barely glance up from their phones.

Now that he's arrived at her place, he's happy that he and Carmel are skipping the pub bit. He stopped off to buy a bottle of champagne anyway, as tonight is definitely worthy of celebration. Already he's feeling unbelievably horny and he can't wait to knock back a few glasses and jump into Carmel's bed.

He jabs her buzzer. 'Hi, come in,' she drawls through the intercom, as if he's an Evri delivery guy. What is this? he thinks irritably. National Nonchalance Day? He steps into the building and there she is, in faded jeans and a loose black sweater, waiting at the open door of her flat.

'Hey, beautiful!' He kisses her and hands her the bottle of champagne.

'Oh, thanks,' she says, as if it's Lucozade. She struts into the flat, plonks it in the fridge and pours him a glass of red wine from the open bottle sitting on the worktop.

'So, how's things?' Perching on a stool at her kitchen island, Joel wonders if something is bothering her today. Normally they'd launch into kissing right away. She'd have him rammed up against her fridge, the brushed steel appliance grumbling and gurgling in his ears as she snogged him in her thrillingly aggressive manner. Then they'd pause for a drink and a bit of chat before heading briskly to bed.

'Since yesterday, you mean?' Carmel asks.

'Uh, yeah.' His mouth sets in a line. Why is she being like this? Not frosty exactly; just sort of *unbothered*. As if they have been married for twenty-five years and it's unthinkable that they might have had sex over her dining table just last week. In fact, Carmel is making her way to the table right now. But what she does there causes Joel's heart to drop.

It's okay, he tells himself. She's only opened her laptop to check her emails quickly, or because she wants to show him something. A shoot, maybe. She's going to show him some pictures she's proud of, and by association he'll be immensely proud of having this 'thing' with such a knock-out gorgeous and talented photographer.

That's how he privately terms it. Not an affair, which would seem tawdry, and even Joel has to admit it hardly constitutes a relationship. His preferred term sounds breezy and modern. *We're having a thing.* No one would haul his arse into a law court over that.

But Carmel doesn't seem to want to show Joel anything on her laptop. Instead, she plonks herself onto a chair at the table. And while he perches there, sipping red wine at her island, she starts reading the *Guardian*.

Joel has lied to his kids and come up with this stupid gallery opening alibi to watch her reading the fucking news!

Well, let her, he decides, irritation mounting rapidly. Finally, when she's finished that fascinating article, she might interact with him? In the meantime he will sit and drink and not say a word. Clearly, she's finding Donald Trump or Vladimir Putin or whoever she's reading about a lot more interesting than the man who's come round expressively to ravish her!

'Carmel?' He can't help it. He can't just sit here being ignored, as if he's… not an Evri delivery guy – he'd have been and gone. More like a plumber who's come round to fit a new mixer tap.

'Hmm?' she murmurs without looking up.

'Anything interesting in the news?'

'Oh, sorry.' She emits a small laugh and closes the laptop and looks up at him. 'Sorry. Been so busy lately and I just wanted to catch up.'

Couldn't she have caught up before he arrived? She hadn't seemed busy last night when she was flicking him with the leathery fringe of her whip.

'Yeah, I'm the same,' he offers. 'When work's full on it feels like I'm living in a bubble.' In fact, Joel never keeps up with the news. He can recognise Trump of course. An embryo would recognise Trump. But he's not sure that he'd know Putin if he was using the next self-service checkout at Sainsbury's – not that Joel ever goes to Sainsbury's (Shelley takes care of all that). His media consumption is pretty much limited to celebrity interviews, tech, fashion and grooming products. He preens and grooms with the enthusiasm of an orangutang, and the launch of a new aftershave balm feels more relevant to Joel than a parliamentary cabinet reshuffle.

'Have you eaten?' Carmel asks, getting up now.

'Er, yeah,' he replies, having quickly stuffed in some stale ciabatta spread thickly with Laughing Cow cheese spread, plus three chocolate tree decorations for dessert. Keen to make his escape, he wasn't about to start cooking for himself.

'I'll just rustle something up then,' she says, proceeding to chop vegetables and throw them into a wok. Soon a second pan – this one containing cubed tofu – is sizzling away, and now she's snipping fresh herbs with scissors. Sorry, but he hadn't planned on coming over to watch *MasterChef*!

Carmel serves herself in a big white bowl and Joel's stomach growls while she tucks in. It's a weird kind of discomfort, he decides, sitting watching someone scoffing their supper when you're not eating. Obviously he doesn't want to stare as she forks in beansprouts and tofu, but what *should* he do? Finally, she finishes.

'Was that good?' he asks.

'Delicious.' She smirks at him. 'So, you're staying over tonight?'

'Only if it's okay,' he says petulantly.

'No, it's fine.'

Fine? The first time ever that they'll wake up together, and it's *fine*?

'I can go home if you want to.' It slips out before he can stop it. 'I mean, if you're busy—'

'Don't be like that.' She frowns in a manner that suggests he's acting like a silly boy.

'I'm not! I'm not being like anything—'

'Well, you seem it.' She slips off the stool and washes her bowl and cutlery and then, agonisingly, both the wok and the pan. Perhaps some floor mopping will follow, he muses. A little light hoover and dusting and—

His thoughts break off as he tries to process what she's just said. 'Did you hear that, Joel?'

His heart seems to stop. 'You… you said you're seeing someone?'

'I said I've *met* someone.'

'"Met someone"? What does that mean?'

'It means it's nothing serious. We're just taking it chill…'

'So who is it?' He jumps off the stool and looms in front of her, face aghast.

She shrugs, like it's nothing. 'Just some guy!'

He gasps, struggling to articulate what he wants to say. 'And you've kept it until tonight to tell me? The first time we're going to spend the whole night together? Well, that's nice—'

'Joel!' She places a hand on his forearm. 'I didn't think you'd react like this. It's just a *thing*...'

'What's a thing? You and him? Or me and you? I thought—'

Carmel is laughing now and shaking her head, as if astounded that he might be a little bit upset. 'You're married, Joel. Or have you forgotten that?'

'Of course I haven't!'

'So did you think I'd just be sitting around, filing my nails, waiting for the rare occasions when you can come over for sex?'

He blinks slowly, feeling as if he has been slapped. Should he storm out? Go home to his kids scoffing their McDonald's or stop off somewhere and get royally drunk in a pub? 'It's not that rare. I was here last night, or was that completely unmemorable for you?'

'For God's sake. That's not the point...'

He looks down at the slate-grey floor. 'I didn't think...' For a moment he thinks he might cry, and Carmel seems to pick up on this as she plants a brief kiss on his cheek.

'Oh, c'mon, honey. Don't be like this. Like I said, it's just a thing.' Another kiss, on his lips this time, which he allows grudgingly.

'What's his name?' *Is he a bigshot photographer? Or one of your clients? Have you used your fringed whip on him too?* Joel wants to know everything – and yet he doesn't. If he did, he thinks he might puke.

'Never mind,' Carmel murmurs. 'It's not important.' Then she smiles, forcing him to meet her gaze, and she tugs gently at his hand. 'Let's just go to bed.'

24

'But the chippy's an hour's round trip,' Pearl protested.

'*Over* an hour,' Shelley corrected her.

'And it's been snowing.'

'Only a tiny bit. And it's stopped now.' She insisted that they would drive to Land's End in a blizzard if it meant fetching dinner for everyone tonight. So with some trepidation Pearl agreed to drive, and she and Shelley set off, leaving Lena at the cottage to look after the guests.

In the village chip shop now, a cheerful woman with pink streaked hair lifts golden battered haddock from the fryer. 'Bit peckish, ladies?' she jokes.

'Just a bit.' Shelley grins.

'So, you've got seven fish suppers...' She turns to the till.

'That's fish and chips, right?' Shelley clarifies, and the woman chuckles.

'That's right. It's a supper up here. A fish supper or a pie supper or whatever kind of supper you fancy.' She looks up at them. 'Salt and vinegar on everything?'

'Yes please.' Pearl turns to Shelley. 'We should get some veggie options too, shouldn't we? Just in case?'

'Oh, yes.' Shelley looks down at the selection of pies in the warming cabinet. 'What are they?'

'Macaroni pies.' The woman says this as if no one has ever had to ask before.

'Macaroni? In a pie?' Shelley exclaims, warming to the concept immediately. In all her years of family meal production, her palate has settled at the heavily carb-laden meals to satisfy a ravenous husband and kids.

'That's exactly it.' The woman closes the cartons of their fish suppers and bags up the required pies. 'Nothing better than a macaroni pie if you want comfort food...' Her gaze veers towards the window. 'Look, the snow's come on really fast. Hope you don't have far to go?'

'It's quite a way actually.' Pearl glances out at the rapidly falling flakes, illuminated by the street lamp. 'We're staying at a B&B. Shore Cottage, I don't suppose you know it—'

'Oh, Michael Lynch's place?' She beams. 'Yes, I know Michael. Lovely place he has. But doesn't he do evening meals?'

Pearl hesitates, wondering if she should explain. 'There's been a bit of hitch,' she starts. 'But it's all fine. He's just gone away on a trip...'

'Ah, he deserves that,' she says firmly. 'Give him my best and take care on the drive home.'

In the car, they package up their enormous order in numerous layers of newspapers brought from the cottage for this very purpose. 'It won't keep it piping hot,' Shelley says, 'but it'll help.' On the slow drive home, snowflakes swirl in the headlights. Who cares if dinner is terribly late and isn't what the guests had ordered? They have decided to present the chippy solution as a fait accompli, and Pearl is more concerned with following the narrow lane in the driving snow than fretting over the guests' reactions.

Back at the cottage, with the Sampsons installed in the lounge, Shelley spreads out the fish and chips on trays lined with baking parchment and slides them into the various compartments of the Aga. Now she's grateful for the numerous ovens. While Lena offers more wine to Frida and Roger, Pearl sets the table with Michael's mismatched vintage china (collected, she suspects, by Rona) and lights candles. Then everything is pulled out of the ovens and the trays are set in the centre of the table. She taps lightly on

Niall's door, announcing that dinner is ready, and calls the Sampsons through from the lounge.

'Oh!' Frida surveys the table in surprise. 'I thought I ordered the moussaka?'

'That did seem a bit retro,' Roger chuckles, already red-faced from the wine. 'Come on, this looks great.'

She purses her lips and enquires about the provenance of the pies. 'It's proper hand-made pastry,' Shelley assures her, 'filled with a traditional combination of, er, *Scottish* pasta and locally produced cheese—'

'That does sound good.' Frida takes her seat, and the others follow and soon everyone is tucking in happily, and wine is flowing.

'So... there was a change of plan?' Niall sets down his fork and looks at Pearl expectantly.

'Erm, yes,' Pearl starts. 'The, um—'

'The Aga's playing up,' Shelley announces. 'More vinegar, anyone? Ketchup?'

'This is *yum*,' Theo announces, feeding Stan a chip.

'It's all right, isn't it?' His father beams at him. Then he turns to Pearl with a frown. 'You say the Aga's not working? Feels pretty warm in here...'

'It's just a bit... temperamental,' she says quickly.

'Really? I could take a look if you like. We have one at home. Just had it installed in the place we've built—'

'Oh, you've built a house?' Shelley interjects. Distraction technique again.

'Can we have a fondue tomorrow?' Theo pipes up. 'Like at Grandma's?'

Roger chuckles and ruffles his blond head. 'Grandma always does a fondue.'

'How lovely,' Shelley enthuses. 'But I'm not sure we have the equipment for—'

'Our *house*, Roger,' Frida says snappily. 'She asked about our house.'

'Ah, yes.' He looks flustered and turns back to Pearl. 'We've just built this place in Northumberland, near the coast. Really, it's been our life's dream—'

'I designed it,' Frida announces, already flushed from her wine.

'Oh, are you an architect?' Lena asks.

'No, I'm a coach. An executive coach. But I knew what I wanted and it's such a joy, being able to create your perfect home...'

'So, shall I look at the Aga after dinner?' Roger cuts in.

'Oh, no need for that.' Shelley dismisses his offer of help with a wave of her hand. 'We can do that. So, what do you do, Roger?'

In explaining that he owns many properties, he seems to temporarily forget about the malfunctioning appliance. 'It's so much harder these days,' Frida announces, 'to run a business like Roger's.'

'Oh, why's that?' Lena asks with genuine interest.

'Well, tenants have *so* many rights these days.'

'Do they?' Pearl asks pleasantly, thinking of Brandon and Abi who, she fears, will be unable to afford to rent a place of their own until at least 2035.

'Oh yes,' she asserts. 'So many regulations now. You have to have the gas checked, the electrics. Smoke alarms and fire extinguishers in multi-occupancy houses...'

Pearl and Niall seem to exchange a silent message. Rather than risk your tenants being fried in their beds?

With dinner over, wine glasses are topped up, and then there's coffee for Roger and chamomile tea for Frida, and in the absence of a proper pudding, Lena locates bars of quality chocolate and a bought ginger cake in the pantry.

'It's been a lovely evening,' Niall announces finally, 'but I think I'll turn in early, if you don't mind.'

Feeling the pace now after the day's events, Pearl would very much love to turn in early too. Are B&B hosts allowed to do that? Or might the unsupervised Theo terrorise Stan? 'No problem,' she says. 'What time would you like breakfast?'

'Erm, how about everyone else?' He looks around the table.

'Eight-thirty?' Frida suggests, and if anyone would prefer a different time, they daren't say.

'Great.' Pearl smiles. 'Eight-thirty it is. Sleep well, Niall.' Then to the Sampsons: 'Would you mind moving through to the lounge while we clear things here?' Off they all drift, with a clearly tipsy Frida clutching at Roger's arm.

'Mmm, wasn't that delicious?' She chuckles. 'Those funny pasta pies! Wonder what we're getting tomorrow night?'

Alone now in the kitchen, the three friends load the dishwasher and perform a final thorough clean of the kitchen. 'We did it,' Lena breathes, looking happily at her friends. 'Well done, girls.'

Pearl and Shelley beam at her, and they hug tightly. 'Well done us!' Lena murmurs.

'I'm done in, though, aren't you?' Shelley adds. Then a whispered, 'When d'you think they'll all go to bed?'

Conscious of Frida chattering away now in the lounge, and Theo becoming whiney through tiredness, the women settle at the table. Does time operate differently up here in Scotland? Lena wonders. Before they booked the trip she'd panicked that Christmas was thundering towards her, with the spectre of Tommy's parents on the horizon, primed to belittle her pigs in blankets and peer around her little ramshackle flat in distaste. But now, with the prospect of looking after Michael's guests until Monday, it feels like an age away. With a pang of missing Tommy, she stands up.

'You two go through to bed,' she says. 'I'll stay up until the Sampsons turn in.'

Pearl frowns. It's only eleven-fifteen but feels later. 'We're not leaving you to deal with everything.'

Lena smiles. 'There's nothing to deal with. Everything's done, isn't it? So off you go. Remember we're up early for the breakfast shift!' Shelley groans and laughs, and hugs her again.

'Thanks, Leen.'

'No problem. Night, girls. I'm just going to text Tommy, okay?' She steps out into the garden where everything is dusted in snow, sparkling under the pearly moon. She strolls down the garden, picking her way carefully over the uneven ground, and gazes out onto the silvery loch.

The sharp night air fills her lungs, energising her instantly. Plucking her phone from her jeans pocket, she goes onto Instagram, wondering if Tommy has posted anything today. He's like a kid with his social media, sharing snaps of meals he's cooked, with jokey captions – *Managed not to poison Lena today!* They both love to wander around different parts of London; little corners off the beaten track. He'll post his picture of a woman with numerous pugs on leads, or of noodles with a comically rude brand name in a grocers. Sometimes Lena rolls her eyes at his boyish humour, but she loves it really. He is uncomplicated, which she finds refreshing. What you see with Tommy Huntley is what you get.

Of course, he was seeing Daisy today, she remembers now. It'll have been good for them to have a dad-and-daughter day, all to themselves. For Tommy to have some company too. He's not the kind of man to do loads of stuff with his mates, or have a raft of activities that don't involve her. From the night they met, he's pretty much wanted to do everything with Lena.

However, it's not one of Tommy's photos that she's looking at now. It's one of Daisy's. An Instagram Story that she must have posted earlier today.

Lena would never think of herself as Daisy's stepmother. She hasn't been around for long enough to earn the title. And Daisy, although pleasant enough, hasn't really let her into her life. Lena has tried her best, asking her all kinds of questions and then holding back in case she was quizzing her too much. She has bought books for her, carefully chosen to hopefully chime with a teen mindset. Although Daisy has always thanked her, Lena suspected that they were slung somewhere, never to be read.

Lena has tried to be Daisy's friend, and if it's felt a little hopeless, then that's fine, she's reassured herself. Catherine is Daisy's mother and she would never try to get in the way of Tommy's family. But now, as she stands stock still in the moonlight, and stares at the picture of Tommy and Catherine together, she feels as if she has been punched in the gut.

Tommy is smiling a little awkwardly, but then his smile is always off-centre like that. And Catherine is beaming and their faces are actually pressed together, cheek to cheek. They are two extremely good-looking middle-aged people with excellent bone structure and great teeth and, Christ, how had Lena never realised how right they must have looked together? How right they *look*, she corrects herself. Present tense. Tommy and Catherine Huntley still look like a happily married couple. Since Lena has known him, the three of them have never gone to lunch together. At least not to her knowledge. It's shocking to Lena, that she's so rattled by a silly photo that Daisy probably put up without even thinking. And they were only having pizza, she tells herself, irritated by this unexpected surge of jealousy.

It was just lunch. It's *fine*. It doesn't mean a thing. That was what Max, Lena's ex-husband, said when she spotted a restaurant receipt tossed casually on the kitchen worktop one evening.

Just lunch with a friend. It was nothing.

She hated herself then for checking his emails and phone, and for rifling through his pockets and desk drawers at home. Everything was remarkably accessible to her: the texts, the little secret codes in his diary, the photos on his phone. Naked pictures of the woman; nudes as they're called now. Max had been so careless about passwords that Lena could only conclude that he didn't care whether or not she found out.

All those years, through the trying for a baby and her pleading with him to try at least one round of IVF, there'd been an affair. And then there was a baby with this beautiful and – Lena had to hand it to her – extremely *flexible* woman (did she do yoga or Pilates, Lena wondered? Or was there some other way of being able to position your legs like that?). Lena couldn't have a child, but that didn't matter to Max, because he'd made one with someone else.

Tommy isn't like that, Lena tells herself as tears flood her eyes. She looks up at the star-speckled sky and breathes in great lungfuls of crisp Highland air, as if that will chase this terrible feeling away.

'It was only lunch,' she mutters out loud. But still, she can't unsee the image of Tommy and Catherine jammed tightly together with Christmas decorations all around them, as she steps back into the house.

25

'Stop freaking out. Don't be an idiot. It's just a little Christmas party.'

That's what Martha had told her little brother Fin, as soon as their dad had gone out earlier.

'But what if he comes back?'

'He won't.'

'But how d'you *know*?'

She exhaled, hoping she could trust him not to breathe a word about what was to happen tonight. Of course he wouldn't. Fin would be part of it as – unfortunately – he lives here too. And much as she'd like to, Martha can't exactly pack him off to a friend's or stuff him into the cupboard under the stairs. So she'll have to accept his annoying presence, and that of his equally annoying friends, and hope that everyone she's invited will turn up. That way, Fin's little group will be so diluted as to be barely noticeable.

'Marth?' Fin prompts her now.

'What?'

'It's just... Dad. He said the thing he's gone to, it might be boring...'

'It won't be boring,' she snaps, and he frowns, looking hurt.

'Yeah, but—'

'Fin, listen to me,' Martha says, adopting a level tone now. 'I know Dad's not coming back tonight 'cause he's taken an overnight bag.'

'Has he?' Fin's eyes widen.

'Yeah. So we're fine,' she states, strutting away from him now and heading for her room, because she can't be around her little brother any more. Not right now anyway. Not after seeing that thing in their dad's bag. Because actually, she wants to tell Fin, to offload it instead of carrying it around in her head like a bomb that could go off at any moment. Equally, she *can't* tell him, because what if she's got it wrong and has misinterpreted the gift tag and the actual gift? Then he'd be freaking out over nothing and it would all be her fault.

It's actually pretty stressful, she decides, being the one in charge. *Holding the fort*, as her dad put it.

Martha necks a vodka shot and studies her face in the mirror. Almost instantly, she feels a little better. She feels better still once she's showered and changed and done her make-up and hair. And her mood continues to improve as she and Fin perform a speedy inventory of the living room, carrying any easily breakable items up to their dad's studio where they'll be safe.

Friends start to arrive, lugging rucksacks filled with beer and wine and various spirits. And now music is playing and Martha's heart lifts as she opens the door to see Izzy, with whom she's in love. They hug and kiss and Martha pulls her into the living room where the table is already covered in cans and bottles and puddles of spilt drink.

Time's a weird thing, Martha reflects briefly as Izzy grabs her hand and they start to dance. This day, with her dad fussing and pacing, seemed to stretch for a hundred years. But now the party's under way, and in a blink it's midnight. Fin and his friends are all crammed onto the sofa, laughing and drinking enthusiastically, a blur of troubled complexions flushed with the headiness of the party. Pablo, who Martha dated briefly, is smoking a spliff in the middle of the living room. Martha wonders for a second whether the smell will linger until morning. So what if it does? They can open the windows; and anyway, her dad won't care because he bought a gold bracelet for someone who's not Mum, and he wrote on the gift card: *Just a little something for you, beautiful.* So fuck him, Martha decides.

That's why she's not overly concerned when a bottle of red wine spills onto the floor, bleeding all over the beige rug, or when a group of unfamiliar young men saunter in without knocking. 'All right!' Pablo says in greeting. There's some laughing and jostling, which signals to Martha that it's okay, they're friends of Pablo's. The fact that Pablo steals car parts to order doesn't concern her. There are no cars in here!

Now the music has changed and is deafening and thumping insistently. Martha panics briefly that the neighbours will hear and might complain to her dad – but it's too late to do anything about that now. And what's he going to do anyway? Ground her? Martha necks another shot, accepts a drag on a joint and allows herself a moment's pleasure that the night is going so well. People are kissing now, in the living room and kitchen, on the stairs and in all of the bedrooms.

The night goes on, and yet more people arrive – to think Martha had worried that no one would turn up! And kitchen cupboards are ransacked, packets of crisps and biscuits torn open. Someone delves into the freezer and starts eating cookie dough ice cream from the tub. Someone else stumbles downstairs to roars of laughter. They've been rifling through a wardrobe upstairs and found these hilarious trousers, like old raver's trousers – yellow with squiggly patterns – and they've put them on.

'Look at these! These are fantastic!' an unfamiliar boy announces, affecting a raver's dance in the hallway.

Fin's friends have surged into the kitchen now, hunter gatherers in search of more alcohol. They have downed all the beers they'd managed to purloin from their own homes and no one will give them anything else. When Fin tried to swipe a bottle of rum, Pablo slapped him on the back of the head.

'Look!' Ajay, aged fourteen but looking around ten, waves the slender bottle he's found in a cupboard. *Red wine vinegar.*

'Don't drink that!' someone shouts. But in his drunkenness the only word Ajay sees is 'wine', and he yanks off the screw top and flings it over his shoulder, into the face of a powerfully built young man drinking vodka from a World's Best Dad mug. Ajay brings the bottle to his mouth and glugs down the vinegar, a rare vintage with a powerful acidic kick.

The instant he's finished, his guts clench and he needs the bathroom urgently. He pushes through all the milling people to get to the downstairs loo. But it's locked. He bangs on the door – a girl yells at him – and then stumbles upstairs, ignoring cries of 'Hey!' and 'Ow!' as he tramples on feet and legs and some girl's long blonde hair.

Although Ajay has been to Fin's house before, he doesn't know which room is the upstairs bathroom. Not this one, obviously. This is definitely a bedroom – it's actually Fin's parents' bedroom – the clue being that there isn't a loo in it but a *bed*, a bed that two people are currently having vigorous sex on. Ajay spins out of the room and clatters up some more stairs, his stomach cramping as he bursts into a room filled with more people and computers, like it's an office or something. In the split second before anyone registers his presence, he sees that there's weird art on the walls. Not pictures – just massive writing. FREE YOUR SOUL, one reads.

Ajay doesn't want to free his soul. He wants to find the bathroom as his stomach is heaving and gurgling in an alarming manner. But he doesn't feel he can ask, as the people in here – all older boys, maybe about nineteen? – are telling him to *get the fuck out, what are you doing up here you stupid kid?* He gawps at them, wondering what's going on in here, what they're doing. Then, amidst their jeers and laughter, Ajay does as he's been told. He gets out.

Martha, who is still dancing with Izzy, knows nothing of the activities in her parents' bedroom and her dad's study. They kiss, and she's so happy she barely registers the cry as someone falls heavily into the lopsided Christmas tree. Down it crashes, tinsel flying and Martha's great grandmother's baubles shattering as it cracks the window and collapses onto the wine-sodden rug.

26

THREE DAYS UNTIL CHRISTMAS

9.20 a.m.

'Hello, hello! Go away silly man!' Theo grabbed the B&B landline before Shelley could race to it and now he won't hand it to her.

'Theo, please. It might be important. It could be someone calling to book a room, and if they can't, my friend Michael will lose a lot of money—'

'Who's Michael?' Still gripping the phone, Theo fixes her with a challenging stare. Breakfast went smoothly and they cleared up with impressive efficiency. Niall offered to help but Shelley assured him that they were fine, and why didn't he head out to enjoy the beautiful day? The sun was shining brightly and everything was lightly sprinkled with snow. Shelley had just begun to believe that they might actually be pretty competent at this B&B lark.

'Remember I told you?' she says sternly. 'Michael's the nice man who owns this house. Now please give me the phone.'

Theo laughs. 'Bye, silly smelly man! Bye bye!' He jabs at a button and flings the phone down onto the kitchen unit. Shelley grabs it, switching on her bright and pleasant receptionist's voice: 'Hello, can I help you?' But the call has ended.

Almost immediately it rings again and Shelley answers quickly. 'Hi there?' comes the male voice. 'It's Michael...'

'Michael, hi! It's Shelley. How's it going down there?'

'Um... okay. Yeah. Okay. It's good...' She catches the tension in his voice. 'But I, uh... lost my phone...'

'Oh no! Where are you calling from?'

'My hotel room. I'm out at Heathrow—'

'Any chance of getting it back?'

'No, unfortunately. I left it on the plane. Totally stupid...'

'What a pain for you.'

'Not the end of the world,' he says briskly. 'So, how are things up there? Everything okay?'

'Er, yeah!' Shelley tries to radiate confidence. 'All of your guests have arrived and they're great, they're *lovely*...'

'Was that the Sampsons' child answering the phone?'

'Oh, yes. Sorry about that,' she blusters. 'Just as well it was you, huh?'

'Er, yeah.'

She can sense him frowning.

'Anyway, we're on top of everything,' she breezes on. 'We've just finished breakfast and everything's cleared up—'

'What, already?' he asks in surprise.

'Yep, all done. We did bacon and eggs – oh, and I found three eggs in the hen house this morning! Three freshly laid eggs! Not that we needed them but so lovely to see. Isn't it magical, the way that happens?'

He pauses. 'The way hens lay eggs? I guess so—'

'Oh, I know that's just normal to you,' she goes on. 'But it's so gorgeous here, Michael. We're loving it. You really are so lucky. Oh, and Frida loved the vegetarian haggis and I tried some too. Delicious! I'm such a *southerner*, aren't I? Never had it before—'

'Well, I'm glad you're enjoying yourselves,' he cuts in.

'I hope you are too,' she says. 'So how are things with—'

'All fine,' he says quickly, and now Shelley gets it. Krissy is there with him in his hotel room.

'Great,' she says. 'Well, I don't want to interrupt—'

'No, I called *you*, remember?'

'Oh yes, of course...' She laughs. 'Well, okay. Just before you go, there is this *one* thing...'

'What's that?'

'The, um... the meals,' she starts.

'The meals?'

'Yes. The dinners. We mustn't have listened properly or taken it all in. Because I'm sure you must have told us—'

'Told you what?' he says, sounding baffled.

'Er, where they are. The tagines and pies and berry crumbles—'

'Oh God. Didn't I say?'

'Maybe not. But it was fine,' Shelley adds quickly. 'We drove to the chippy instead. I hope you're not mad with us—'

'Mad? Of course I'm not mad!' He exhales loudly. 'I'm *so* sorry. Can't believe I didn't tell you where the other freezer is...'

'The *other* freezer?' Shelley repeats.

'Yeah. I don't what I was thinking. It's in the woodshed,' he adds.

Shelley blinks slowly. 'Right.'

'That's the main freezer where all the evening meals are,' he clarifies. 'I really am sorry—'

'Honestly,' she cuts in, 'no need to apologise. It all worked out in the end and everyone loved it. The fish and chips – the *fish suppers* – were amazing, and Frida loved the macaroni pies. She had two—'

'You had macaroni pies?'

'Yes! My God, they're delicious. What a fantastic invention – carbs encased in carbs. So it was actually quite fun, figuring it all out. Like some kind of challenge.' Shelley chuckles. 'Like we were being filmed for a reality show.'

She senses him smiling now.

'Are you always as positive as this?'

'I try to be,' she replies.

'Even so,' he ventures, 'I'm sure it was a challenge you could've done without.'

'Well, never mind,' she says quickly. 'You were in a hurry and you had other things on your mind, didn't you?'

'Well, yeah.' A small silence settles between them and Shelley wonders why he's still on the line, chatting to her, when surely he has company.

'So, erm... I hope things are working out for you?' she ventures.

She hears him moving around the room. 'I actually feel a bit stupid,' he starts.

'Why?' She frowns.

He sighs heavily. 'I wasn't going to say because you've been so brilliant. You all have, in making this possible for me. And I'd already decided I was going to say it's been great—'

'Michael,' she cuts in, frowning, 'you don't need to *lie* to us...'

'Okay.' He clears his throat. 'I s'pose I just feel a bit ridiculous, taking off on a whim when obviously, it was never going to work...'

'Hasn't it? Oh, I am sorry. So, what happened?'

'Erm, well...' He tails off, and she wonders whether she should have asked. 'It was obvious right away,' he starts, 'that what we'd had over all those thousands of miles wasn't... well, I don't know *what* it was,' he adds. 'Just that it didn't translate into real life.'

'Oh, Michael,' she murmurs.

'It really is okay,' he continues, feigning brightness now. 'We had a few drinks and a perfectly nice time. But there was this unspoken thing that it wasn't going to happen. What is it that they say?'

Shelley frowns. 'That there wasn't a spark?'

'Yeah.' A wry chuckle. 'Maybe we should've just kept it as a long-distance thing...'

'But you had to try, didn't you?' she suggests.

'I s'pose so. But it still feels...' He breaks off. 'Kind of mortifying.'

She stands at the window, looking out over the white-topped hills as she takes this in. Niall and the Sampsons have all headed out to enjoy the bright, snowy morning and Lena and Pearl are out walking Stan. 'You shouldn't feel like that,' she says now. 'Not that I'm *telling* you how to feel...' She pauses, wondering how best to put it. 'I just mean there's no shame in it. It was always going to be risky, wasn't it?'

She senses him pacing around and wonders what the view from his hotel is like. 'Guess so. But I should've approached it with a lot more care and thought...'

'What were you supposed to do? Perform a risk assessment?'

He laughs. 'Maybe.'

'Well, I don't think that's any way to live your life,' she adds, 'personally speaking. Not that it's anything to do with me, but we all make cockups sometimes, don't we? We all jump in with both feet because we believe in something – or someone – and we have to take that chance—' She stops, catching herself, and laughs. 'Oh my God. I'm spouting memes at you. I'll be saying "we all have the same twenty-four hours in a day" next—'

'Who came up with that?' Already, he's sounding happier.

'Just some woman off *Love Island*.'

'Oh.'

Shelley smiles. 'I'm guessing you've never watched *Love Island*.'

'Can't say I have—'

'Okay, so what are your plans for today?' she asks.

'Well, I'm just going to come home,' he replies, as if it's obvious.

'But aren't you booked in at the hotel for two nights?'

'Yes, but I don't care about that…'

'And what about your flight? Aren't you meant to be flying home tomorrow?'

'I'll get another flight,' he insists. 'I'll get one today if I can. If not I'll take a train. Honestly, it's the best thing. The way we left it…' He coughs dryly. 'It was a bit awkward. A bit, well… we both knew we wouldn't be doing stuff together today.'

'Yes,' Shelley ventures, 'but you could still *do* stuff, couldn't you?'

'By myself, you mean?' he asks in surprise.

'Well, yes!' She smiles. He really does sound like a fish out of water down there.

'I don't really know what kind of stuff,' he admits.

'Oh, Michael,' she exclaims. 'Come on. You might live in the wilds but you do still remember how to operate in a city, don't you?'

'Well, yes. Of course I do.' She senses him frowning. 'But I'm not in actual London. I'm at a Heathrow hotel and people don't come here for fun, you know? They come for stopovers and layovers, or because they're catching an early flight—'

'Yes, but you're not incarcerated there, are you?' she interrupts. 'I mean, they will let you out—'

'Yeah, of course!'

'So you could sit there in your hotel, where I bet there's a kettle and a miserly selection of teabags and skinny Nescafé sachets and tiny cartons of UHT milk—'

'There is actually—'

'—And you could make a cup of tea and sit at the window, watching the planes...'

She breaks off as he laughs. 'You make it sound so enticing.'

'I do, don't I?' She grins. 'Or, instead of that, you could treat it like a not-exactly-ideal hotel that you only booked because it's cheap. Like when you were young and went away with your mates and didn't care that the apartment was crappy and there was a single bare bulb and your mattress was so thin, it was like sleeping on a slice of bread—'

'I remember those places.' Michael chuckles.

'Me too. And didn't you still have a brilliant time?'

'Well, yeah. Of course.'

''Cause you just made the best of it,' she continues. 'So what you could do is, you could leave your miserable little room and take yourself into London for the day and do the kind of stuff you could *never* do up here...'

'Like... what?'

'Oh, come on,' she splutters. 'It's London! One of the greatest cities in the world! On the last Sunday before Christmas. It'll be *amazing*. Just get on the train and get off somewhere central and walk around. Soak it all up like tourist—'

'But I *am* a tourist,' he reminds her.

'Well, that's good then, isn't it? You're in the mindset.' She laughs. 'So just enjoy it. Enjoy the contrast...'

'The contrast?' he repeats.

'From what it's like up here,' she clarifies, 'to what it's like *there*. Walk down Regent's Street and look at the decorations, everything all lit up and wonderful. Go down to Trafalgar Square and look at the enormous Christmas tree. Get yourself a drink in a nice bar and take yourself off to the Natural History Museum and go ice skating—'

'Oh, I don't think so—'

'And then, if you're feeling energetic, walk all the way back along Piccadilly, and go into the Rivoli Bar at The Ritz—'

'The Ritz?' he splutters. 'I can't go there!'

'Why not?'

She senses him trying to scrabble together a reason. 'Well, my clothes for one thing—'

'You don't have to wear a suit,' she teases. 'You have a nice shirt and trousers with you, don't you?'

'Yes, but—'

'—so go in and order one champagne cocktail—'

'But isn't that—'

'It's a fortune, yes. And that's the point. Have more than one if you feel like it. Get yourself sozzled on champagne cocktails, and then come back to your airport hotel and fall into drunken slumber. And then, when you wake up tomorrow with a fuzzy hangover...' She catches herself. 'I'm sorry. I've just spouted a whole load of instructions at you, haven't I?'

'Yes, you have.' He sounds bemused now, and a little stunned. 'So, if I do all that – if I follow your instructions – then what do I do next?'

He's teasing, she realises. Pretending he can't operate without her telling him what to do. 'Oh, that's easy,' she says with a smile. 'When you've done all of that and had a brilliant day exploring London on your own...' Shelley hesitates. '*Then* you can come home.'

27

As Joel steps out of the Tube station and starts to walk home, he tries to make sense of his sleepover at Carmel's.

It went okay, in the end. All right, so she could have dredged up a tad more excitement over the gold bracelet, which he'd taken ages choosing in a cool little designer jeweller's in Soho. For all the gratitude she showed he might as well have grabbed her a bangle at Camden Market. And she'd had nothing to give him in return. But Joel isn't a child – even though he might act like one when out Christmas shopping with his wife. And he wasn't going to throw a tantrum over the lack of gift.

What Carmel *had* given him was a thorough going over in the confines of her bedroom like nothing he'd experienced before. It was as if the very existence of this other man had added a whole new dimension. Jealousy, humiliation, even rage; it was all swirling inside him and he wanted her so much. He wanted her more than this other nameless man could ever want her, and although he's not one to brag, he reckons he gave her the performance of his life last night. And she was mad for it, flipping him around and throwing him about and biting him like he was a fucking sandwich. Utterly spent, he'd finally fallen asleep at around 5.30 a.m.

As Joel turns into his street, he reflects that Carmel could have been a bit *nicer* to him this morning. He wasn't expecting a favourable performance review, or even a 'good boy' sticker – but she might have been a bit keener to hang out together. He'd looked forward to a leisurely breakfast – pastries, eggs, her excellent coffee – and hopefully some more sex. But that was not forthcoming. She had to 'get on', she explained. She was busy-busy-busy! He wasn't even offered toast. But the worst of it was that she asked if he'd mind having his shower at home, rather than at hers, as she needed to head out right away.

Head out where? To see her other man? Feeling grubby and a bit smelly, out he was flung into the cold December morning. He feels a little *used*, frankly. Shattered too. Once he's showered and made himself respectable, he might slip off to bed for a nap.

Towards him now comes a person dancing along in a Christmas tree outfit, her spherical head poking out of the top of it. She's a vision in green fake fur and tinsel, and he knows for certain that she is going to try to interact with him. *Keep walking. Don't look at her.* 'Morning, Scrooge! Cheer up, love!' she bellows, stopping to rattle a charity tin in his face.

'Sorry, no cash,' he mutters, trying to avoid eye contact.

The woman seems to peer at him in an odd way. 'Ooh, *naughty*.' Her eyebrows – one red, one green, how very festive – shoot up. 'Someone's been having a fun time!' Instinctively he touches his head, trying to flatten down his hair as he hurries onwards, keen to get away from her as she's obviously mad.

His house is in view now and Joel exhales in relief. But his relief dissipates quickly as now he thinks… No, no. He must be mistaken. It'll just be a reflection or a trick of the light. The living room window *can't* be broken. Joel quickens his pace, his chest tightening as he approaches his home and registers that his first assumption was correct. The Victorian sash window is definitely not as he left it yesterday. There's a bloody great crack in it. And the Christmas tree which stood at the window, decorated by Shelley with her grandma's precious baubles, has gone.

Burglars, is Joel's first panicked thought. Burglars have stolen our tree!

A sickening feeling surges up in him as he swings in through the gate and up the short path. He opens the front door and steps into the hallway and for a moment he cannot move or speak or do anything at all.

Joel stands there, mouth agape. Then: 'Martha? Fin?' he bellows. 'Come here *right now!*'

* * *

On this cold, bright, snow-dusted Sunday morning, Pearl believes that she is actually in the most beautiful place on earth. It's so still and quiet, and after the hectic activities of yesterday and today's breakfast, she is relishing the solitude.

Her heart sinks a little when Niall appears in the distance, rucksack on his back, clearly setting out on a hike. She wanted to sit here alone on this rock at the lochside, taking in the calm, still water, blue as the sky, and the white-topped mountains in the distance. But now he's striding towards her, and he stops as they exchange pleasantries. 'Nice spot you've found here,' he remarks.

'It's gorgeous, isn't it?'

He nods and smiles. 'I, um, couldn't help overhearing Shelley on the phone earlier,' he adds.

'Oh, really?' Her heart quickens.

'Yeah, talking to Michael, I assume. The owner? Something about there being another freezer in the woodshed?'

'Ah, right. Yes.' Pearl senses blood rushing to her cheeks and then catches his eye, relieved to see that he's amused by their deceit. The 'temperamental' Aga. The hurriedly changed dinner plan. 'You must think we're a bunch of incompetents,' she adds. 'And you're writing about all this, aren't you?'

'Yeah, and very positively too.' He picks up a smooth pebble from the shoreline and sends it skimming over the water. 'They're easily the best fish and chips I've ever had,' he adds.

Pearl's shoulders relax. 'Glad you enjoyed them. But you'll be pleased to know that tonight, everyone will be having what they ordered. There won't be any surprises.'

'Oh, I was kinda looking forward to seeing what might happen.' Niall grins, and Pearl registers the intensity of his blue eyes behind the glasses.

'Sorry to disappoint you.' She smiles.

Niall picks up another pebble and skims it, then sits on the rock beside hers. 'I also owe you a bit of an apology.'

'Really? What for?'

'For being such a grump yesterday, when you were asking me about Christmas...'

'It was none of my business,' she says quickly. 'And you saved the day with those towels, you know. That was some arrival, wasn't it?'

He chuckles. 'Yeah. Poor kid. I was just glad I still had them. I'd been meaning to get rid of them.' A small pause. 'I had the world's most carsick dog,' he adds.

Pearl frowns in sympathy. 'But you don't any more?'

'Oh no, he's still very much going, is Barney. No, my ex has him now.' Another pause, and the pebble is skimmed. 'Bit of a custody battle,' he explains with a dry laugh.

'That must've been difficult,' Pearl offers, but he shrugs off her sympathy.

'People go through far worse things. It's all fine now.'

Pearl takes this in, figuring that it isn't all fine, and also that this might explain why Christmas was a sensitive issue. Damn Christmas! She'd looked forward to it so much, all those years when it was the three of them: Pearl and Dean and Brandon. And possibly even more so when it was just her and Brandon, her little mate – because it gave them something to plan for and focus on. *We can't feel all jaded and sad because Christmas is coming!*

'The thing is,' he continues, 'I s'pose one of my main motivations for arranging this trip, and persuading my editor to go for it, is because...' He breaks off, as if figuring out how best to explain it.

'Well, it's work, isn't it?' Pearl suggests. 'It's your livelihood—'

'Yeah, there is that.' He looks out over the water. It's as still as glass until a bird swoops down, skimming its surface. 'But there's another reason too.'

Pearl glances at him, waiting for him to offer more. When he doesn't, she lets the silence settle and looks along the shoreline. She notices a small wooden jetty and a little rowing boat lying on the rough grass above the pebbled shore. There are oars too, jutting out of it. She's glad now that Niall stopped to talk, after the awkwardness of yesterday. Her curiosity is piqued and she senses that he might actually want to open up to her.

'Look,' she says, getting up from the rock. 'That must be Michael's boat. You don't fancy a row on the loch, do you?'

Niall seems to hesitate. 'I'm actually not the best at rowing. Bit embarrassing. I realise it's one of those things men are instinctively supposed to know how to do—'

'No, I can row,' Pearl tells him, 'believe it or not.'

Niall looks quizzical. 'Why the "believe it or not"?'

'Oh, I don't know,' she says quickly. 'Maybe I don't look like the type—'

'I don't really judge people like that,' he says lightly, and briefly, their eyes meet.

'Right.' Pearl smiles. The morning is so still and quiet, the blue sky streaked with wispy clouds. When she'd told Elias about the rowing – what a big part of her childhood it had been – he was amazed. 'What, a dainty little thing like you?' Feeling patronised, she'd quickly changed the subject. 'My dad had a boat on the river Weaver, close to where we lived,' she explains now. 'He taught me to row and it became the thing we did together, Dad and me. I was mad about water, being on the river...'

'Let's go then,' Niall enthuses. And so, between them, they lift the wooden boat and carry it down to the water's edge and push it into the loch. On the weather-worn jetty, Niall holds its rope tightly as Pearl steps into it, and then he follows her. Pearl uses an oar to push them away.

'So, you were saying,' she prompts him, emboldened now that she has something practical to do. 'About your reasons for coming up here?'

Niall catches her glance and she smiles encouragingly. He watches as she takes both oars, allowing herself a moment to look around and assess the direction they'll head in. 'I guess,' he says, as they glide away from the shore, 'what I really wanted to do was avoid Christmas.'

28

Like a grim-faced police officer who's first at the crime scene, Joel patrols the downstairs of the house. The kitchen is terrible. The sight and stench of it makes his stomach heave. Bottles and cans and dirty glasses have been dumped on every surface, some with cigarettes stubbed out in them. There are sticky puddles of beer and smashed crisps all over the floor. The smell of weed and smoke, with a base note of stale booze, evokes the heady fragrance of student parties from his youth. But he's not a student now. He's a fifty-two-year-old man – and a father. He thought he could trust his kids! He bought them a KFC and McDonald's and this is how they thank him!

From there, sensing that it will be even worse than the kitchen, he steps into the living room. There he surveys the Christmas tree lying broken, the baubles smashed, pine needles everywhere and the window cracked. The rug has been liberally doused in red wine, and the presents, wrapped so carefully by Shelley, have all been torn open and scattered about.

A reusable coffee mug, which he remembers Shelley being determined to buy that day at the shopping mall, is sitting in the middle of the floor filled with some kind of murky liquid. He doesn't know who the other presents were meant to be for. Shelley had taken care of all that. To Joel it's just a load of random stuff lying in a sea of torn wrapping paper and shiny ribbon and bows.

He sits gingerly on the sofa, taking care to avoid the various spillages on it as he's still wearing his best trousers, the ones he'd picked out for his night with Carmel. Martha and Fin hover, looking pale and queasy, at the door. 'This,' Joel announces, 'is a nightmare.'

'I know,' Martha murmurs. 'I know, Dad.'

'I can't believe you did this.'

Fin sniffs and peers down at his trainers. 'Sorry, Dad.'

'Sorry?' Joel glares at him. 'As if that makes it all right?' He jumps up and gestures wildly. 'Look at the state of this place! The pair of you – I don't know what to say. But there's going to be consequences, I'll tell you that. If you think you're getting off scot-free then you're very, very wrong. Because I'm going to—' He breaks off because he doesn't know what the consequences should be. Where is Shelley when he needs her? She always knows what to do. The kids are *her* area. But she's living it up in Scotland with her friends!

'We did try to clear up,' Fin says in a small voice.

'Really?' Joel scoffs. 'You mean it was actually *worse* than this?'

'Yeah.' Martha nods. 'We did try. We've been up for hours, Dad, cleaning and—'

'When's Mum back again?' Fin croaks.

'Christmas Eve. I've told you already—'

'We're *sorry*, okay?' Martha interrupts, fixing her father with a look. Although she's clearly a little shellshocked – and hungover – now there's a flicker of something else too. Defiance is what it is. Why is she looking at him like that? 'It was only meant to be a little gathering,' she adds. 'But then all these other people came—'

'Oh, so big boys did it?' he barks.

'Some of them *were* quite big,' Fin mumbles.

Joel blows out air as he tries to wrestle his thoughts into order. Nothing has gone right since Shelley decided to book herself a little holiday with five minutes' notice, leaving him to deal with this crap. Well, fuck it, he decides, stomping upstairs now to see what else is in store for him on this, the shittiest of days – actually the worst day of the year so far. But maybe something else has yet to top it? There's still time.

He flings open the bathroom door. There's vomit in here – obviously – and he wonders briefly what young people drink these days, because when he was a teenager his was never neon orange like that.

Joel doesn't bother checking the kids' bedrooms. If they're trashed then they can live in them like that. Serves them right. Instead, he hoofs up to his studio, his heart racing now. Surely no one's been up here in his lair, his precious space? Not at the top of the house. Why *would* they?

He opens the door with some trepidation and his gaze sweeps his desk. The slab of teak the size of Kent is littered with more bottles and cans and there are several little dark brown marks on it. Burn marks where cigarettes have been stubbed out on it, he realises. Sheer and utter vandalism! He feels as if he might cry. But now fury has surged up in him again.

'Martha!' he yells. 'Get up here now!' Joel squeezes his eyes tight shut, hoping that when he opens them again everything will be normal and it was just a terrible mirage. Surely no one would burn the desk of a renowned graphic designer who once delivered a keynote speech at Glasgow School of Art?

But it's not a mirage. His studio with its thousands of quids' worth of tech has been used as a party den. He spots a few items from the living room in here: the tall ceramic vase, the pink glass candlesticks and the ailing cheese plant. Stranger still, some vaguely familiar yellow patterned fabric is draped over his ergonomic swivel chair. On closer examination it would appear that these are his trousers from the nineties – his phat pants – which would suggest that someone has also been in his bedroom, raking through his wardrobe!

'MARTHA. FIN. GET UP HERE NOW OR I'LL KILL YOU!'

He hears them whispering, either conferring or trying to apportion blame, as they approach. 'That's nice,' Martha mutters, 'threatening to murder your children.' They appear in his studio doorway, pale as snow.

'Oh, shit,' Fin breathes as he surveys the room.

'Yes. "Oh shit" indeed.' Joel notices now that, although his guitar is still sitting on its stand as he left it, two strings are broken. He exhales and looks around again, his gaze stopping suddenly. He steps forward and stares at the small expanse of bare desk, in between all the party detritus. 'My new laptop,' he says.

'What?' Martha frowns.

'My laptop! Where is it?'

'I don't know, I wasn't up here—'

'I didn't do anything!' Fin says quickly.

'Then who *was* up here? Who did this?'

'Honestly, I have no idea...' Martha shrinks back as he storms around the room, checking shelves and desk drawers in the feeble hope that it might just have been 'moved'.

Joel pushes past his kids and flies down the stairs. Where the hell is it? Not in the bathroom, he's been in there, unless some joker dropped it into the cistern? As he's less than keen to see the state of his kids' rooms right now, he swings into his own room, the room he shares with Shelley, who should be here right now. Here to help and support and *do* something more useful than get pissed with Lena and Pearl—

'Dad?' He's conscious of his daughter hovering next to him, giving him a curious look. It strikes Joel that someone else looked at him that way today: that preposterous dancing Christmas tree woman in the street.

'What?' he shouts.

'That thing there...' Martha seems to recoil, and at the same time Joel becomes aware that not only is the bed unmade, duvet and pillows and even the sheet tossed around as if in a storm – but that someone is *in* the bed. A small young male with dark curly hair. A child, for Christ's sake.

As Ajay stirs, feeling much better now after his sleep, Joel feels as if he might faint. Not because there's a kid here – a kid he semi-recognises but God knows what his name is – but because Martha is staring right at him and, with a wave of horror, he realises what it must be.

'*Daaaad*,' she says slowly. 'What's that on your neck?'

29

'Theo, come here, darling!'

Frida's shrill tone cuts through the early afternoon stillness as Pearl and Niall head back towards Shore Cottage. Then: 'Theo, please stop that for a moment, sweetheart. Isn't this beautiful? You must come and look at this view!'

Pearl catches Niall's glance. 'He's six.' He chuckles. 'I don't think he's interested in views...'

'She might as well say, "Come and see this fascinating tax return, darling",' Pearl adds. But then her expression drops as Stan barks sharply and she sees what's happening in front of the house. 'Theo!' she cries out as Niall runs ahead.

'No, you can't do that to Stan,' he says firmly. When Pearl catches up he is already disentangling a length of frayed old rope that's been wound in a complicated fashion around the dog's collar and forelegs.

'What were you doing, Theo?' she exclaims.

'I made a harness.' He grins proudly.

'Yes, but he doesn't need a harness.' Niall stuffs the rope into a jacket pocket.

'Yes, but I want to ride him—'

'Yes, but Stan doesn't want to be ridden,' Niall says firmly.

'Yes, but I *want* to ride him—'

'Yes, but he's a dog' – Pearl has jumped right into the yes-but game – 'not a pony.'

'Come over here and see how the water ripples in the sunshine, Theo!' his mother trills, to no effect.

'*I want him to be a pony.*' Theo's dark eyes beam fury.

'He's not, though,' Niall says lightly. 'Sorry, but it's biologically impossible.'

'And Theo, it's not kind to do that to Stan.' Pearl bobs down to his height. He has the look of a sculpted cherub: plump-cheeked and pouting, face so pale as to be almost translucent, crowned by light blond curls. She pictures him in a museum, on a plinth, with a little label on it: *Irritating child, mid-2020s, marble.*

His bottom lip protrudes. 'But he likes it.'

'Hmm, I'd say that evidence suggests otherwise,' Niall remarks as Stan mooches away, head dipped, back into the house.

Theo looks around for his mother. However, it's his father who appears, excitedly brandishing an Ordnance Survey map. 'What d'you say we go for a nice big walk, Theo? Just me and you, let Mummy have a rest?'

'Where to?' The child glowers.

'Well, I thought we could climb that big hill there?' He points in some seemingly random direction.

'What's there?' Theo peers over as if there might be something he would like to see.

'Well, it's just a hill, but—'

'There's nothing there!'

'Yes but we could climb it and see the amazing view—'

'No.'

'Or just... walk *towards* it?' Roger says brightly. 'So we could look it—'

'No.'

'Well, how about we just go to the end of the lane?'

'What's *there*?'

'You know, just sheep and things. This is the countryside, Theo—'

'I want to go to Happy Castle,' Theo announces.

'Oh, there is a castle,' Pearl announces. 'You'd probably need to drive there, but it's not too far. We could pack you a picnic...' *Get you off the premises for a while, dog molesting little monster.*

'It's not a real castle,' Theo growls.

'No, it is,' Pearl insists. 'It's hundreds of years old. A proper historical castle with a moat and—'

'Erm, the one Theo's talking about isn't a real castle.' Roger grins apologetically. 'Happy Castle is a soft play centre near where we live.'

'Can we go there?' Theo brightens.

'Not today, darling.' Roger pats his shoulder. 'But we're going home tomorrow, so very soon—'

'Hurrah!' Theo punches the air.

'I'll second that,' Niall murmurs as he and Pearl leave father and son in intense negotiations over what to do next, while Mummy 'rests'. 'I mean, for them,' he adds as they step back into the cottage. 'I could happily stay here for longer, couldn't you? Although I realise this is hardly the kind of break you'd planned...'

'No, I love it here,' Pearl says. 'And it's fun, you know, helping to run this place, even just for a weekend. Like nothing I've ever done before.'

'That's good to hear,' he says with a smile.

She stops and looks at him. 'And I really needed to get away. We *all* did.'

Niall nods, and she knows that, for whatever reason, he did too. And later, as they amass what's needed for dinner from the woodshed freezer, he tells her a little more about his life in Derbyshire, and the cottage he's bought there and is doing up. And in turn, Pearl finds herself telling him a little of her own story. How Dean was the love of her life, and how, over the past eleven years, she has tried to build a different kind of life. And how that life now includes Abi.

Later still, as they fetch more wood for the fire in the lounge, Niall fills her in on why he'd decided to do Christmas alone this year. 'So, my wife and I split up a year ago. She's French and her parents still live in Rouen, where she grew up. And last year she decided to go over on a pre-Christmas visit with the kids...'

'You have kids?' Pearl isn't sure why this surprises her.

'I do, yes. A boy and a girl. I couldn't go – I had a work assignment to finish – and Helene didn't seem to mind.' He pauses as the new firewood catches light. 'In fact she seemed quite pleased that I couldn't join them. She just needed a break, she said. A little break from...'

'Christmas?' Pearl suggests.

'More like me, I think. Or our marriage. At least, that's what I assumed because off they all went. And then came the announcement that they were in fact staying in Rouen for Christmas. And then...'

Niall rubs at his face. Clearly, this is still painful for him, and Pearl isn't sure how to react. 'I'm sorry,' she murmurs.

He exhales. The fire is crackling comfortably now, drawing them close with its warmth. 'We started this year with Helene telling me she wanted to split,' he goes on. 'And that she planned to move back to France permanently, with the kids.'

'Oh no!' Pearl's gaze meets his.

'Yeah. It was all a bit... y'know.' She doesn't know – she can't imagine – but she touches his arm, encouraging him to go on. 'And then the kids were being enrolled into French schools,' he adds quickly, 'and that was that.'

She searches his expression, trying to imagine how she'd feel if Brandon had been whisked away to another country. She's certain that her heart couldn't take another loss. 'But what about their life at home?' she asks. 'Their school, their friends... and *you*? Were they okay about all that?'

He seems to consider how to answer this. 'The thing is, they'd always had a life out there too, with their grandparents. Every year, they'd spent huge parts of their summers there and they loved it. So...'

'Yes, but what about you? Didn't you have any say in it at all?'

'I did. Of course I did. But it's what they all wanted, so we set up an arrangement where they'd spend their school holidays with me. The whole summer, for one thing. They're old enough now – thirteen and fourteen – that we can travel together, so we did that this year and it was *great*.'

Pearl nods, resting her gaze on the glow of the fire. Although she barely knows him she can tell he's being stoical, and that he's found a way to make the best of the situation. 'It still must be difficult, though,' she ventures, and he nods.

'We've made it work. And they're happy there living in Helene's family home with the pool and ponies. They've grown up bilingual so that's not an issue...' But what about other issues? she wants to ask. What about you missing them, and vice versa? 'And Helene reckons I get the best of them,' Niall adds, 'away from the school schedules and homework, the tedium of the everyday. A whole two months to do fun stuff. And in a way, she's right.'

Pearl wants to say how admirable it is, how he seems to have managed this. And also that, compared to what Niall's been through with his children, it seems churlish to be upset about her current home situation. What does it matter if Abi hogs the bathroom and mashes up her Tom Ford lipstick? Because at least Brandon is still with her. She makes a mental note to be extra tolerant of Abi because, if and when they do move out, she'll miss him terribly.

'You seem like a really good dad,' she tells him, 'wanting what's best for them.'

He shakes his head, dismissing the compliment. 'Oh, I don't think so. Not really—' Then there are voices in the kitchen and he breaks off, perhaps relieved by the distraction.

'Don't worry, Frida,' Shelley is saying. 'Dinner will be *exactly* as advertised tonight...'

'It's not that I minded the surprise change of plan, but—'

'No, you can trust us,' Pearl says as she strides through to join them. 'Everything's in full working order now and we'll have dinner on the table by seven.'

'On the dot?' Frida raises a sharply plucked brow.

'On the dot,' Shelley says firmly. Then she steps outside into the gathering dusk where, for the first time since she arrived here, she plans to call her husband.

30

'Must be some kind of rash,' Joel told his kids. 'Probably that fragrance I was sent, remember? When I redesigned that product range?' Of course they didn't remember. They probably think he doodles with crayons all day. 'I think it's reacted with my skin,' he added.

Martha's laser gaze drilled into his head. 'You had a good time, though? At the boring gallery thing?'

'It was all right,' he muttered.

'Did you take a present for them?'

Joel's stomach lurched. 'For who? Who's "them"?'

'*I* don't know,' she said with a shrug. 'For the artist whose exhibition it was?'

"Course not,' he growled defensively. What *was* she going on about? Had she been delving through his bag? No, surely not. He was just being paranoid. Even so, he had to get away from his kids. He couldn't take any more interrogation. So he hotfooted it to the sanctuary of his studio at the top of the house.

However, it doesn't feel like a sanctuary now as he sits gloomily at his desk. For one thing, it's still disgusting, all sticky and smelly and littered with bottles and cans. But it's not just the state of it that's bothering him. Now this room feels like a prison cell, where he'll be forced to remain until

Shelley comes home, in order to minimise any interaction with Martha and Fin. Because how can he operate normally with the new household dynamic at play? It's as if they are now the superior ones – because they *know*. They haven't stated said as such, but since they spotted the mark on his neck there have been no further mentions of clearing up the mess. There's not a drop of contrition now. They are behaving as if they had nothing to do with what happened here last night.

Martha especially has the measure of him. She came home with a love bite once, a livid bruise on her neck. Although visibly upset, Shelley was determined not to make a big thing of it. 'It's awful, Joel, but that's just part of being young. And I suppose worse things can happen.'

Now, as Joel sits here at his desk, he's not sure that worse things *can* happen. His laptop has gone and there's not a damn thing he can do about it. If he called the police, then it would all come out about him leaving the kids alone overnight and then Shelley would be bound to find out. No, that's far too messy to contemplate. Instead, he must switch his brain into practical mode because hiding up here, twitching and panicking is doing no good whatsoever. After all, Shelley will be home in two days' time, full of the joys after her little holiday with her best friends. So the whole house will have to be put back to normal by then.

One small glimmer of positivity is that Joel has managed to contact a glazier who's promised to come round tomorrow at a colossal cost. 'Sorry, mate. It's the week before Christmas!' As if Joel didn't know. In fact, he'd have festooned the man with gold bars if that's what it had taken to entice him round.

Now he checks his phone, trying to build himself up to sending a cheery message to Shelley. *Hope you're having fun! We're all having a great time here with our smashed fucking window in our stinking house!* But before he's even typed a word, a message appears from Martha. His heart quickens and he snatches his Citalopram from his desk drawer – mercifully, the laptop thief didn't steal them too – and pops one into his mouth, even though he's already had today's dose. With the lack of anything else to wash it down with, he grabs an open can and gulps down flat tepid lager, choking as something solid lands in his throat. He coughs and splutters, spitting the vile thing onto the floor. It's a soggy cigarette butt.

> **MARTHA**
> Are you upstairs?

Joel's heart thuds like a drum.

> **JOEL**
> Yes

As he hits send, his phone rings and he yelps, as if electrocuted. It's Shelley. Christ. 'Hey! How are you?' he shouts.

He senses his wife frowning all the way up there in the frozen north. 'Hi, Joel,' she says levelly. 'Everything all right there?'

'Er, yeah! Hi, babe. All good. How are you?'

'Great.' Shelley still sounds hesitant. 'Yeah, we're all having fun here... So, the kids are okay, are they?'

'Yeah, they're fine. They've been great.'

'That's... great!' The pause hangs. Joel tries desperately to dredge up some news to tell her. But as his 'news' lately has concerned only Carmel and the kids' house party, he's stuck for words.

'So you'll remember to pick up the turkey tomorrow morning, won't you?' Shelley starts, and for once Joel is grateful for practical matters to focus on.

"Course I will,' he says.

'It's just, the butcher has his slots, y'know? And he gets a bit funny if we don't pick up the order on the day we said—'

'No, I remember that,' he fibs. It occurs to Joel that lying comes instinctively to him now, like breathing.

'There should also be chipolatas and bacon and sausage meat in the order,' she goes on, 'and the ham for Boxing Day. D'you mind checking it's all there? He forgot the sausages last year and I had to use those cheap ones from the freezer, remember? Not the butcher ones your mum likes? She was in a bit of a sulk...'

'Yeah, haha. How can I forget?' The quality of their Christmas Day chipolatas is the least of his concerns right now. He touches his neck, aware of the tenderness lingering there. What was Carmel thinking? She knows his situation here and, much as Joel still thinks of himself as a teenage raver, aren't they a bit *old* for love bites? He gives her a £275 gold bracelet. She gives him a prominent bruise. He hates to be petty but it hardly feels like a fair exchange. It also occurs to him that he hasn't bought Shelley anything, apart from a Superdrug voucher he picked up when he was buying shaving foam. Will the kids have any ideas? That'll mean conversing with them, which he'd rather avoid. Perhaps he'll be able to casually quiz the glazier on acceptable presents for wives?

'Anyway, love,' Shelley adds, as if catching herself, 'I didn't call you to fire off a load of instructions...'

'I'm relieved about that,' he says jovially.

Another pause. 'So, we're all having a fun time here,' she adds, somewhat pointedly. Joel realises he's supposed to be asking all about her trip so far.

'Oh, yeah! So what've you been up to?' She tells him then about the owner guy rushing away suddenly, something to do with a flight attendant, and feeding some hens and then guests arriving, and something about an emergency dash to the chip shop? And some writer guy writing something or other and some kid trying to ride Stan like a pony—

'Stan's the kid?' Joel is struggling to make sense of it all.

'No, Stan's the collie!' She chuckles. 'Theo's the child. And he doesn't want what we're doing for dinner tonight. He wants a fondue like he has at his Swiss granny's—'

'A fondue? What is this, 1976?'

Shelley laughs, and Joel laughs, amazed that he still has it in him to make a joke. Perhaps he sounds normal after all. Perhaps he can deal with the party devastation here, and by the time Shelley comes home, if he tries his hardest to be super-nice and totally reinvents his personality, everything will be all right.

'So, it's Christmas Eve you're back, isn't it?' He knows this. He just wants reassurance that she won't bowl up tomorrow morning before the darn window's fixed.

'That's right. Flight lands at three-thirty. So, by the time I've caught the train into London—'

'No, I'll come and get you.'

'What? At the airport, you mean? You don't need to do that...'

'No, I'd like to. I'll come out to Stansted and bring you all into town. I'll drop off Pearl and Lena at their places too—'

'Really?' she gasps.

'Yeah. 'Course I will.' He feigns hurt at her surprise that he can do something nice for other people. 'It's not a big deal,' he insists, really embracing the role now. Because somehow, it feels that this single act will cancel out all the lying and deceit and awfulness. Somehow, it'll turn Joel into a *decent guy*. 'They'll want to get home and enjoy Christmas Eve, won't they?' he goes on. 'Lena will want to see Tommy, and Pearl will be keen to see, er, thingie...' A minor slip-up there – he can never remember Pearl's kid's name – but Shelley doesn't seem to notice.

'Wow. That's really sweet of you, honey. I know they'll appreciate that.' He senses her smiling. 'And thanks for manning the fort there. Honestly, it's amazing here. So beautiful and lovely to have this time with the girls. It's doing me so much good to be away, you know? After all the worry at work, the job cuts and everything...' He starts to faze off. He has never managed to be interested in Shelley's job. '...And thanks for the other stuff too,' Shelley adds.

'What stuff?' he croaks.

'Just those last bits I asked you to do. Dropping off the neighbours' Christmas cards and wrapping those presents...'

'That was no trouble.' His voice is oddly high pitched. 'No trouble at all.'

She clears her throat. 'So you managed the wrapping okay?'

'Yeah, fine!'

'The Sellotape didn't try and attack you—'

'No, the Sellotape's been very well behaved.'

But I haven't, Joel reflects when the call is over. *I have been appallingly behaved.* And now he sees that Martha has messaged him again, and with a thudding sensation in his gut, he reads it.

MARTHA

Dad we're not stupid. We know someone bit your neck last night and you've been lying to us. Don't really want to think about what else you've been doing. Don't want that in my head. So we're going out tonight – Fin's staying over at Ajay's and I'm going to Lizzie's. We need to get away.

Oh, do they really! Seemingly, the whole sodding world needs to get away! No matter that Christmas is hurtling towards them—

He catches himself and reads on.

MARTHA

So the deal is we won't say anything when Mum gets home and you can cover up the bite with something or do whatever you have to do. Just don't say anything to Mum about the party and we won't say anything about your neck. We're just going to pretend none of it happened. Is that a deal?

Joe senses sweat pulsing from his forehead as he mutters under his breath. Blackmailing him like this! What sort of monsters has he raised? He looks around his trashed studio, and again his fingers go to the tender part on his neck.

JOEL

Deal.

And then, for the first time in his life, Joel heads downstairs, pulls on rubber gloves and cleans the entire house.

31

TWO DAYS UNTIL CHRISTMAS

Before Shelley has even opened her eyes she knows everything is different. It feels and sounds and even *smells* different as she lies there in bed. Everything is still and quiet, as if muffled. And she thinks: what's happened?

Could it be that, in this short time she's been away from home – although it's hardly been restful – her head has cleared, and by tomorrow she'll be ready to return to her real life? Already she feels as if she is firing on all cylinders again. That day last week, when the chilli had been scoffed and she'd glugged a bottle of sauvignon for dinner, at least one of those cylinders had felt broken.

She opens her eyes and lies there in the quiet room. Beside her, Pearl is still asleep. And over in the little fold-out bed, Lena mumbles and repositions herself.

Shelley looks up at the ceiling as she replays her conversation with Joel yesterday. Okay, he only said he'd come and meet them at the airport. He didn't say he'd whisk them all home on a flying carpet – but still. It's unexpectedly generous of him. Shelley realises she can't remember the last time Joel did anything kind for her.

Her eyes prickle with unexpected tears and she quickly blinks them away. It's probably done him good, she reflects as she slips quietly out of bed. Her coming up here means he's had to manage the kids, their home, and the last bits of Christmas. And rather than shirking his duties he's risen to the challenge. Okay, wrapping a few presents for his own parents is hardly heroic – but in all their years together she can't recall him ever wrapping *anything*. Not even for her birthday or Christmas. It's been vouchers in envelopes, or a bottle of perfume clearly bought in haste and handed to her unwrapped.

Once he really pushed the boat out and presented her with a family meals-type cookbook in a gift bag. *Just* what she'd needed. New ways to make flipping sausage and mash! She knew Martha had had a hand in the gift bag element, as she'd overheard her telling him off. 'Are you just going to give it to her like that? For God's sake, Dad!' Joel doesn't get the whole ribbons, gift tags, wrapping paper thing. But now he's coming to meet her at the airport! And this must mean one thing.

That he loves and appreciates her after all! Because driving out to Stansted Airport for her benefit is, by Joel's standards, akin to traversing Siberia wearing only his socks.

Shelley pads across the room, parts the curtains a little and blinks at what's before her.

Snow! So much snow, thick and white and covering the garden and the hills beyond. So much white that land and sky have merged. Only the loch is a different hue, gleaming silvery grey. The world is monochrome and Shelley stares, transfixed.

Perhaps, she thinks, Joel is coming to the airport because he wants to make it up to her. Finally, she decides as she dresses quickly in jeans and a sweater – and then, at the front door, pulling on a pair of Michael's green wellies – he's realised that being in possession of a penis means you still have to pull your weight. And that his isn't so colossally huge that it makes it impossible for him to stand at the sink and wash up. That it's not so exhausting to drag around all day that evenings must be spent, near comatose, on the sofa.

Shelley steps outside, blinking as the dazzling whiteness tingles her eyes. *That's it,* she realises. *It's taken me coming up here for Joel to remember that I am an actual person.* She's wondered sometimes, these past six months especially. Because he's seemed different. Even more distant and blasé than usual. Preoccupied too, as if he's had something – or someone –

on his mind. There have been nights out with friends, which he's been vague about. And when he's come home from these nights, he's slipped into bed and turned his back to her. She's known he was awake, that he was lying there with his eyes open. She could just sense it.

What was he thinking about? What was going on?

'Joel?' she murmured one night. She touched his back and he flinched. 'Are you okay?'

'Just really tired.' He exhaled slowly and then his breathing deepened and settled, as if he was asleep. But she knew he was faking it. When you've been with someone for twenty-five years you just *know*.

Snow crunches underfoot as Shelley makes her way to the edge of the garden. Trees are clotted with snow, and fence posts jut out from the thick white blanket like pencil lines. It's a Christmas card, right here. Did Joel really remember to drop off the cards to their neighbours? She catches herself fretting about home, and mentally shakes herself out of it. Is she too controlling, wanting her grandma's decorations brought down from the attic and a holly wreath for the front door? Is *that* the problem? Her thoughts break off as someone groans quietly where the cars are parked.

'Roger!' She smiles and tramps over towards him. More snow is falling now in soft flakes.

'Morning, Shelley.' He smiles, hot-faced in a brown bobble hat and a thick padded jacket. He tweaks at his beard. 'This is something, isn't it?'

'It's incredible.' She spots the shovel, propped up in a drift of snow. 'Are you trying to dig out your car?'

'Hmm, yes. Quite a job but we need to get back today. In fact we should have left by now. It's the local kids' Christmas party later and I still need to finish Theo's costume—'

'You mean fancy dress?' she asks, and Roger nods. '*You* do that?' she exclaims.

'Well, yes.' He looks bemused by her reaction. Yet for a moment, this man's willingness to make his kid's fancy dress outfit is more astounding to her than the vast quantity of snow that fell during the night.

'Well, Theo and Frida come up with the idea,' he clarifies. 'The *concept* is theirs. They're very good at that.' He says this jovially, with no trace of bitterness. 'But I tend to do the construction.'

'Right.' Momentarily, Shelley tries to picture Joel being put in charge of such a task. But it's impossible to imagine. Switching her attention back to the snow, she looks around to where Roger has been digging. Of course, if the Sampsons' car needs to be dug out of the snow, then Niall's will too. All of the guests are supposed to be leaving today. What if they *can't* dig their way out? And what if the snow is still lying tomorrow – on Christmas Eve! – and she and Lena and Pearl can't get to Glasgow for their flight home? No, that can't happen. Shelley pushes the thought aside and turns back to Roger. 'D'you think you'll manage this?' she asks.

'To dig us out?' He grabs the spade. 'Have to. No question about it. There's a prize for best fancy dress and we won it last year. Theo went as a cracker! And this year he'll be a Christmas pudding.'

'But how—' she starts.

'Not as tricky it sounds actually. I built a wire frame and covered it with papier-mâché. Layers upon layers of the stuff. Had to buy extra newspapers, even the trashy ones we can't abide, haha—'

'No, I actually meant how—'

'So the basic structure's done. A huge papier-mâché sphere that'll be suspended from his shoulders, and all I need to do is—'

'Roger,' Shelley cuts in, 'I meant, even if you *can* dig out your car, how are you going to get up onto the road?' Her gaze follows the track. Or rather, where the track lies beneath a thick layer of snow. 'We'll all help you. Of course we will. But what will the actual road be like? Will it be possible to drive safely?'

'Oh, the gritters will have been out,' he says firmly as he starts digging again.

Shelley frowns. 'D'you think gritters come all the way out here?'

'Of course they do!' Frida announces, stomping towards them now in a thick sweater and pyjama bottoms stuffed into wellies. And now Niall appears, followed by Lena and Pearl.

'Oh my God,' Lena breathes. 'We're snowed in!'

'No, we're not,' Frida exclaims. 'This is twenty-first century Britain and we need to get home. Theo has a party to go to—'

'Mummy! Snow!' Theo hurtles out of the cottage and grabs handfuls of snow, which he flings ineffectually towards the adults.

'The snow plough'll be along soon,' Frida says firmly, as if that's the matter settled. 'We might as well go in and have breakfast while we wait.'

Shelley bites her lip. 'I think we should call Michael...'

'Yes, call Michael,' Frida commands.

Lena frowns, ruffling Stan's head as he bounds out to join them. 'I'm not sure he'll be able to do much about this from London.'

'But he'll know when the gritters and snow ploughs are likely to arrive.' Frida stares at her.

'We could try digging up to the road,' Niall offers, 'but if *that's* blocked...' He blows out air. 'It's ten miles of single-track lane, Frida.'

'Yes, but this can't be a one-off event, can it?' she counters. 'Surely it happens every year, and they're prepared for it—'

'Who's prepared?' Lena looks at her. 'I mean, who's going to come to a remote place like this?'

'The council people!' Frida turns to Roger, as if expecting him to back her up. 'The snow team. The *army*...'

'The army?' Shelley splutters.

'Oh, I don't know.' Frida glares at her husband. 'I *said* you should paint the pudding before we came up here. Then we'd be all ready.'

'But Frida—'

'Why didn't you? What was the problem again?'

'I forgot to get brown paint,' he mutters. 'I thought there'd be time today—'

'We're not doing any good all standing around, are we?' Shelley offers.

'No,' Frida agrees. 'There must be something we can do to clear this snow...'

'I'll fetch my hairdryer,' Pearl murmurs, and Nail's mouth twitches into a smile. 'Oh, but we can't call Michael,' she adds. 'He's lost his phone.'

'I'll try him at the hotel,' Shelley announces, and as the others head indoors she plods through the thick white covering to the end of the garden. Here the whiteness is punctuated by the hen house and a glimpse of dry-stone wall. She stops and googles the airport hotel, calls the number and is put through to his room. 'Thank God you're there,' she exclaims when he answers.

'Shelley? I was just about to call the house. How is it up there?'

'You know already?' She steps carefully over a snow-covered log.

'Yeah. I had the news on just now. Caught the weather report. So, it's really bad, is it?'

'It's actually beautiful,' she replies. 'But yes, I guess it's not exactly ideal—'

'No, it's not. I'm sorry.' He exhales. 'This is going to be difficult for you, isn't it? If the guests can't leave today?'

'We can look after them,' she assures him. 'And hopefully it'll all be cleared tomorrow, so we can still catch our flight—'

'Shelley, I hate to say it but—'

'We'll just get through today,' she says briskly, unwilling to even consider that they might not be able to fly home, as planned, on Christmas Eve. 'Frida's not happy,' she adds. 'She's had Roger digging for hours already, but their car's stuck...'

'Right,' Michael murmurs. 'Like that, is she?'

'Yes, she's used to things happening the way she wants them to.' She breaks off. 'But what about you? I'm sorry, I've been so caught up with things here, I've just realised. You're flying home today, aren't you? I'm so sorry. This is my fault...'

'Your fault?' He sounds bemused now. 'How are you to blame for this?'

She watches as a small feathered head appears at the door of the hen house, and quickly pops back indoors. 'You wanted to change your flight and come yesterday. And if you had, you'd be here now and everything would be okay—'

'Hey,' he says, 'it's happened. As long as you're all okay, then it's fine.'

She pauses, still trying to quell her guilt. 'So will you still fly to Glasgow and stay there until the weather clears?'

'Actually,' he starts, 'I thought I might as well stay in London...'

'What, forever?' she teases. 'Come back, Michael! We need you here—'

'I mean until the thaw comes.' He chuckles. 'I think I can amuse myself here.'

Shelley smiles, despite everything. 'I should've asked. How did yesterday turn out?'

'I had a great day actually. Walked for miles, taking it all in. All along the South Bank and then through Covent Garden and Soho, and there was this amazing place with a huge courtyard, Somerset House, and I sat there and had a coffee and got chatting to all these tourists on a Christmas shopping trip. Then I found a little bar on the Strand…'

'Oh, that's great. I was worried about you mooching around, all on your own.'

'No, quite the opposite. I must've talked to more people than I've talked to all month, probably.' A pause. 'I haven't been ice skating though.'

'There's still time.' She smiles. 'But I'm glad you've been out and about. Sorry, that makes it sound as if you're about ninety—'

'I feel it sometimes.' He laughs. 'But actually, not so much right now. It really has been pretty good. And that's why I thought I'd stay here a little bit longer. I don't care about the flight. I did buy a cheap phone though, in case you need me…'

'Great. So have fun, won't you? Sounds like you're loving it down there…'

'I am. It's…' She senses him smiling too. 'It's… well, it's *different*.'

'You can say that again.' She laughs. Then Lena calls out that breakfast is nearly ready, and over at the cars Frida snaps at Roger, 'Don't be so defeatist. The party's happening at four and that pudding's not going to paint itself!'

'What was *that*?' Michael asks.

'Just your guests,' Shelley says, 'having a mini crisis. But we're all fine here. Honestly, there's nothing to worry about.'

'But what about you and your family?' he asks. 'How will they feel if you can't get back home tomorrow?'

Shelley forms deep footprints in the snow as she heads back to the cottage. 'Oh, I'm sure the snow will be gone by then,' she says firmly. 'It's got to be, hasn't it? It'll be Christmas Eve.'

32

No magical snow plough arrives. No gritter either. There are enough shovels to go around, so everyone – Frida and Theo excepted – digs away at the snow around the cars. However, Niall and Roger do the lion's share and by lunchtime the two men are visibly spent as they all return to the kitchen.

'Well, we had to try,' Niall says, catching Pearl's eye, 'but there's no chance of getting out of here today.'

'No, I realise that,' Pearl says. Hours before, the three women had reassured each other that of course the snow would clear for tomorrow. Now Pearl isn't so sure. 'Thanks for all that digging, though,' she adds, aware of Frida's rising agitation.

'We're the ones with something to get back to,' she retorts, and Lena appears from the lounge. Her hands are filthy with ash and soot from cleaning out the fireplace.

'What d'you mean?' she asks Frida.

'Well, Christmas!'

'We *all* have Christmas coming,' Shelley points out. 'We all have things to do and people back home…'

Niall disappears briefly and returns brandishing a basket of logs from the woodshed. 'Let's try and stay positive,' he says. 'If there's a thaw tonight, then we can all leave first thing in the morning, can't we?'

'In time for Christmas!' Frida announces.

'But what about Stan and the hens?' Niall turns to Shelley. 'With Michael not being here, who'll look after them if we leave?'

'He's planning to catch a flight to Glasgow as soon as the thaw comes,' she explains. 'And if there's a delay, he said his friend Harry from the farm down the road can take care of things here. So that's not a problem.'

'So, we're all sorted then?' Frida looks hopeful.

'Not really,' Lena starts, frowning. 'There's a huge amount of snow out there, Frida. There's no guarantee it'll melt away overnight—'

'But it's Christmas Eve tomorrow!' she exclaims.

'Yes, but the weather doesn't know that,' Lena says. 'We can't *wish* it away, much as we'd love to—'

'I do realise that,' Frida snaps, grey eyes flashing. Lena's heart rate quickens as she quells her urge to snap back. She is unused to dealing with this kind of lack of logic.

'I'm just saying,' she says, trying to remain patient, 'that if there's no thaw overnight, and no gritters or snowploughs come up this way, then it's likely that we're all going to be here for Christmas…'

'Oh, God, Leen.' Shelley looks at her. 'Let's not even go there.'

'How would Joel react, if you're stuck here?'

Shelley shakes her head. 'I don't even want to think about it. You know he wasn't best pleased about me going away so close to Christmas.'

'How about you, Pearl?' Niall asks. 'How would your crew manage without you?'

'Brandon and Abi?' Her heart seems to squeeze at the thought of spending Christmas apart from her son. 'I'm sure they'd cope. But…' She breaks off as her eyes mist. 'I feel so responsible, suggesting this trip in the first place. Coming up to the Highlands in winter…' She looks at her friends. 'Of course it could snow! Why didn't I think of that?'

'Hey, we were *all* in on this,' Shelley says, wrapping an arm around her shoulders. 'We're all responsible.'

'…Or irresponsible,' Pearl mutters, focusing now on making teas and coffees for everyone, because Niall is right. Lamenting their situation isn't helping.

It's only Lena who isn't exactly feeling desolate at the prospect of spending Christmas at Shore Cottage. In fact, she decides, as she takes herself off to their bedroom, it's becoming more appealing by the hour. Here in the stillness of their airy room, she perches on the chair at the window and looks out over the silvery loch.

If they're snowed in for Christmas, she reflects, there'll be no William and Annabelle making barbed comments about her 'background' and peering around her flat in disdain. (She once heard Annabelle telling Tommy that she 'could *never* live in a flat'). And there'll be no stressing over how to cram a turkey, a joint of beef and a trough of roast potatoes into her poky little oven. In his gamely fashion, Tommy has assured her that things can be 'kept warm under foil' and then 'given another hot blast near the finish'. But the logistics are still making Lena's head spin. And managing to serve up a piping hot meal to her future in-laws isn't really the issue. It's about their disdain and judgement of her.

'And what does your father *do*, Lena?' Who even asks that, in this day and age? She knew what Annabelle was getting at. That she expected Lena to say he ran a corner shop.

'He's an accountant,' she replied.

'Oh!' Annabelle hadn't known what to say after that. And now Lena stands up at the window, gripping her phone, wanting to call Tommy, but also *not* wanting to. They spoke first thing and she broke the news about the snowfall. 'Let's just hope it thaws,' he said. 'There's still time, isn't there? And then you'll still be able to catch your flight?'

She agreed that there was, and told him a little about the snow-covered hills and the cosiness of Shore Cottage. 'That sounds lovely!' he enthused. Yet there was an awkwardness there, as if there was more than physical distance between them. As if he was holding something back. She didn't mention seeing Daisy's photo of the festive family lunch. It didn't matter, she told herself. Tommy was only having pizza with his family. What was wrong with that?

She calls him again now, wanting to reassure herself that everything is okay. 'Snow still bad, darling?' he asks.

'Just the same,' she replies. 'It's freezing out there and the forecast isn't looking good...'

'Oh God, really?'

'Yeah. I do feel a bit stupid coming up here the week before Christmas. What was I thinking?'

'Honey, you needed a break with your friends,' he insists. 'You've been working so hard. And you weren't to know this would happen...'

'I guess you're right. Anyway, I haven't asked about you,' she adds.

'Oh, all's good here. I'm missing you of course. Can't wait to see you. But I saw Daisy yesterday—'

'And Catherine,' Lena blurts out before she can stop herself.

She feels him take a breath. 'Yes, um... she came for lunch too. Bit of a surprise. But Daisy wanted her to join us and I couldn't really say no—'

'No, there was no reason to,' Lena says quickly, feeling ridiculous to be so rattled by a casual photo on Daisy's social media. What's wrong with her? It's not Catherine who's the problem. It's Tommy's parents – and the way he bends to their wishes every time. And now Lena wonders if it might be easier for him to entertain his parents on Christmas Day at her place without her being there.

She doesn't exactly love the idea. Not because she imagines Annabelle and William rifling through her private things – she has absolutely nothing to hide – but because the flat is hers, hard won and cherished, a place of refuge after her divorce. The thought of the Huntleys marching in and occupying it, even just for one night, feels very wrong to Lena. However, she's starting to think it would be preferable to the alternative.

She finishes the call rather curtly and gazes out at the snow-covered landscape, almost willing more snow to fall. Just enough, she thinks, to keep them here for a couple more days. So she can avoid the Huntleys.

Lena knows it's mad to think like this, and that it'll be awful for Shelley and Pearl if they can't fly home for Christmas. So it's selfish of her really. So horribly mean to wish they'd be snowed in.

She also knows she should tolerate Annabelle and William with an eye roll and not let them get to her. After all, in April, Lena is marrying Tommy at High Gables and Annabelle has already booked the string quartet. Lena's parents and siblings will all travel down to the Berkshire pile from their red brick terraced house in Manchester. It has already been decided that there will be a formal sit-down meal, which Lena wouldn't have chosen, and of course all of Team Huntley will be there: the braying brothers and the glossy wives, and their children – not that Lena doesn't like children, but these are a *type*, feral-with-privileges, tangle-haired and grubby-faced, but with cello lessons and cricket whites and a surefire entry into Eton.

Fucking hell, she breathes out loud. People shouldn't feel that way about their forthcoming wedding, but Lena is having the kind of wedding she never wanted to have. How did she allow this to happen?

Still, it's too late to do anything about it now, she decides, her gaze fixed on the distant hills all swathed in snow. Christmas comes first. That's the first hurdle to get over.

And now, as if by magic, fat snowflakes start to fall, coming thicker and faster by the second. And Lena's heart lifts as she watches from the window of the cosy room.

'Thank you, snow,' she whispers. 'Thank you *so* much.'

33

CHRISTMAS EVE

By the following morning the snow is falling so hard that Shelley decides this must be a blizzard. Has she ever been in a blizzard before? Possibly, although you're pretty much insulated from the weather in London. It doesn't lash at you in the same raw way as it is now, the snow driving into her frozen face as she hurries towards the hen house.

By the time she's fed and checked on the hens, and is back at the cottage, everyone is up and gathered just inside the front door, staring out. 'You'll need to start digging now if we're going to have any chance of getting home,' Frida barks at Roger. But it's Niall who responds.

'Frida, we might as well try digging to the centre of the earth for all the good it'll do. Look how fast it's falling.' He hands around mugs of coffee and a hot chocolate for an excitable Theo, who at least seems delighted by the fresh snowfall.

'Yep, without a doubt,' Roger agrees. 'Frida, we're just going to have to accept this...' As tempers flare between the Sampsons, Shelley, Lena and Pearl go to confer in the lounge.

'This is it,' Shelley announces. 'We're all stuck here for Christmas. There's no way around it, is there?' She has called Michael's new mobile already, and assured him, stoically, that they'll all be fine. But she doesn't feel fine as she imagines Joel's reaction.

'Haven't you told him yet?' Pearl asks with a grimace.

'That he'll have to manage Christmas Day with the kids and his parents, all by himself?' Shelley rubs at her face, as if that might erase the terrifying vision of Joel juggling the making of a proper turkey-stock gravy while sautéing sprouts and hoisting out the turkey, stuffing, roast potatoes and pigs in blankets from the oven, all at the correct time. And what about the home-made cranberry sauce that his mother always expects? 'No, I haven't dared to call him yet,' she says, shuddering. 'I don't know how he's going to cope...'

'He'll just have to,' Pearl insists. 'There's literally nothing we can do now.'

'You could dispense instructions over the phone?' Lena suggests, trying to lighten the mood. 'Literally talk him through making Christmas dinner, like the emergency services when someone's having a baby at home?'

Shelley musters a weak smile. 'Maybe his parents will pitch in. The kids too. They might even peel a potato!'

'It could even be good for them,' Lena suggests.

'Maybe. You do realise my name will be mud, though?' Shelley wishes she didn't care about how she'll be viewed by her own family and in-laws. But she can't help it. For seventeen years her overriding aim has been to be a good mum, and guilt comes over her now in a wave. But gradually, as snow continues to fall, a sense of acceptance begins to settle over the group. Because really, what other option is there? They can hardly be helicoptered out of here, and there is certainly no sign of a thaw.

Before tackling breakfast, the three women and Niall escape the intensity of the cottage by walking Stan to the lochside. Here, as they stop at the water's edge, they try to figure out how their somewhat unlikely group might manage Christmas Day together. 'If it was just us,' Lena offers, 'it'd be great.'

'Y'know, I think it actually would,' Shelley agrees. 'And maybe you were right when you said it might be good for them. They're just going to have to get off their backsides and all pull together for once. And perhaps I'm being unfair on Joel, assuming he won't be able to cope.' She bends to ruffle Stan's soft black and white fur, reminding herself that her husband seems to have changed, since she ran away to Scotland. And that the new improved Joel has been nothing but pleasant on the phone – even offering to pick them up at the airport. It hardly seems possible that this is the man who let her drag a Christmas tree down the street, all by herself. So yes, of course he can roast and carve a turkey and dish up sprouts. 'It's funny,' she continues. 'When we booked this trip, if I'd thought there was even a chance that I wouldn't be back home for Christmas, then I'd have said no way—'

'And now here we are, trapped together in the frozen wastes,' Niall remarks with a grin.

'And actually, it doesn't feel like a disaster...' Shelley breaks off, gazing across the loch to the snowy peaks beyond. 'It feels... *okay*.'

'Christmas is only a day, after all,' Niall offers with a shrug.

She chuckles. 'Funnily enough, that's what my husband always says. That I make far too much fuss, wanting everything to be perfect and the house all decorated. But yes, it *is* only a day. And anyway, there's nothing we can do to change things.' She turns to Pearl. 'But what about Brandon?'

Pearl brushes a fresh flurry of snowflakes from her auburn hair. 'I'll miss him. I've never had a Christmas without my boy...' Like Shelley, she's dreading calling home to break the news. 'But with Abi there...' She doesn't want to say, *It wouldn't be the same anyway. Not like our Christmases have always been.* But it's true. 'Maybe it'll be good for them to have the place to themselves,' she continues. 'And actually, it'll be fun to spend it with all of you.'

Lena wraps an arm around her shoulders. 'All these years we've been friends and we've never spent Christmas Day together. And look where we are! It couldn't *be* any more Christmassy...' They all fall silent for a moment, taking it all in. Not just the snowy landscape, sparkling now in the weak sunshine, but the realisation that they will definitely be spending Christmas Day together, right here. Then Shelley remembers that the hens' water bottle might be frozen, and they all make their way back to the cottage, where Niall offers to check it.

Pearl finds herself watching as he marches away through the freshly formed layer of white. 'He's great, isn't he?' Shelley remarks, catching her friend's eye.

Pearl nods. 'Yeah. He really is.'

'And you two seem to be getting on well,' Lena suggests with a smile.

Pearl chuckles, shrugging off the suggestion that there might be a spark between them. 'He's just a nice guy. Down to earth. A decent man...'

'Single, right?' Lena asks.

'Yes, his wife left him this time last year. Took his kids over to live in France.'

'Wow,' Shelley murmurs.

'So he's not a big fan of Christmas,' Pearl adds. 'Not now anyway.'

'I wonder how he feels about spending it with us?' Lena muses as they head back indoors and start to prepare breakfast. Busying away in the kitchen, they are already working instinctively. Shelley is main cook, Pearl the sous-chef and Lena the table setter and Director-in-Chief of toast, ensuring that a steady supply is produced. And breakfast today is a reasonably jolly affair, despite Frida declaring that 'it's a complete disaster' as she reaches for Michael's home-made plum jam. But there's a resignedness to her tone now. And when Niall reminds her that they have everything they need here, she doesn't disagree.

'Most importantly, we have wine,' Shelley announces.

'And plenty of food,' Niall adds. 'We won't have to drill holes through the ice and fish in the loch...'

'...Or eat each other,' Lena says with a grin.

'But what if we eat all the food?' Theo blurts out. 'Will we have to kill the hens?'

'Of course not,' Pearl exclaims.

'The woodshed freezer's practically full,' Lena assures him.

'Oh, more hedgerow berry crumble?' Frida groans, and Roger pats her hand as if placating a child.

'The crumble's excellent, darling.'

'But a bit of variety would be nice...'

'Well, how about we build a fire down by the loch later, and we can cook sausages?' Niall suggests.

'Great idea!' Pearl enthuses.

'But what about Christmas Day?' Frida asks, forehead furrowed now. 'We don't have a turkey, do we?'

'We'll just have to improvise,' Shelley says firmly.

She's not exactly sure what she means by this, and perhaps, if this goes on for days – or even weeks – they'll be resorting to fish fingers garnished with sweetcorn kernels after all. But it'll be okay, she decides, trying to dampen down a flurry of nerves as she steps outside to call home. *It's not your fault,* she reminds herself. *You didn't cause the snowfall.*

'Joel?' she starts when he answers. 'It's not good news, I'm afraid…' Her chest seems to tighten as she awaits his reaction.

'You mean you're definitely snowed in?'

'Yep, totally. There's no chance of getting out of here, I'm afraid. So we can't catch that flight.'

She senses him absorbing this new information. 'Oh, darling,' he murmurs. 'You poor things.'

This catches her by surprise. She hadn't expected sympathy – even from the new Joel. 'I do feel kind of stupid,' she adds.

'Don't worry,' he says firmly. 'I'm gutted, of course I am. I can't believe we're not going to be together tomorrow. But as long as you're all warm and safe, that's all that matters.'

'We are,' she says. 'We'll be okay. But I'll miss you all…'

'We'll miss you so much,' he exclaims. 'But it's not your fault…' Her gaze skims the line of fence posts jutting from the snow-smothered field. She's relieved of course. But something about his stoical tone stirs a pool of uneasiness in the pit of her stomach. She shrugs off the feeling, reminding herself that this is what she's always wanted. For Joel to be a willing participant in the family, rather than acting as if it's a terrible party he's been forced to attend.

He hands her over to Fin and then Martha. Their chats are brief but at least they are cordial. 'We'll miss you, Mum,' Martha says. 'It won't be the same here without you.'

Shelley's heart seems to twist. 'Oh, darling. I'll miss you too. I'm so sorry it's turned out like this…'

'It's all right.' Her daughter's voice wavers. Her headstrong daughter who has barely given Shelley the time of day these past few months sounds genuinely upset. Shelley rubs away sudden tears as they finish the call, reassured that at least Christmas will still happen back at home, even without her being a part of it. To think she was so worried about them fending for themselves. New Year's resolution number one, she decides, is to stop fussing and worrying because her family is wonderful. She's been far too critical lately, and too quick to rise to small misdemeanours.

And resolution number two? To be grateful for what she has. Because Shelley has a husband and children who love her and the best friends in the world.

What more could she possibly want?

* * *

So Joel is going to have to manage Christmas alone, with intense hostility pervading the house. Brilliant. Just *brilliant*. Whatever happened to goodwill towards all men? Frankly, it's a nightmare. He doesn't even know where to start with the raft of issues he's been left to deal with here.

However, a glimmer of positivity has cut through the gloom. In fact, Shelley being trapped up in Scotland is something of a Christmas miracle because yesterday, despite his promises, the glazier didn't turn up. Glaring at the cracked window, Joel left several panicky messages, his anger mounting as the man failed to respond. He tried other glaziers, to no avail, and was starting to fear that he'd have to figure out how to replace the glass himself. Christ, he can barely hang a picture without injuring himself! Could he lie and say that some passing vandal had lobbed a brick at it? But now, minutes after Shelley has finished the call, there's a sharp rap on the door and Joel runs to it, overcome with relief when he sees the glazier standing there. 'You're here, finally!' he announces.

'Yeah, sorry about yesterday.' The man scratches his meaty forehead, seemingly unconcerned by the anguish he's caused. 'Ended up having a bit of an impromptu Christmas lunch with the team.'

'Team? What team?' Joel barks. He has already decided not to offer him coffee or tea.

'Just colleagues.' He shrugs.

'Oh, a *glaziers'* Christmas party,' Joel sneers. 'Hope it was smashing.' The joke falls flat. In fact, he doesn't care about the tradesman's social engagements. All he wants is for him to fix the living room window and stop sniggering at the state of their Christmas tree. Yesterday Joel made a zillion calls in an attempt to locate a replacement. There were none left; not a single fir or spruce or whatever they are – he's not good on tree varieties. So on top of fretting madly about the window and his love bite and daubing on toothpaste – hadn't that worked in 1988? – he's had to fix the cracked tree with brown parcel tape and prop it back up in its pot. 'Come a cropper, did it?' The man smirks.

'It had a small accident, yes.' Joel watches in a supervisory role as, finally, the glazier turns his attentions to replacing the broken glass. Job completed, he tots up the bill and announces that he'd appreciate payment right now, if that's okay – Visa or Mastercard will do.

As soon as he has cleared off, Joel glowers at a succession of delightfully festive emails he's received this morning.

Hi! I will be right on point, is the gist of these things. *You visit 18+ sites. Your devices are compromised and I have seen you pleasuring yourself. Don't worry we all do it! But I created a double screen video (you have good taste lol) and I can access your contact lists on email mobile socials etc. Unless you pay 3000 $ in bitcoin I will share masturbatory video to all on your list including mother. Amount: 0.28 BTC (approximately).*

Joel isn't an idiot. He knows it's a scam and even before his laptop was stolen, he never did anything of that persuasion at home. Instead he's been bottling up his sexual tension like a demijohn of home-made wine until he's round at Carmel's and the great uncorking happens. Carmel who, incidentally, seems to be blanking his messages at the moment. But still, he is unnerved by these emails, and now his kids – his own flesh and blood – are acting like bitcoin scammers after everything he's done for them. Firstly, there was no helping to clear up after their house-wrecking party. Now Fin is hinting that he'd like to go on a ruinously expensive school trip to Rome and is he okay with that? Of more immediate concern is the fact that neither he nor Martha have lifted a finger to get ready for Joel's parents arriving tomorrow, and are clearly not planning to do anything he asks, possibly ever again.

'Just popping out,' he calls upstairs, to zero response. He's picked up the butcher's order already – it was like lugging a bison in a cardboard box down the street – but he still has to figure out how to replace Shelley's granny's smashed antique baubles (*and* explain where they've gone), and buy paper to wrap not only those last remaining gifts, but also the ones that were all torn open at the party. And Shelley's present! He can't just hand her the Superdrug voucher. At the very least, he'll have to buy her a box of chocolates too. As he marches to the shops he remembers that he's also supposed to have delivered the neighbours' Christmas cards. But sod them. What have they ever done for him? Insisted that he'd taken in a parcel for them when he hadn't.

And now, in the distance, he registers a woman in a pink padded jacket whose neutral expression seems to flash to one of anger as she spots him. 'Hello!' he says brightly, realising she's vaguely familiar but he can't place her face.

'You're Fin's dad, right?' she snaps.

'What?' Joel backs away from this madwoman.

'Leaving the kids alone to run riot in your house!'

'Erm, I'm sorry, I'm not sure who you—'

'I'm Ajay's mum. He's fourteen, you know. He could've had alcohol poisoning thanks to you. You think it's fine, do you? Supplying alcohol to minors?'

'I didn't *supply* it,' he protests. 'They brought it when I was out. I didn't realise—'

'Does Shelley know about this?'

'Yes. No. I don't know!' What *is* the correct answer here?

'Well, you should be ashamed of yourself!' Off she stomps, leaving Joel glancing around nervously as if the police, or a team of Ajay's fierce uncles, might be closing in.

At least there is wrapping paper and Sellotape – his nemesis – at the corner shop, plus a decent-looking box of chocolates that he's sure Shelley will appreciate. Back home, he gets stuck into the wrapping. The Sellotape only attacks him twice and at least the window's been fixed, *and* the tree, after a fashion.

You can do this, Joel tells himself. All he needs now is for that damn love bite to fade and everything will be all right.

34

Shelley and Lena and Pearl huddle close together as the fire crackles and glows on the shore. Its fierce heat is welcome and the Sampsons have gathered at its other side. Niall is setting out sausages on a wire grill he found in the cottage's utility room. However, it was Pearl who got the fire going at the lochside as Niall and Roger went off to scavenge for more wood.

'Oh, you can build fires?' Roger asked, surprised that it had leapt into life in their short absence. Pearl explained that she'd grown up in the Cheshire countryside where she and her father would go on walks and toast marshmallows on a fire. But she knew why he was taken aback. Because when the Sampsons arrived Pearl was her usual pulled-together self, with make-up immaculate and hair freshly styled.

Today though, the auburn curls that she usually insists on taming have been stuffed under a woolly hat. Her face is bare too. It wasn't that she was too busy with breakfast to apply her face. More that it felt ridiculous to bother with make-up when surely she'd be out in the snow, just as she'd have been as a little girl. Something about being here in the Scottish winter – even the snowed-in part – is making Pearl feel young again, as if all her cares and stresses are falling away. It hardly seems possible that, just a week ago, she was crouched in her little north London flat peeing into a Celebrations tub.

And she has no need for make-up here, that's clear to her now. Her cheeks are glowing and her green eyes are shining brightly in the firelight. Pearl doesn't know it, but she looks beautiful. Niall thinks so, although he's busying himself with arranging rocks to support the grill, so the sausages can be sizzled.

Pearl can't help watching him. As she catches Niall's eye across the fire, it occurs to her that she hasn't felt like this since Dean died. That she is absolutely fine, just as she is. That she can be comfortable in her own skin. Amidst the chatter and laughter she closes her eyes briefly, enjoying the fire's warmth on her face. What is happening to her up here in the Highlands? She isn't devastated to be separated from Brandon for Christmas. She has accepted that she'll be here at Shore Cottage and, just as startling to her right now – *she isn't wearing any mascara*. She looks around the fire and thinks, I'm with my best friends and Niall, who I think is becoming a friend. And the Sampsons – well, they're the Sampsons. They're fine. We'll all get through this together. Pearl can sense herself glowing tonight, as if something is wakening in her: the country girl she once was, and the younger woman who breezed down to London at twenty, when virtually nothing intimidated her.

She is unfazed now when a figure appears in the distance and plods heavily towards them. After all, they're not doing anything wrong. Michael had mentioned that he often has fires here.

'Hi!' Pearl says, jumping up.

'Hi there.' Bar the small area around his eyes, the man is entirely bundled up in a thick hooded jacket and muffler.

'We're staying at Shore Cottage,' Pearl starts. 'D'you know Michael?'

'Of course I know Michael,' he says gruffly. 'Thought I'd come down to meet you all...' His gaze skims the group.

'Oh,' Lena says quickly. 'We thought it'd be okay to light a fire here. But if it's not we can put it out—'

'No, no, you're fine,' the man assures them. 'I just wanted to see how you are. With the snow situation, I mean. I live on the farm over that way —' He jabs a finger a little way inland. 'We met, remember? When you'd just arrived?'

'Oh, yes!' Pearl says. 'With the sheep—'

'Aye, that was it.' The man tugs down his hood and muffler, exposing his weathered face now, and smiles. 'I'm Harry.' Pearl does a quick round of introductions, but more through politeness than any expectation that he will remember everyone's names.

'So how's it been, managing the place by yourselves?' Harry asks. 'With Michael running off to London like Dick Whittington?'

Pearl laughs, realising that everyone must know everything around here. 'We're doing fine,' she replies.

'Well, that's good to hear. So, I was thinking, what are your plans for Christmas Day?'

He looks around at them expectantly, nodding his thanks as Niall hands him a roll stuffed with a freshly grilled sausage. 'We, er, don't have any *firm* plans,' Lena admits.

'We don't have a turkey either,' Frida announces.

'Or stockings or presents!' Theo exclaims, as if he has only just realised this. He turns to his mother. 'Father Christmas will go to our house and I won't be there!'

'Hey, it's okay, Theo,' Pearl assures him. 'He knows you're here.' She glances at Shelley and they exchange a silent message: *Presents! What are we going to do?*

'So it's going to be a pretty rubbishy Christmas,' Frida adds, and Harry frowns.

'It needn't be. Come over to our place tonight, if you like. We always have a few people over on Christmas Eve.'

'What people?' Frida asks, and Harry laughs.

'There are people around here, you know. We do socialise. Sometimes we even manage to have fun.'

Pearl chuckles and she sees Niall trying to suppress a laugh.

'Even in this weather?' Pearl asks. 'I mean, people will come out in the snow?'

'Aye, 'course they will.' Harry nods and pulls a small silvery flask from a pocket and hands it to her. 'Have a nip. It'll warm you up.' Tentatively, she takes a sip of whisky and senses its warmth spreading through her.

'Mmm, that's lovely.'

'Ten-year-old malt, that. Pass it around, if you like—'

'I'm not drinking from that.' Frida shudders. '*Hygiene—*'

'Maybe don't give any to the kid.' Harry chuckles. 'But yeah, we're used to walking in snow. You have torches, right?'

'Yes, of course,' Shelley asserts. So Harry gives them directions and later, when the fire has died down to its glowing embers, the entire Shore Cottage contingency tramps along the snowy lane with Stan trotting at their side. Soon they find the track that leads to Harry's farm. They are all beckoned in, and Pearl's heart seems to swell at the warmth of the welcome here. There is chatter and music and drinks appear miraculously in their hands. A fire is glowing in the hearth and tinsel has been tacked along the wooden ceiling beams. A real Christmas tree is an explosion of gaudy colour and there are people here – actual *people*, Pearl reflects with a smile as she catches Frida's surprised expression. But soon, as more drinks are drunk and the music is cranked up, everyone – even Frida – seems to relax. Mince pies are abundant and Theo is handed a bowl of foil-wrapped chocolate coins.

Although they have no idea where these places might be, they meet Isla from the post office, Kevin from the bakery and Pam – Harry's wife – who runs a cheese shop. 'A cheese shop!' Frida exclaims. 'Where might *that* be?' There's the local taxi driver (it seems there's just the one) and a small, elf-like man who runs a campsite and says they're welcome to stay any time: 'No charge for friends of Michael's.' There's Jimmy from the next farm, and his long-haired twin boys, gangly and liberally tattooed and not what Pearl would have imagined as farmer's sons.

Then Roger suggests that Theo – who so far has been remarkably pleasant – is looking terribly tired. And as the Sampsons are leaving, Shelley and Pearl and Lena decide to head home too (Shelley realises she has actually referred to Shore Cottage as 'home'). And so, together with Niall and Stan, they all thank Harry and Pam, who insist that they take two frozen chickens plus some kind of peculiar ginger wine and a tub of Celebrations, which they insisted was 'going spare'. 'Handy for Pearl,' Lena whispers, grinning, 'if the bathrooms are all occupied?'

'Chicken?' Frida mutters as they make their way along the snow-covered lane. 'Not turkey?'

Pearl chuckles, surprised at how happy she is that Niall is walking with her while the others march a little way ahead, laden with Harry and Pam's gifts. 'I actually prefer chicken,' he admits with a smile.

'Me too!'

They fall silent, a little fuzzy from whisky as their boots crunch into the snow. The moon hangs low over the faint black outline of the mountains. 'I think Christmas is going to be perfect,' Pearl announces suddenly, turning to look at Niall. At some point – she's not quite sure when – she must have slipped her arm in his, just to steady herself in the snow.

'I think it will be too,' Niall says. And then they stop suddenly. His arms are round her now and they hug, and then kiss. It's the briefest brush of the lips, as tender as a snowflake. Pearl's heart seems to soar like a shooting star, and as he takes her arm again, and they trudge slowly back to Shore Cottage, everything feels just right.

35

'Oh, Dad, that doesn't feel right at all.' Tommy has taken Daisy out for their customary Christmas Eve movie night at the cinema close to her home. Now, at 9.45 p.m., they are walking together back to her mother's place.

'It'll be fine, darling,' he assures her.

She looks at him as they pass a cocktail bar with achingly beautiful choral music drifting out. It's more Bach's 'Christmas Oratorio' than Slade's 'Merry Xmas Everybody' around here. 'Grandma and Grandpa and you, all together in Lena's flat?' Daisy reiterates, as if still trying to make sense of it. 'Without Lena?'

'Well, yes,' Tommy says lightly. 'It can't be helped. She's totally snowed in up there.'

'But... won't it be weird?'

'I don't see why. It's a perfectly nice place, isn't it?'

'I don't mean that,' she says quickly. 'Of course it is. It's lovely.' Daisy seems to be mulling something over as they pass a bookshop, its window filled with twinkling silver lights. 'I just think they'll find it really odd, that's all.'

'They probably will,' he agrees. 'But you know, darling, we'll just have to make the best of it.'

'Hmm, yeah. I guess so.' He senses her quizzical look. 'So, are you all ready?'

'Yep, the big shop arrived this morning and the turkey came from a little butcher in Hackney. And believe it or not, I've made a Christmas pudding—'

'Wow, Dad!' she exclaims. 'That's impressive...'

'It's not rocket science.' He grins. 'But I did drench it in booze to anaesthetise Grandma—'

'You *are* bad.' She laughs. 'But seriously, it's a shame you're going to be doing the whole thing yourself.'

'Well, you know I love cooking,' he says, and it's true. He always has, especially after a full day at the office. He doesn't mind working in recruitment, and he supposes he's pretty good at it as he's organised and affable. But he also enjoys the rhythm of an ordinary domestic life. Ordinary in that it's how most people live, when they don't have cleaners and nannies and gardeners and a sprawling home with a library and a snooker room, as is the case at High Elms.

Tommy had never wanted to be like his dad. He certainly hadn't wanted to follow his lead when it came to fathering: hiding away in a study, or shielded by the *Telegraph* when forced to occupy a family space. When he and Catherine were together they had shared the workload equally. There was no question of Tommy shirking any of his parental obligations.

He glances at Daisy in profile. Her shiny blonde hair is secured in a tidy ponytail, and her neat little nose and curve of her chin are so similar to her mother's, it could be the young Catherine's face. Daisy even dresses like her mum, favouring classic cashmere in shades like Elephant's Breath (Tommy grew familiar with the Farrow and Ball paint chart during his marriage). He treasures their time together and, as they approach the little late-night cafe that's a favourite of Daisy's, he has a sudden urge to prolong the evening a little.

Over these past few years, Tommy has grown used to the fact that Daisy always spends Christmas Day with her mum. It's the way they want it, and Catherine, it has to be said, is Queen of Christmas with all her family amassed. But this year, with Lena being stuck in Scotland, he feels differently. He'd love to be with Daisy tomorrow, and the thought of being separated from her triggers something of an ache in his gut.

Tommy stops as they reach the cafe. 'Will Mum mind if we stop off for a hot chocolate?'

Daisy beams at him. 'Of course she won't!' So they step into the cosy warmth of the cafe with its berry red interior and mistletoe decorations on the tables. As Daisy chatters away about the art prize she won at school, Tommy tells himself that he's lucky to have this as their annual ritual: he and his beloved daughter together on Christmas Eve. But still, Tommy can't help thinking that tomorrow she won't be with him. She'll be at home, where there'll be *three* Christmas trees: the vast ten-footer in the living room, a second one in the hallway and a mini one in the sleek kitchen.

There won't be any cheap decorations of the type that Lena likes. Catherine has an aversion to tinsel and multicoloured lights. Instead, everything is beautifully coordinated in silver and gold, and sprigs of natural holly and fir adorn the mantlepieces. And around the festive table there'll be Daisy and her mother, and Catherine's parents and brother and sister-in-law and the two nieces. There'll be a turkey so large it would barely fit through Lena's doorway, let alone into her oven. And not just a Christmas pudding, or a pavlova – as Daisy has always favoured – but a *pudding buffet*. For Catherine, Christmas prep kicks off in early October and by 25 December, everything is perfect.

As for Tommy, it'll be him and his mum and dad, cramped around Lena's little table with the wobbly extendable leaf. As he and Daisy sip their delicious hot chocolates and eat their mince pies, he tries to reassure himself that this will be perfectly okay. It's only a day after all. But still, he makes a point of savouring the last fragment of buttery pastry, just as he wants to savour every last moment of Christmas Eve with his daughter. And now the cafe is about to close, but they still sit there.

Daisy looks across the table at her father. She seems hesitant as she twirls the teaspoon in the empty hot chocolate mug. Tommy can sense that she's building up to something, but he can't figure out what that might be. 'Dad, I just want to say,' she starts. 'About tomorrow... about Christmas Day...'

'It'll be fine, darling,' he says firmly, but she shakes her head.

'I'm sure it will be. I know you'll be brilliant at doing it all.' The young waitress comes over and he pays the bill. Tommy is grateful for the small distraction because he doesn't really want to think about Christmas Day in Hackney and how bizarre it's going to feel without Lena being there. When he said it would be fine, he was lying.

They leave the cafe and make their way along the quiet street. There are few people out now, and less traffic than usual around here. *That's because people like to be home and cosy on Christmas Eve,* Tommy reminds himself, *with the people they love.*

Now he senses Daisy about to say something else. And then she does, just as they turn off the main street. 'Dad,' she starts, 'what if we ask Mum if you and Grandma and Grandpa can come over to ours tomorrow?'

'Oh, I don't think so,' he blusters.

She looks at him, eyes round and bright. 'Wouldn't that be lovely, though? All of us together?'

He exhales forcefully as they turn into the even quieter residential road, where Catherine and Daisy live. Catherine will invite him in, he's sure of it. Just for a glass of wine before he takes an Uber home to Hackney. 'No, Daisy,' he says. 'It's a lovely thought but it's far too short notice for Mum. We couldn't just descend on her like that. And anyway, I have everything in at the flat, all ready—'

'But you could bring it all over to us tomorrow.' She smiles hopefully. 'We could blend our Christmases—'

'*Blend* our Christmases?' He can't help smiling at that.

'Yes! Wouldn't Grandma and Grandpa love that? Being with me?' She grins cheekily.

'Yes but—'

'I'm not saying I'm their *favourite* grandchild,' she teases. But she is. Of course she is, because she's charming and clever and she knows exactly how to handle them. And Catherine is their favourite daughter-in-law, and Tommy knows that they would have a far better time at her beautiful apartment tomorrow than in a little flat in Hackney.

Why had they insisted on coming to Lena's anyway? To check her out, he suspects. To see her under duress, struggling to make Christmas Day run as smoothly as possible and then watching her fail. Lena has already mentioned to his parents that cooking isn't exactly her forte. Yet Tommy's mother has already asked, 'D'you prefer the brining method for your turkey, Lena? Are you Team Delia or Nigella?'

'Oh, Tommy takes charge of all that,' Lena replied cheerfully.

'Lena is *Team Lena*, Mum,' Tommy added tightly. Now he can picture his parents heading home after Christmas, with mission accomplished – agreeing that he really is marrying beneath himself.

Realising all of this causes fury to fizzle like a firework in Tommy's gut. Not just towards his parents but towards himself too, for allowing his parents to run roughshod over their lives. What must Lena think of him? Well, their plans have been upended now, Tommy tells himself as they arrive at Catherine's apartment. Their little game – his mother's game really – has been scuppered by extreme weather in Scotland. Because without Lena there, is there any point in them coming to Hackney after all?

Daisy goes to ring the doorbell, but Tommy stops her with his hand. 'If Mum's okay about this,' he starts, 'and I do think it's an awfully big ask—'

'It's not. Of course it's not!' Her face brightens.

'Will there be room, though, for three extras?'

'"Extras"?' Daisy laughs, showing her perfectly even white teeth. 'Are you crazy? We're all family, Dad.'

He beams then, filled with happiness. 'Then I think that spending Christmas all together is an excellent idea.'

36

CHRISTMAS DAY

Perhaps it's the way the sun shines brightly onto the snow, making everything sparkle. Or just being here all together in Shore cottage, on Christmas Day; unexpected, yes, but surely there are worse places to be. Pearl looks around the table laden with a vast breakfast, and what she sees gives her a little jolt of surprise.

Everyone, she realises – even Frida! – looks happy. Niall is topping up coffees and Lena is making Buck's Fizz and a lemonade version for Theo. The kitchen is filled with chatter and there's something else in the air, Pearl realises. A sort of charge, like static. She keeps catching Niall's eye and is enjoying the frisson between them. It's so liberating, Pearl decides, being 500 miles from home. Of course she misses her son but this is something just for her: a flirtation at least. 'You deserve some fun,' Lena said firmly when Pearl told her friends about the kiss last night. They'd made hot chocolates and whispered and giggled at the fireside like the young women they once were.

However, now they are firmly in practical mode, clearing the breakfast table as Theo lays out the spoils from his Christmas stocking. 'Look at all this!' he commands, and everyone coos over the gifts that were hastily assembled and stuffed into one of Niall's thick red walking socks. There's a paper 'fortune teller', of the type Shelley used to make for Martha, when

Martha was perpetually glued to her side. Pearl made a little story book, entitled *Stan of the Highlands*, in the way that she'd made books for Brandon when he was little. Shelley had found paper in a box stashed under the coffee table, plus felt tips, a kid's paint set and glittery snowflake stickers, presumably a rainy-day kit for young guests. Her heart snagged at the thought of Michael putting this together. When Lena was shovelling away snow at the front door she found a toy racing car, presumably left by a previous guest. Niall made a little garage for it from a cookie box and Roger's offering was a whittled stick to be used for toasting marshmallows, should the opportunity arise. And Frida's contribution had been to pick out Theo's favourites from the Celebrations tub.

'I'm so glad you like your stocking,' Shelley says now.

'Yeah.' Theo grins up at her. 'So when are we getting the *real* presents?'

She laughs tightly and turns away, and after a flurry of dishwasher loading she pulls on wellies and FaceTimes Joel in the garden.

'Happy Christmas, darling!' He beams at her.

'Happy Christmas, honey. I'm missing you all...'

'Missing you too,' he says. 'So how are things up there?'

'Actually pretty good,' she says. 'It's not what we planned but we're still having fun...'

'I'm so glad to hear that,' he enthuses.

She smiles. He's in the kitchen and, as with their last call, she finds herself having to adjust to his newfound buoyancy. 'So the turkey's in the oven? You remembered to get up early—'

'I'll have you know I was up at seven to put it in,' he teases, radiating pride.

Shelley studies his face on the screen, bright eyed and flushed, presumably from the morning's exertions. He looks different, she decides. And he's wearing a black polo neck sweater that she doesn't remember seeing before. Joel isn't a polo neck kind of guy. 'So I guess your mum and dad'll be arriving soon?' she remarks.

'Yep, they're on their way.'

'Great. Well, I hope the kids are helping,' she adds.

'Yeah, they've been brilliant so far. Peeling, chopping, making pigs in blankets...'

'Wow! That's... amazing.' Shelley is stunned by this. It's great, of course it is. But why can't Martha and Fin be willing and eager when she's around?

'I know,' Joel agrees. 'They've been really, really amazing. Marth peeled tons of potatoes...'

'Have you drugged them?' Shelley exclaims, laughing now.

'Haha, no. They're just high on life, I guess. High on Christmas!'

She blinks at him. She hasn't seen him this happy and excited since he won a design award in 2015. 'I'm so glad to hear that,' she says. 'So you haven't done presents yet?'

'Actually, we have,' Joel admits with a small wince of discomfort.

'Oh, really? Why's that?' The tradition is that they always wait until Joel's parents arrive before opening presents. Every year, it's a sticking point with the kids: *Why do we have to wait? No one else does!* But that's how things were done when Joel was growing up. Presents sat under the tree, not to be touched until his aunts and uncles arrived. Shelley knows Joel's parents will be disappointed that the great unwrapping has happened, without them being there to witness it.

'Just thought we'd change things up a bit this year.' Joel seems to have developed a twitch in his jaw. He tugs at the polo neck.

'Right,' Shelley remarks, 'so I'm out of the picture and everything's different!'

'Haha, yeah...' He laughs uncomfortably.

'I wonder what else you've been up to while I've been away?' she teases, and his cheeks blaze.

'Nothing!'

'Joel,' she exclaims. 'I'm *joking*, okay? And it's up to you how you manage the day. It's your parents who'll be horrified that the best part's already over—'

'D'you think they will be?' Now he looks positively frightened.

'*I* don't know.' She smiles. 'And to be honest, I don't blame the kids for wanting to tear into their presents first thing. I always thought it was a bit...' She wants to say 'joyless' but holds back. 'Anyway,' she adds, 'sounds like it's all going great, so—'

'It is. It's really, really great. And thanks for the guitar amp, honey. Honestly, what a present! You shouldn't have...'

'You're welcome.' Shelley brushes off the fact that he chose it and sent her the link.

'Your presents are all waiting for you here,' he adds.

She remembers the John Lewis voucher he gave her last year, which hardly filled her with festive cheer. Petulantly, she spent it on a non-stick frying pan. 'Can't wait,' she says. Then he passes her on to Martha – 'Thanks for my presents! They're *amazing*. Love you, Mum!' And then comes Fin, who despises FaceTiming. There's still that look of abject horror as if he's defending himself at the Old Bailey. But he tries at least. 'Happy Christmas, Mum! I love my stuff. Yeah, all of it. We miss you!'

It's all so unexpected that after their call, Shelley has to take herself away, down to the end of the garden, just to absorb what's happening.

She chose to run away to Scotland in the week before Christmas and now she's stranded here. Joel isn't angry or accusatory; in fact, she believes now that he'll rise to the challenge and that this unplanned situation might make things so much better between them.

She watches as one of the russet hens potters out of the hen house and takes a drink. Her heart seems to swell as she pictures her family, rallying to prepare for Christmas Day without her. Pulling her phone from her pocket, she pauses, and then texts Joel.

SHELLEY

Thank you darling for managing everything at home. I love you. S xxx

Immediately Joel's message pings back.

JOEL

Love you too

Back inside the cottage, she shows it to Pearl. 'D'you think it's really him?' she jokes.

'Maybe you should go away more often,' Pearl chuckles, on something of a cloud herself after a blur of happy Christmases with Brandon and Abi, despite

Abi reminding her that the loo seat is still broken. They've seemed fine each time she's called, if a little unforthcoming until today. But this morning Brandon was full of how they were preparing Christmas dinner together, and if the kitchen is trashed in the process, well, Pearl can handle that.

Now Harry and Pam's chickens are roasting in the Aga, along with potatoes, and the cottage is filling with delicious aromas. Soon stuffing will be added, improvised with breadcrumbs and onions and whatever herbs they can find in the pantry. Niall is busily doing something with carrots and butter and honey on the hob, and Roger is announcing, 'I don't want to boast but my gravy's really something, isn't it, Frida?' No one seems to care that there aren't any sprouts or cranberry sauce. In the absence of Alexa or any means of accessing Spotify playlists, Shelley has got to grips with Michael's rather antiquated stereo, and now a festive complication CD tinkles away in the background.

'Oh my favourite!' Frida enthuses when 'Do They Know It's Christmas?' comes on.

'The last time I heard this was when I was out Christmas shopping with Joel,' Shelley remarks.

'Ahh, how romantic,' Lena teases, feeling pretty loved up herself after an exchange of affectionate texts with Tommy.

LENA

> Happy Christmas darling. I know you'll be busy getting ready for your parents so let's call later ok?

TOMMY

> Yes sweetheart, happy Christmas to you my love. I adore you xx

'I actually wanted to kill him that day,' Shelley chuckles. 'But now there he is, manning the fort in a black polo neck like some sixties jazz guy—'

'Wow.' Pearl laughs. And now, with heat rising in Shore Cottage's kitchen, Lena opens the front door and steps outside. The sky is clear blue, the air sharp and crisp and everything is sparkling white, as if lightly glittered. Lena inhales, fixing her gaze on the snowy mountain tops, until she feels fortified enough to call her mum and dad in Manchester. They want to know all about the Highlands, and make jokes about bagpipes, and has she been chased by any haggis yet? Her heart seems to twang at the sound of all the jollity there.

'We miss you, Lena,' her dad announces.

'I miss you too, Dad. I'll be up straight after New Year, okay? I promise.' Then she's passed around to speak to her brothers and sisters and by the time the call has ended she feels quite dizzy.

So when she sees Daisy's Instagram she thinks, Oh, that picture must be from years ago. God knows why she's put it up now. Still, it's unsettling to be faced with a festive scene of this kind. Of Tommy sitting next to Catherine at a lavishly decorated Christmas table. And there's Daisy looking stunning in a deep blue dress, and Tommy's parents, William and Annabelle, grinning and raising glasses to the camera.

Then it dawns on Lena that this isn't an old photo. Because this isn't how Daisy looked a few years ago. It's Daisy *right now*.

She blinks at it, feeling sick to her gut. What's going on? Why aren't Tommy and his parents at her flat in Hackney? Lena doesn't understand. For one mad moment she thinks: Is this real? Or AI generated? Is it a *joke*? There are other people too – Catherine's brother, she thinks. And that must be her sister-in-law and their kids. But as soon as she registers these other people, they seem to melt away. And all Lena can see is the two people in the centre of the picture. Tommy and Catherine, beaming happily on this Christmas Day, 500 miles from her. And as she reads Daisy's caption, her heart seems to freeze.

Christmas Day with the fam. Love them so much!!!!!

37

What a morning Joel's had. First – without any consultation – all of those hastily re-wrapped presents were torn open in a ramshackle fashion, with no sense of occasion and no grandparents present to enjoy the spectacle. Then he'd asked, 'Could you peel a few spuds for me, Marth?' She'd glared at him as if he'd told her to eat the turkey's giblets for breakfast.

Now Joel's parents, Ken and Kathleen, are here in their best clothes. For Ken this means 'slacks' and a rather cardboard-looking blue shirt, still bearing the creases from the packaging. Meanwhile, Kathleen looks overheated in a violently flowered dress and a purple cardigan buttoned up to the neck. She is already in full flow about stabbings in schools.

'They're taking knives into classrooms now,' she says festively. 'They've having to put in metal detectors at the entrances.'

'Even round our way it's getting bad,' his father announces. 'An elderly couple were found tied up and gagged in their house, did you hear?'

No, Joel didn't hear. He's been too occupied lately to pay any attention to the news. Now he is simultaneously checking that the turkey isn't burning while carrots are bubbling on the hob. Is he too early with the carrots? He has no idea. Only that he has peeled so many vegetables this morning that a sharp pain is shooting up his wrist. He wishes his parents would bugger off to the living room where Martha and Fin are lying around like lords. When he caught Martha pouring herself a glass of champagne at 9.45 this morning he didn't dare to comment.

As his mother describes how the intruders at the old couple's house urinated into their fish tank, Joel decides he should make a start on the pigs in blankets and stuffing and gravy.

'So, when are we doing presents?' she asks.

'Oh, I'm sorry, Mum. The kids have already opened theirs.'

'Really?' She looks aghast, and then sighs loudly and glances around the kitchen, as if only just registering that things are very different this year. 'So Shelley's stuck up there in Scotland, is she?' As if she has only just remembered that he has a wife.

'Yeah. Crazy isn't it?' He bobs down to check the turkey, burning his forearm on the scorching tin and yelping in pain. 'Shit!' He rams the tray back in.

'Maybe you could've just got a chicken?' his father offers.

'Funny time of year to go away,' his mum remarks, patting her hair, 'if you ask me.'

I'm not asking you, Joel thinks, glaring at her. And also, what's with the snail's pace at drinking? His mum is still sipping the small sherry he pressed into her hands ninety minutes ago. Evaporation would be more effective. However, Joel's parents are moderate people who like to spin out the single alcoholic drink they have all year. Stuff that, Joel decides. As far as he's concerned there's only one way to survive this day.

He will *drink* his way through it. He will get absolutely smashed and sod the consequences. And so, as culinary preparations continue with his parents still welded to the kitchen chairs, he slugs a half pint tumbler of red, and then another, feeling the alcohol coursing straight to his face and setting his cheeks on fire. Potatoes come out of the oven and go back in and come out again, several times over. How can he tell when things are ready? Joel's approach to anything technical that's not working properly is to turn it off and on again and hope for the best. But obviously that won't work in this situation. 'You look awfully red,' his father remarks, crunching a crisp.

'Yes, aren't you hot in that polo neck?' His mum frowns.

'No, I'm fine.' Sweat drips from Joel's forehead onto the potato tray.

'Have you had your blood pressure checked?' she asks. And then, as if he is nine, 'Why don't you go and put a T-shirt on?'

'*I'm capable of choosing my own clothes, thank you!*' he barks, and she shrinks into the chair. 'Sorry,' Joel mutters. 'There's just quite a lot going on here right now.' How does Shelley manage all of this by herself? 'Look,' he adds, 'I think everything's under control' – like hell it is – 'so why don't we go through and do your presents?'

Reluctantly, as if transfixed by a particularly riveting episode of *Hell's Kitchen*, Joel's parents troupe after him to the living room where their grandchildren are currently sprawled. Joel's father splutters again at the sorry state of the Christmas tree. 'Been at the sherry, has it?'

'It fell over,' Joel says flatly. 'Sit down. Eat some nuts. I'll just nip upstairs and fetch your gifts...'

Up he trots like a drunken pony, gripping his tumbler of vicious red wine and slugging it on the hoof. He takes a moment on the landing to check his phone in case Carmel has wished him a happy Christmas. Still not a peep from her. He messaged her again this morning, keeping it cool. *Have a lovely day babe*, he wrote, realising that he didn't know who she was planning to spend it with. The unnamed man, perhaps? Or are they too new for that? Forget that for now, Joel decides as he locates his parents' presents neatly stacked at the bottom of Shelley's wardrobe. He lays out the sweater for his dad, plus some spy novels – an entire series by the look of it – plus soft leather gloves and a definitely non-moulting scarf for his mum. All chosen and bought by Shelley because he never has any idea of what to buy them. They're just two quiet people living in a pebble-dashed semi-detached house in the direst of suburbs. So how can he possibly know what they'd like?

Still slurping his wine, Joel chastises himself for forgetting to wrap these gifts. He was too busy re-wrapping everything else, and now he realises there's no Christmas paper left. So he storms upwards into his studio, but all there is here is plain white copier paper and even Joel knows that won't do. Defeated, he carries the unwrapped gifts downstairs and presents them, steeped in shame, as both his mum and dad try to appear pleased. 'Thank Shelley for us, won't you love?' His mum raises a small smile and Martha shoots him a frosty look from the sofa. Then Joel is thrown back into kitchen duties, stirring and carving and lifting searing hot trays from the oven. There's the table to lay and he hasn't chilled the wine or made any stuffing. There's none of Shelley's famous home-made cranberry sauce either – this isn't his fault! – but sod it. With his life crumbling around him, and his kids currently in bitcoin-blackmail mode, it hardly matters that they won't be dolloping what's basically jam on their turkey.

A little wobbly on his feet now, Joel dumps everything on the unadorned kitchen table and calls his family through. There are no crackers (was he meant to buy crackers?) and the potatoes have cooled, inexplicably, within seconds of being brought out of the oven. Yet a single chipolata incinerates his dad's mouth.

'Well, this is nice, isn't it?' Joel hoists his tumbler and forces a smile.

'Yes, it is,' his mother manages. 'The carrots are lovely...'

Joel glares down at them. They're okay, he reckons. But who gets excited about carrots? The turkey has the texture of an old horsehair-stuffed mattress and the scorching sausages are virtually raw inside. And gallingly, after the many, many hours of intense preparation, the whole meal is devoured in what feels like about eight minutes. Without a single offer to help him, everyone surges back to the living room leaving a billion plates to wash and the kitchen destroyed.

It's like sex with Carmel, Joel reflects as he launches into the massive clean-up operation. He doesn't want a prize or even a burst of applause. Just some acknowledgement would be nice – that he tried his best. That he *exists*, even. That he is a real man with actual feelings.

Is this his life now, he wonders, as he wipes roast potato grease off the kitchen floor? Will he be beholden to his kids forever, and what will Shelley make of all this?

The day creaks on interminably with TV and snacks. His parents enjoy Monopoly, so they play that. But Martha keeps flashing him a look so Joel 'forgets' to charge her rent on Vine Street and at one point, as banker, he slips her an extra £500 note. Mercifully, at around eleven, his parents announce that they're off to bed, and the kids slope away to their rooms. Finally Joel can pull off this wretched sweater and inspect his neck.

At last something good has happened. When he checks in the downstairs bathroom mirror he sees that the livid bruise has almost faded away. So by the time Shelley comes home it should be all gone.

Buoyed up by this, he strides to the kitchen and refills his wine glass, and then settles on the sofa, revelling in the calmness. Brazenly, and missing Shelley a little now, he fires off a text.

> JOEL
>
> We survived it! Had a great day and Mum managed to spin out a single glass of sherry for nine hours. Must be a record huh? How are you?

Then, while he waits for a reply, he goes to Carmel's Facebook page. He gazes at her profile picture and fiddles with his phone, seized by an urge to text her. What should he say? He doesn't want to seem maudlin because actually, he's feeling pretty sanguine now. If she's dumped him for whatever reason then he'll be cool with that. Maybe, Joel figures, he should turn over a new leaf and start to behave like a decent human being. Life would be a lot less stressful for one thing. And maybe, if they both made an effort and Shelley stopped wearing those nan-curtain pyjamas, they could resurrect some semblance of a sex life.

Joel drinks more wine and ponders on this. Then all in a rush, before he can overthink it, he types out a message:

> JOEL
>
> Hey babe happy Christmas! Haven't heard from you since our sleepover and wondering if all ok? You were magnificent that last time. Like a goddess on top of me. Understand if you want to cool it but I think we should talk as I'd like closure. xxx

He rereads his message and thinks yeah, that's good. That's pretty eloquent considering he's sunk something in the region of two bottles of red wine over the course of the day. Then he wanders through to the kitchen figuring that he might guzzle some leftover roast potatoes to soak up the booze.

Funny, he muses as he shovels in the cold spuds, that leftovers are often the best part of Christmas dinner. Perhaps next year they should cook double the food so there'll be acres of leftovers to keep them going for days? Joel decides he'll suggest this when Shelley comes home. He'll help of course. He won't have her doing all that by herself.

Thrilled with his genius idea – to go leftovers crazy! – he strides back to the living room and grabs his phone, intending to share it with Shelley. His vision is a little squiffy as he frowns hard at the text he sent her just fifteen minutes ago. No, no, no. This isn't right. He is sweating now and shaking too. He thinks he might actually throw up. It's not the wine or the under-cooked chipolatas or his usage of the word 'closure'. It's the fact that he was so wrapped up in getting the words right that he wasn't paying full attention as he sent it.

With sickening horror Joel realises what he's done. In his sozzled state, he didn't send Carmel's message to Carmel. He sent it to his wife.

38

'I'm sorry,' Tommy is saying. 'I know it sounds mad but I just didn't know how to tell you. It just sort of *happened*. I took Daisy out last night, like I always do on Christmas Eve. And she said, "Why not come to us?" Then her mum opened the door and Daisy blurted it out and Catherine said—'

'Tommy, it's not that,' Lena cuts in, although it *is* that. It's all of it. 'It's the fact that we've been messaging and even spoken today. We spoke this afternoon! And you said it had all been lovely and I just assumed—'

'I know, darling. I'm an idiot. I just didn't know what to tell you.' He stops then, saying nothing more. And Lena shivers in her jumper in the darkness of Michael's garden and remains silent too.

Moments stretch. A light wind rustles the trees. Lena picks up a handful of snow, barely noticing that it numbs her hand as she scrunches it into a tight lump.

Because really, all of her feels numb now. Tommy spent Christmas Day with his ex-wife and her beautifully coordinated baubles and his parents loved it. Of course they did. They would also love Tommy and Catherine to reconcile, and perhaps this is the first step towards it? With a start, Lena realises she is crying. She tries to wrestle her emotions under control, but as a russet hen juts her head out of the little wooden house, she emits a sob.

'Lena, you're upset,' Tommy says, sounding choked himself. 'Please don't be upset.'

'Don't tell me whether or not to be upset!'

'Okay, okay! I'm sorry...'

She rubs at her face but can't stop crying now. Briefly, she wonders why, when it's so extremely cold out here, her tears aren't forming speckles of ice.

'I don't want to talk any more tonight,' she murmurs, stomping back to the cottage now.

'Please don't go. Please talk to me, Leen. I just wish you were here with me now—'

'Where are you?' she asks, although he has already told her he's back at the flat, and that his parents are spending the night at Catherine's. But she wants to hear him say it again.

'I'm here at the flat by myself.'

She rubs at her cold nose. 'What happened to all the Christmas food you'd ordered?'

'I took everything over there this morning. And then when I came home tonight I poured myself a whacking great drink.'

'Right.' He's trying to lighten things, but she isn't biting.

'And I'm sorry but I had a cigarette in the garden,' he adds.

'Did you,' she says flatly. She bites her lip. 'It hasn't just been today, has it? There was your lunch date too—'

'That wasn't a date!' he protests. 'I told you, it was just—'

'I *hate* this,' she exclaims, anger rising up in her suddenly.

'I know you do. But honestly, there's nothing for you to—'

'Tommy, do you understand?' Lena snaps. 'I hate the way this has made me feel. As if I'm a jealous and insecure person, which I'm not. Even after what Max did, cheating on me all that time. It still didn't make me like that because that was about *him*. It was him being pathetic and weak and needing his ego stroking by a younger woman. But even he didn't turn me into a jealous and insecure woman and you're not going to either—'

'Lena!' Tommy cries, and she realises she's been shouting. 'I don't want to turn you into anything! I think you're perfect just as you are.' She realises he is crying too. And now Shelley appears in the doorway, her face awash with concern. She steps out into the snow and touches Lena's arm. And Lena finishes the call abruptly and Shelley puts her arms around her, pulling her close.

'Come inside,' she murmurs. 'Come on, honey. It'll be all right.'

Lena blots her face on her jumper sleeve. They step into the kitchen where Pearl and Niall are drinking tea at the table.

'Leen, are you all right?' Pearl asks, jumping up.

Lena shakes her head and Niall gets up too, about to leave the room. 'No, Niall, it's fine. No need to rush off.' She rubs at her stinging eyes. 'Just a bit of a thing with my boyfriend—'

'Oh, Lena.' Pearl hugs her tightly. 'I'm sure it was nothing. Daisy probably just wanted him there...'

She nods and Shelley hands her a glass of wine. 'What a Christmas,' Lena announces, shaking her head.

Niall still looks as if he's walked into the wrong room at a hotel and a conference is going on. 'I'm sorry there's stuff going on at home, Lena.' He pauses. 'But look, I just want to say you've all...' Now he glances at Pearl. 'Somehow, you've managed to make this a brilliant Christmas.'

'I'm glad you've enjoyed the day.' Lena manages a smile.

'Yeah.' He clears his throat. 'It's been... pretty memorable.' He smiles then, and without needing to say anything, both he and Pearl step outside into the sparkling garden, away from the others. Here, as they walk down towards Michael's snow-covered vegetable patch, Niall takes her hand. The simple gesture feels so natural and right – Elias wasn't the hand-holding sort – and Pearl's heart seems to soar as she smiles up at him. 'I wonder how long we're going to be snowed in?' she asks.

Niall chuckles. 'Another few days would be bearable, wouldn't they?'

'They would,' she agrees. 'Honestly, I think I could cope with that—'

'Pearl,' he cuts in suddenly. 'I just want to thank you...'

'For what?' She is genuinely surprised.

He shrugs, as if unsure how to express it. 'For helping me through this time of year, corny as that sounds. Honestly, I was dreading it.'

'I'm glad,' she says. 'I mean, I'm glad you've been here with us. It's been...' She breaks off, and they look at each other in the glow of light from the cottage. 'It's been wonderful,' she adds. Then she reaches up and kisses his cheek, and then her lips are on his and they are kissing in the crisp, cold night, his hands wrapped around hers.

As they pull apart he looks hesitant. 'I'd love to see you,' he starts, 'when you're back in London. Would that be okay? I'm sorry, I don't even know how you feel about all of that. If you even want to meet someone. It sounds as if your life's pretty full—'

'I was seeing someone,' she cuts in, 'for a few months. It's just finished...'

'Oh, I understand,' Niall says quickly. 'It's not what you want. I totally get that. I haven't seen anyone since the split...'

'No, what I mean is,' Pearl clarifies, 'I finished it because it wasn't right. Because I didn't want to be with someone just for the sake of it, you know?'

Niall nods and their footsteps crunch into the snow as they make their way back to the cottage. 'Yes, I do know.'

She looks at him as she pushes open the front door. 'But yes, I'd like to see you,' she adds, 'when we're all thrown back into our real lives. I'd like that very much.'

* * *

At ten to midnight on Christmas night, the three women settle by the fire in the lounge. Everyone else has gone to bed but they need time together, just to reflect on the strangest Christmas they've ever had.

Christmas night always feels weird to Shelley. It's the end of a whirl of a day, when the enormous dinner is over and the furls of wrapping paper have all been swept up and stuffed into bin bags. All the preparations and fuss, and it's over in a blink. She wonders momentarily if Joel's mother has done her usual thing of gathering up the biggest pieces of wrapping paper to be taken home and ironed and reused next Christmas. And if in fact Joel really did remember to buy more wrapping paper for his parents' gifts, as she'd asked him to. Not that it matters now, she decides as Stan jumps up and settles on the sofa beside her.

'Leen, it'll be *fine* when you get home,' Pearl assures her.

She shrugs. 'Will it though?'

'Of course it will,' Shelley says firmly. 'Tommy adores you. You know that.'

Lena inhales, her head filled now with the image of a lavish wedding at High Elms, with the string quartet and the tables all set out with napkins folded in that particular way that Annabelle likes. 'Maybe he does,' she says. 'But I'm not sure how I feel any more.'

'Oh, honey.' Shelley touches her arm and Lena gets up to fetch the wine bottle from the kitchen.

While she's gone, and as Pearl puts another log on the fire, Shelley picks up her phone. It's been so busy today that she's barely looked at it. But now she sees a text notification. There are two from Joel; one joking about his mother nursing a single drink throughout the day. She smiles at that.

However, the second message doesn't make Shelley smile. At first she thinks there's something wrong with her phone or that it's some kind of scam. Because it doesn't make any sense. But no, it's definitely from Joel. Her heart seems to stop as she reads it again.

> JOEL
>
> You were magnificent that last time. Like a goddess on top of me.

It's a message that, clearly, Joel didn't intend to send to her. And at one minute to midnight on Christmas Day, Shelley knows for certain that her marriage is over forever.

39

BOXING DAY

He did it because the snow's gone, he says. That's why Theo snuck into the kitchen and found scissors in a drawer and cut down Michael's beaded curtain. 'I don't understand,' Pearl exclaims, gathering up the red, gold and orange beads. They are everywhere: under the table and fridge. Some have even landed in Stan's basket.

'I was bored,' Theo states, hands plonked on hips, ''cause there's no snow any more.'

'Well, there's still *some*,' Lena points out.

'You didn't mean to do any harm, did you, sweetheart?' Frida asks.

'No.' He pouts, looking down at his slippered feet.

'What d'you mean by that?' Shelley rounds on her. *I didn't mean it!* That was something Joel said earlier. Or was it, *It didn't mean anything?*

'I mean it's just the kind of thing children do,' Frida clarifies.

'It's not, though, is it?' Shelley glares at her. 'This is Michael's place and we're supposed to be looking after it for him. And that curtain came all the way from *India*—'

'Don't shout at my mummy!' Theo wails.

'I'm not shouting!' Shelley shouts as, horrified, Theo turns and clatters out of the house.

'Oh my God.' Shelley places her hands over her face. 'I am *so* sorry, Frida. I don't know what I'm saying—'

'Shell, it's okay,' Lena murmurs, squeezing her arm. Niall and Roger appear briefly, having taken it upon themselves to clear out the fireplace and make everything shipshape in the lounge.

'Oh,' Roger says with a grimace.

'Everything all right here?' Niall asks.

'Not really, no,' Frida announces, stomping to the front door and stepping out. 'Theo, you shouldn't be outside in your slippers!' However, she makes no move to go after him, adjourning instead to the family room as she needs to pack. Everyone is leaving today: Niall, the Sampsons. Shelley, Pearl and Lena too. Only Pearl can be reasonably confident that her life will be pretty much as she left it when she returns home. Shelley and Lena are dreading it. If it were possible, they would stay here forever. Shore Cottage would be a perfect place to hide from life.

However, they can't do that. Because things have to be sorted out. This realisation has turned Shelley's heart into a cold, hard stone as, in their room now, she starts to pack. Lena is gathering together her things too, and keeps asking Shelley if she's all right, if she wants to go for a walk or should they leave right away? Would that be better? Shelley doesn't know what would be better. She can hardly think as she glances out at the clear blue sky and the smudge of purplish mountains beyond.

'Shell, I promise you I'll never see her again,' Joel said when she called earlier, her hand shaking as she gripped her phone. 'I've been so stupid. I was just flattered, I suppose. Flattered that someone like that would be interested—'

'Someone *like that*?' she shot back. 'You mean someone beautiful and successful – a glamorous photographer – and not a clapped-out middle-aged receptionist in a care home—'

'You're *not* clapped out. God, Shell, of course I don't think that! I think you're amazing, with all you do for everyone else. For us, I mean. For me and the kids. You *never* think of yourself and I love you, darling. I'll do anything to make it up to you.' Joel swore that Martha and Fin know nothing about this other woman, but surely they've picked up that something's going on?

When they touched on the kids she couldn't talk to him any more, so she finished the call abruptly. And now Pearl and Lena are sitting with her in the calm of their bedroom, away from the guests. They bring her tea and gently pick over what's happened. Then Shelley doesn't want to talk about Joel any more because she needs to go home and get on with the business of dismantling her marriage. New flights have been booked, leaving from Glasgow this afternoon. Shelley clicks into practical mode, gathering up the last of her things. It's easier than trying to figure out how Martha and Fin will react when they find out what's happened. Anything will be easier than that.

Ever the organised one, Pearl's case is already packed neatly, ready to go. Her special hair-drying towel and vast collection of skincare and make-up products have barely been used, bar the first day or so. It was silly to bring them, she decides as she steps outside into the bright winter sunshine and she and Niall wander towards the end of the garden to check on the hens. 'Oh,' he says suddenly. 'Why's that hen out?'

They stop and look around wildly. 'The hen run's open!' she announces, and they run towards it, aware of Theo watching gravely as they try to round them all up. 'Did you let them out, Theo?' Pearl asks as they coax the last hen – the speckled black and white one – back into the run.

'Yes,' he announces.

'But why?' Niall asks incredulously.

'Because...' His bottom lip crumples and tears spring from his pale blue eyes.

'Oh, Theo,' Pearl cries. 'No need to be upset—'

'Shelley shouted at Mummy,' he whimpers, rubbing at an eye with a fist. 'I don't like Shelley.'

'Look, darling.' Pearl crouches down and takes his hand. 'She wasn't really cross at you. Well, she *was*, but she only reacted like that because...' She tails off and looks up at Niall. 'She was upset about... other things.'

Theo is staring at her, eyes as round and glossy as marbles as she straightens up. Niall exhales and locks the hen run, and Theo slips his small, cold hand into hers as the three turn back towards the cottage. 'Oh, your slippers,' Pearl murmurs, looking down at them.

'They're wet,' Theo observes.

'Yes, darling. But they'll dry out.'

He seems reassured by this. Then: 'I missed the Christmas party.'

'I know, honey. It's such a shame. But there'll be other parties.'

'I had a costume,' he adds.

'Yes, I know. But you can wear it next Christmas—'

'But what if I don't want to be a pudding then?' he exclaims, and Pearl catches Niall trying to trap in a smile.

'Then you can come up with another brilliant idea!' she announces. 'I'm sure Daddy will be able to make whatever—'

'Are *you* a mummy?' he cuts in suddenly.

She smiles at that. 'Yes, I am. I have a son called Brandon.'

'How old is he?'

'He's twenty-one,' she replies. 'So all grown up.' Earlier today she called him to dispatch the weather report. He sounded relieved that she was coming home. 'How's Abi?' she asked, as she has each time she's called. Brandon muttered something unintelligible, seeming keen to finish the call, and with a niggle of unease, Pearl managed not to quiz him. Better to catch up face to face.

'Brandon's a nice name,' Theo says now.

'Thank you.' She squeezes his hand gently. 'I think it is too.'

Pearl senses him looking up at her, frowning. 'Where's Brandon's daddy?'

Something catches in her throat as they stop. 'Brandon's daddy isn't here any more,' she replies. As they walk on through the melting snow, stepping around the puddles of slush, Niall puts an arm around her shoulders. She looks up at him and musters a smile.

It's okay, his expression seems to tell her. Everything's going to be okay.

Theo is still gazing up at her. 'Did Brandon's daddy die?'

A cool gust catches her throat and, for a moment, Pearl can hardly breathe. 'Yes, Theo. He died.'

Then they walk on, and she worries now that she might have upset him. Will he be scared now that his own dad might die? Or his mum?

'Is he in heaven?' Theo asks.

Brandon asked this once, because at ten years old he still struggled with the concept that it might not exist. And Pearl gave him the answer that felt right. *I'm not sure, darling. But he's still here with us, even though we can't see him.*

'But where *is* he?' Brandon wanted to know.

The answer Pearl gave then is what she truly believed. And that's why she tells Theo, 'I actually believe that Brandon's daddy is still all around us, darling. I think he's in the stars.'

* * *

They are ready to leave now but Shelley is striding down the lane, away from Shore Cottage. She has taken herself off, not because she doesn't love her friends. But actually, they have talked it all out, and in the aftermath of the terrible conversation with Joel this morning, Shelley needs to be alone.

There is some snow left, but it's thawing rapidly. She stomps along, still trying to make sense of everything Joel told her. That he hates what he's done to her and his family. That he'll do anything to make things right.

What he didn't do was blame her in any way. 'This is 100 per cent down to me,' he told her tearfully. Shelley has never known Joel to cry about anything before. 'Please,' he begged her. 'Just get yourself home as soon as you can and we'll figure this out.'

Can they do that? It might be possible, Shelley thinks, as he swears he's told her everything. Not just about this photographer in Finsbury Park, but Martha and Fin's house party – 'That was my fault, not theirs, I should've *known*' – and the broken window and stolen laptop and the fact that her grandma's baubles were smashed. They could have some couples counselling and things might change for the better. Hasn't she read that an affair can actually help the relationship? That it can shine a spotlight on the problems that caused it and what's really important?

Shelley marches on, past Harry and Pam's farm. With the snow nearly gone it seems so much closer to Shore Cottage than it had on Christmas Eve. A cool wind gusts into her face now, and her ponytail has come loose in the wind. 'Give me a chance,' Joel implored her, 'for the kids as much as anything else. For our *family*.'

Now she sees a car in the far distance, heading towards her along the winding unmade road. She keeps walking, sploshing through puddles of melting snow as it comes closer. There is barely any traffic around here. Just the occasional farm vehicle or tourists getting lost, hoping that the satnav will spring to life. But the car has nearly reached her now, and Shelley steps back onto the verge to let it pass.

It doesn't pass her. Instead it stops, and the driver lowers his window, and despite everything, Shelley senses her heart lifting, and she smiles.

Michael is home.

40

He listens as Shelley fills him in on the events over Christmas. Practicalities come first: how Harry and Pam welcomed them all into their farmhouse on Christmas Eve, and supplied them with chickens for Christmas Day. How things all worked out in the end. 'So it's really gone okay?' he suggests as he makes her a coffee in the kitchen. The sunshine is dazzling now, transforming the landscape into a glittery wonderland, and everyone else has taken themselves out for one final walk.

'It really has,' Shelley says. 'At least, things have gone well *here*. At home, not so much...' And then it all tumbles out, about Joel's affair and how Shelley is adamant that her marriage is over. 'It's not just the other woman,' she explains, surprised by how comfortable she feels, chatting over the kitchen table with this man with whom she'd barely spent any time before he rushed away to London. He really listens, she decides. And listening has never been Joel's forte. Really, *Joel* is Joel's forte, and that will never change. So they talk and talk, and a second cup of coffee is made and Shelley is grateful that it's just the two of them for now, in the cosy warmth of Michael's kitchen.

'Enough about all that,' she says abruptly, freeing her ponytail from its band. 'What actually happened with Krissy? Or would you rather not talk about it?'

'No, it's fine,' he says. 'I'd like to actually, to make some sense of it.' He tells Shelley then that he *knew*, the moment they met face to face. He explains how the hotel receptionist had called Krissy's room, and she'd come down to where he was waiting in the bar. 'Hi, how are you?' There'd been a big glossy professional smile, as if he were a passenger on her flight. They'd hugged and Michael felt as if he'd staggered in from a field.

He hadn't, of course. Although he exists in sweaters and jeans and thick insulating jackets at home, for this trip he had put on his best shirt, carefully ironed late the night before (with all those sheets, Michael has become excellent at ironing), plus smart trousers. He'd dug out shoes that were actual *shoes*; not boots for walking or gardening or cleaning out the hen run.

Yet he still felt utterly wrong. And he sensed Krissy – immaculate, smelling strongly of a floral perfume – pulling back and appraising him, and he knew that *she* knew too.

That the man she'd spent countless hours talking to, and FaceTiming, wasn't how she'd imagined the real-life version. Of course he *was* the same person: a divorced forty-seven-year-old B&B owner with a dog. But he wasn't the Michael she'd built up in her mind. 'I think,' he ventures, 'that she was disappointed.'

'No,' Shelley exclaims, frowning. 'How could she be?'

He smiles awkwardly. 'With all those thousands of miles between us, I think Krissy had an idea of me, of the single man in the Highlands, in my cottage, with my dog and my hens, surrounded by lochs and mountains covered in purple heather...' He breaks off. 'D'you really want to hear all this?'

'Yes,' Shelley says truthfully. Since their chats when he was alone and somewhat lost in London, she's started to genuinely care for Michael. Plus, his story is distracting her from the almighty mess awaiting her back at home, at least a little.

'I used to take Krissy out on walks,' he explains. 'That's what we called it: going on a walk together. I knew the routes to take where there was a decent phone signal.' Michael tells Shelley how he showed Krissy the waterfall streaking like silvery hair down the mountain. How he took her out onto the loch in his rowing boat and circled the thickly wooded island.

He took her to villages consisting of a few huddled white cottages and an old red phone box, which she found so quaint, so *amazing*, and a wooden village hall and an old chapel, its roof long gone, its crumbly stone walls thickly covered in moss. He has shown her deer and feral goats and even an eagle once, soaring above. Krissy has seen Michael's little corner of Scotland in dazzling sunshine and misty rain and a crazy sudden hailstorm. And one magical night Michael took Krissy out and sat with her on a rock at the lochside, and together they watched the Northern Lights.

'It was about this place really,' Michael says. '*That's* what Krissy loved.'

Shelley shakes her head, taking all of this in. 'So,' she says gently, 'what happened then? After you'd met, I mean?'

He smiles ruefully as he describes the grim airport hotel with its artificial Christmas tree with integral lights blinking feebly in a corner. How Krissy has teased him about leaving his phone on the plane: 'You need to get up to speed with travelling, Michael. Honestly! When's the last time you flew anywhere?' And how he'd been relieved when she'd suggested an early dinner in the hotel restaurant. It was clear now that there was no romantic spark, but here was something they *could* do together. He went to fetch laminated menus from the bar, and as they made their choices he kept glancing at her nails. They were long and glossy and shaped into perfect ovals; pink with very white tips. 'No one who stays at Shore Cottage has nails like that,' he says with a smile. And then their food arrived and Krissy, a little altered now by a couple of wines, was short with the waiter, barking, 'Is that it? No sides?' And as Michael ploughed his way through a burger and greasy yellow fries, Krissy scowled down at her risotto.

'Is that okay?' he asked.

'It is if you like eating wallpaper paste,' she retorted. Michael looks at Shelley now and pushes back his wavy hair. 'So that's about it. She said she was jet-lagged and we decided to call it a night.'

'I'm so sorry,' Shelley murmurs.

'Oh, don't be.' He smiles. 'Harry and Pam had been on at me to get out there, to sign up to the dating apps and just give it a go.' He laughs dryly. 'They're worried about me frittering my life away…'

'I wouldn't say you're doing that,' Shelley says firmly.

'Well, I shouldn't have gone. It was mad to act so impulsively like that.

I'd looked forward to getting to know you all. It sounded from Pearl as if you all needed a break, and what did I do?'

'Abandon us!' Shelley teases, and she senses the spark reappearing in those dark brown eyes.

'Even though things didn't work out, I'm still grateful to you all. I really am.'

'You know, we actually loved it,' Shelley says.

'I'm glad. But I don't just mean looking after this place. I mean...' He pauses, colouring slightly. 'Those chats we had while I was away. Honestly, I didn't know what to do with myself. But you helped me to enjoy London...'

'I'm so happy to hear that,' Shelley says.

'I'm just sorry you had to do the chip shop dash that first night,' he says with a smile.

'And I'm sorry we forgot to ask everyone to fill in the visitors' book,' she adds, and he laughs.

'Don't worry about that. Maybe they'll be back someday, and they can do it then...' Michael stands up now, and she sees his expression change as he seems to focus on the opening to the pantry.

'Oh, the beaded curtain's gone,' he remarks. 'I thought it was just pushed aside but—'

'Michael, I'm so sorry,' Shelley blurts out. 'It was Theo. He chopped it down. But I'm not blaming a five-year-old child. It was our fault really, we should have kept an eye—'

'Don't worry. You had enough to do here,' he says, shaking his head. 'And actually, it was from a holiday a very long time ago...' He smiles then, and despite the fact that her life has been upended, Shelley senses a glimmer of hope somewhere deep in her very core.

'I'm glad you're not upset,' she ventures, and he hugs her reassuringly, as any friend would.

'No, not at all,' he says. 'It was just an old thing. And sometimes it's good to let things go.'

41

It's Tommy who meets them at the airport. He'd called Lena, saying they had to talk about the wedding and that he needed to see her as soon as possible. They drop off Pearl first, and then Shelley. She looks pale and stressed as she strides to her front door. But there's a sense of determination there too, Lena decides as she watches her friend step into her house.

She and Pearl know that Shelley can handle this, and that they'll be there for her every step of the way. So as Shelley greets her kids, and then whisks Joel upstairs to their bedroom for a talk – to ask him to move out, and give her space for the time being – Lena senses that something is different in Tommy too. Even so, she's not quite ready to forgive the fact that he lied by omission when she was in Scotland. That's how she views it; that he wasn't open with her. It's so confusing to her, and so unlike the man she loves.

'It's just the way I am,' she says as, alone now, they pull up close to her flat. 'I suppose I must still be insecure, even though I pretend I'm not.'

Tommy's eyes gleam with sudden tears. 'You're making out this is your fault and it's not. It's all down to me and I'm so sorry. There are no excuses, darling. I was just swept along, and I realise that sounds pretty pathetic. I should've told you what was going on, and then you'd have been fine.'

They climb out of the car and she glances at him, a wry smile playing on her lips now. 'Well, maybe not *fine*...'

He exhales, taking her hand as they make their way to her block and upstairs to her flat. 'Well, it's made me realise something important.'

'What's that?' She fixes her gaze on his as they step into the hallway.

Tommy reddens and looks down. 'That I need to stop snapping to attention when other people want me to do stuff. My parents, I mean. And even Daisy—'

'Tommy, I never want to get between you and Daisy,' Lena exclaims.

'No, I know that. But even so, I reckon we should do things *our* way now. Me and you. What d'you think?'

She nods. 'That's... that's good to hear,' she says cautiously.

In the living room now, Tommy pulls her close and kisses her. 'I missed you so much on Christmas Day,' he tells her. 'And I'm sorry you were upset...'

'Tommy, it's okay now,' Lena says firmly. 'Being logical, I knew Daisy wanted you there with them. You're her dad. It's natural. I just...' She winces. 'Please, let's just be honest with each other from now on.'

'Yes, definitely.' His dark eyes radiate kindness as he steps back. 'And you're right. Daisy wanted me there. But you're my family too, Leen.' He glances towards the tree and then goes to pick up a small tissue-wrapped gift from beneath it.

'What's this?' she asks. She and Tommy exchanged presents before she headed to Scotland.

'Just a little something for you from Daisy.'

Lena blinks in surprise. Daisy has never given her a present before. She peels off the turquoise paper, gasping at the delicate beaded earrings. 'I love them,' she exclaims, and Tommy smiles.

'She made them herself. We conferred on colours, although actually...' He laughs. 'She didn't listen to a word I said.'

Lena strides to the mirror and fixes them on, examining the beads in bright blues, greens and pinks. The joyous colours she loves. 'They're perfect,' she says, welling up now and already picking up her phone to call Daisy.

'They are,' Tommy agrees. 'And so are you.'

* * *

Joel moves out two days later to a friend's across town. He takes his studio kit so he can work from Mark's, holed up in his dingy box room for God knows how long. It's shameful of course, having to crash at a mate's. But what hurts Joel most is that Martha and Fin – although certainly surprised – accepted the new situation without copious tears or even saying very much at all. But then, separation is hardly unusual among their friends' parents. And Shelley has handled it with her usual thoughtfulness, suggesting that she trims her work hours so she's always around for the kids after school. Not that they're little ones, of course. 'But it feels important,' she explained to them all, when she chaired their excruciating family meeting, 'that I'm around as much as I can be at the moment.'

Her job seems safe for now but Shelley suspects it's time to try something new, to stretch herself and spread her wings. A more senior role at another care home is coming up later in the year, and she plans to go for it. Hopefully by then, everything will feel more steady at home. But for now, as the days and then weeks spin by, her family settles into its new shape, and a new way of doing things. Running their home is a team effort now – between her, Martha and Fin.

'They've risen to the challenge,' she tells Michael when they chat. They have fallen into a pattern of texting, just light and friendly messages that always make her smile. Somehow, one always seems to land when she is feeling wobbly. Then every week or so, usually late at night when his guests have gone to bed, they'll talk at length. She's found herself looking forward to these calls, when she'll curl up on the sofa with a glass of wine. 'Martha will be leaving home next year and Fin won't be far behind her,' Shelley tells him now. 'Really, it was time to stop running around after them. I keep telling them I'm giving them life skills,' she adds, and he laughs.

'Good for you. You know they're going to thank you in the long run.'

'I do hope so.'

'You *know* so,' he says, and her heart seems to lift. 'Honestly, you're amazing. They're lucky have such a brilliant mum.' At times like this

Shelley can hardly believe that she's spent so little time with Michael, face to face. Because now it feels as if she has known him forever.

Meanwhile, when Joel sees the kids it tends to be out at a Vietnamese place, where they order copiously and chatter away, strangely more open and relaxed with each other than when he was at home. Perhaps they feel a little sorry for him, now that he no longer has his studio or even a proper home of his own. He doesn't know. They certainly don't go into the ins and outs of the split, and he's relieved about that. As far as he is concerned it should remain a taboo subject whenever they're out together. Of course Joel misses his family but in time, when he's found a flat and he and Shelley have dealt with the finances, he reckons he'll be okay. After all, as he wrote in his secret document: *We only have one life to live and everyone owes it to themselves to squeeze the maximum fun and joy out of it. Once your one life is gone, it's gone.*

He's musing on this now as he and Martha and Fin leave the restaurant, full of noodles and tofu and spicy peanut sauce. And that's when he spots her. Carmel with a ridiculously good-looking man strolling along the street towards them.

He's way younger than Joel. He'd put him at mid-thirties tops. Joel quickens his pace, aware of Martha shooting him a curious look, and he turns his face away to avoid eye contact with the dazzling couple. But somehow his gaze is still pulled around to the left, and as they pass each other, he sees a small smile playing on Carmel's crimson mouth. And then they're gone.

42

APRIL

Lena didn't want to get married. At least, she didn't want to get married at High Elms, with the poached chicken in tarragon sauce and a load of terrible speeches and Annabelle Huntley making disparaging comments about her dress.

His mother had only said it as a joke, Tommy insisted. But that had been the final straw. They'd been up in Berkshire on a visit and Annabelle had badgered Lena about her wedding dress, asking to see a photo, saying it would be 'their secret'. 'We don't want our outfits to clash, do we?' she'd said. Heaven forbid, Lena thought darkly. And finally she'd given in and shown her a picture of the beautiful knee-length velvet dress she'd chosen, with the help of Shelley and Pearl, in a little vintage shop in Hackney.

Get married in red, wish yourself dead.

Lena was glad, actually, that she'd said it because her mind was made up then. The High Elms wedding was cancelled and, with Tommy in full agreement, they planned a small, casual ceremony at the registry office in Hackney Town Hall. Tommy's parents refused to attend but he said sod them, silly fools. 'We'll have a far better time without them there. Let's do it our way.'

And that's what they're doing on this bright and blue-skied April morning. Pearl stands next to handsome Brandon as confetti flies all around them like snowflakes. He and Abi broke up at Christmas. Although Pearl has managed not to grill him about it, she gets the feeling that Brandon had been swept along into a living-together situation, way before he was ready. Perhaps he'd been flattered that someone as loud and confident as Abi had wanted to be with him. But he'd seemed overshadowed, she realises now. He is obviously happier now – more like his old self – and is busily applying for better paid jobs with the plan to move into a house with his mates in the summer. Pearl will miss him of course, but it's time. He is twenty-two now and the image of his dad. He loves Abi as a friend but he's ready to do things his way now.

'Thanks, Mum,' he said, after Abi had moved in with a girlfriend.

'What for?' Pearl asked, although she knew of course. A week or so later a brand new Tom Ford lipstick arrived in a jiffy bag addressed to Pearl. *Love A xx*, was all the note said. But it meant so much more.

After the wedding ceremony everyone adjourns to a bar where they've booked a room for the reception. There's a casual buffet and everyone drinks and laughs and Shelley makes a brilliant speech, kicking off with reminiscences about when the three women met, on a magazine in Soho, when the world was at their feet.

'That was really good, Mum,' Fin murmurs when she sits back down.

'You think so?' Her eyes are shining with tears.

'God, yeah. You were amazing. I never knew you could speak in public like that!'

Martha beams at her and Shelley squeezes her hand. The party revs up then, growing more boisterous as dusk falls because, even though they're all grown up now, everyone still loves to party. Lena's parents and brothers and sisters especially. There's no stopping the Manchester contingency tonight. Pearl dances with Lena's dad, and Shelley dances with Lena and Tommy and Brandon and Daisy. Then suddenly it's Pearl and Niall who are dancing together. He protests that he's not much of a dancer, but is giving it a go anyway. And Shelley, ever keen to document everything, takes photos with her phone and sends them immediately to Michael at Shore Cottage. He replies straight away.

> **MICHAEL**
> Looks brilliant! Really looking forward to seeing you next week and meeting the kids. Sure they'll be okay being stuck out in the wilds for a week?

> **SHELLEY**
> They'll love it.

And they really will, she thinks. Because the Highlands in winter was beautiful but Michael has assured her that it's gorgeous in springtime too: lush and verdant, so different to how it was in the snow. Just as Shelley 'showed' him London via her instructions, he is looking forward to showing her his wild and untamed landscape, properly this time. Michael has mentioned that the Sampsons are keen to visit again too, as apparently Theo has talked of little else since Christmas. 'Perhaps we won't coincide this time,' Shelley laughed.

Will anything happen between her and Michael? Not this time, she thinks. This trip is about her and the kids doing something fun together. But she feels that something is there, and that they have grown close over the past few months. And the thought of seeing him again fills her with happiness.

And now Lena and Tommy are leaving amidst cheers and frantic waving, heading off on their honeymoon to a little cottage on the Cornish coast. The party disperses with hugs and tears, and suddenly it's all over.

Outside the bar now, Pearl takes Niall's hand. 'Shall we do it then?' she asks.

He nods. 'Yes, let's do it.'

She grins broadly. 'You really want to see it?'

'Of course I do,' he says. So they take a bus into Soho and she looks out as they pass the scruffy old bar where Dean proposed to her. Then they get off the bus, and they wander the streets together, hand in hand, and she shows him the magazine office where she met her best friends so very long ago. It's not a magazine office any more. It's a smart boutique now, but that doesn't matter because she can still feel it: her young life, her past.

They stop at a newsagent where Niall buys a copy of the travel magazine and shows his Highland supplement to Pearl. Shore Cottage is featured prominently, illustrated by Niall's own photographs. *The perfect hidden bolthole,* he's written. *A secret nook on the shores of the sparkling loch.* 'He's going to love this,' she enthuses.

'I hope so.' Niall smiles. 'It was pretty special up there, wasn't it?'

She nods. 'It really was.' Then they stop and kiss, right there on a warm evening with people milling all around. Kissing like young people. Like they never want to stop. And then they do stop and Niall says gently, 'That thing you said, when Theo asked where Brandon's daddy is now. D'you remember?'

'Yes.' She nods. And then wordlessly she looks up to the night sky. There are no stars to be seen because this is London, not the wild landscape around Shore Cottage. But Pearl knows, as she squeezes Niall's hand, that just because she can't see them, doesn't mean they don't exist.

Because the stars are always there.

ACKNOWLEDGEMENTS

Thanks as ever to Caroline Sheldon, my fabulous agent, and to all at RCW, especially Safae, for making me feel so welcome. A huge shoutout to my editor, Rachel Faulkner-Willcocks – I'm thrilled to be working together again! Thanks to Amanda Ridout, Nia Beynon, Jenna Houston, Hayley Russell and the fantastic Boldwood team. I'm so excited to join you. Thanks to Candida Bradford for excellent copyediting and to Jennifer Kay Davies for eagle-eyed proofreading. Hugs to fellow authors Shari Low (you helped me to make the leap!), Jenny Colgan for the generous quote, and Sarra Manning for keeping my pecker up with #atwwc (all the work while crying). Cheers to Lisa Wood for flight attendant info, to the brilliant Rachel Gilbey for blog tour expertise, and to Barbara Copperthwaite for setting up the 'we can do this!' Facebook authors' group. Thanks to my ever brilliant friends: Jen, Kath, Riggsy, Susan, Ellie, Cathy, Michelle, Wendy V, Maggie, Jennifer, Mickey and the Currie clan – I don't know where I'd be without you. Thanks for your plotline wizardry, Jackie Brown. Sure you don't fancy writing my books for me? Finally, all my love to my wonderful readers for such loyal support, to Jimmy for cooking a zillion meals when my deadline was breathing hotly down my neck – and to Sam, Dexter and Erin for everything.

ABOUT THE AUTHOR

Fiona Gibson writes bestselling and brilliantly funny novels about the craziness and messiness of family life.

Sign up to Fiona Gibson's mailing list for news, competitions and updates on future books.

Visit Fiona's website: www.fionagibson.com

Follow Fiona on social media here:

- facebook.com/fionagibsonauthor
- instagram.com/fiona_gib
- bookbub.com/profile/fiona-gibson
- x.com/FionaGibson

Boldwood

Boldwood Books is an award-winning fiction publishing company seeking out the best stories from around the world.

Find out more at www.boldwoodbooks.com

Join our reader community for brilliant books, competitions and offers!

Follow us
@BoldwoodBooks
@TheBoldBookClub

Sign up to our weekly deals newsletter

https://bit.ly/BoldwoodBNewsletter

Milton Keynes UK
Ingram Content Group UK Ltd.
UKHW041859290824
447475UK00002B/14

9 781836 172147